TO THE
EDGE
of
SORROW

TO THE
EDGE
of
SORROW

———

Aharon Appelfeld

Translated from the Hebrew by
Stuart Schoffman

SCHOCKEN BOOKS

New York

English translation copyright © 2020 by Schocken Books,
a division of Penguin Random House LLC

All rights reserved. Published in the United States by Schocken Books,
a division of Penguin Random House LLC, New York, and distributed
in Canada by Penguin Random House Canada Limited, Toronto.
Originally published in Israel as *Ad Khod Hatza'ar* by Kinneret, Zmora-Bitan,
Dvir Publishing House Ltd., Or Yehuda, in 2012.
Copyright © 2012 by Aharon Appelfeld and Kinneret, Zmora-Bitan,
Dvir Publishing House Ltd.

Schocken Books and colophon are registered trademarks
of Penguin Random House LLC.

Library of Congress Cataloging-in-Publication Data
Names: Appelfeld, Aharon, author. Schoffman, Stuart, translator.
Title: To the edge of sorrow / Aharon Appelfeld;
translated from the Hebrew by Stuart Schoffman.
Other titles: 'Ad ḥod ha-tsa'ar. English.
Description: First edition. New York: Schocken Books, 2020.
Identifiers: LCCN 2019011548. ISBN 9780805243420 (hardcover: alk. paper).
ISBN 9780805243437 (ebook).
Subjects: LCSH: Jewish soldiers—Fiction. Holocaust,
Jewish (1939–1945)—Fiction.
Classification: LCC PJ5054.A755 A62513 2019 | DDC 892.43/6—dc23 |
LC record available at lccn.loc.gov/2019011548

www.schocken.com

Jacket photograph by Ildiko Neer/Arcangel Images
Jacket design by Linda Huang

Printed in the United States of America
First American Edition
2 4 6 8 9 7 5 3 1

TO THE
EDGE
of
SORROW

I

―――――

M y name is Edmund, and I'm seventeen years old. Since last spring we've been inching our way over these hills: most of them bare, some sparsely wooded. The bald patches in the forest make our life difficult, but we've gotten good at camouflage and deception, and we've learned how to stay close to the ground, utilizing blind spots to surprise the enemy. The enemy knows it is dealing with damaged, resolute people; it unleashes its well-trained fighters, assisted by gendarmes and local farmers, who act as informants. We will not be easily defeated.

Daylight is a problem, but the night belongs to us. We also need to be very cautious at night, but over time we've learned the advantages of darkness. There's nothing like lying in ambush on summer nights: you're on high alert, picking up every sound, poised to strike like a panther.

At the end of the summer, the commander decided that we had to leave this place and head toward the wetlands, to the swamps and the lakes. Such a move would distance us from the fields and orchards that provide our vital needs but would give us several clear advantages: stagnant water is an obstacle, and an army is not eager to plod through swamps, cut off from its headquarters.

During the day, we are dug in and camouflaged, and we advance at night. Progress is slow but steady. Each day brings us closer to the goal. On the last few nights we could smell the water and celebrated quietly. But we must never rest on our laurels; the enemy is vigilant and follows us always. They try to outflank us and block the way to the wetlands. We outsmart them and ambush them. Our calculations have worked out so far, and we haven't suffered many casualties, but who knows how this bitter struggle will end.

At the beginning of September, we arrived at the ridge overlooking Lake Tanura, a long lake surrounded by boulders. The previous day, the commander had sent an experienced squad to prepare rafts; they reached their destination, cut down trees, and when we arrived, a few small rafts awaited us on the water.

Several fighters went out on the first raft to check the opposite shore. We watched them row, ready to provide covering fire and to help them. The crossing was undisturbed. We saw them land, spread out, and carefully survey the area. After two hours, they signaled us to launch the remaining rafts.

The little rafts floated back and forth, carrying people and equipment. By the way, our equipment is not minimal; it includes hammers, knives, axes, saws, cooking utensils, and food. Not to worry, everything is well packed and travels with us from place to place, supervised by Hermann Cohen, about whom I will have more to say when the time comes.

By midnight we were all on the other bank. We saw right away that this was different territory, covered with thick vegetation and smelling heavily of dampness.

2

Ever since I joined the fighters, I've changed beyond recognition. The commander promises us that if we try hard, train diligently, and follow orders precisely, at the end of the course we'll be fighters. Fighters do not complain; they grit their teeth and do not pity themselves.

Just one year ago I was a student, a teenager of average height with eyeglasses, and until last year I excelled at school. I don't want to talk now about last year, when I was a tangle of contradictions. Presumably things will become clear when the time comes, but I will say this, my parents were greatly pained by the decline in my studies.

My report card glittered with high grades during my time at high school. I was my parents' pride and joy, but suddenly my life veered off course, and their quiet happiness turned into shame. They were periodically called to the school and stood mutely before the vice principal, unable to offer a word in my defense.

The teachers grieved alongside my parents over my failure, especially the math and Latin teachers.

"What happened?" my humiliated father would ask in despair.

"Nothing," I would say, over and over.

"Why aren't you studying like you used to; something must have happened."

The war was at our doorstep. People ran around in the streets, trying to escape the trap, but my parents were sunk in their depression. The decline in my studies concerned them more than the imminent danger. In those days I was blind and merciless. I felt that my parents were drowning in their own world and blocking my way. I didn't speak up or make excuses, but without meaning to I was pouring salt on their wounds.

NOW THEY ARE far away from me, and I'm here. Sometimes it seems that everything that has happened to me in these past months is a nightmare to be deciphered in the future. I will undoubtedly be found guilty, which is why I try hard to obey orders and be a flawless fighter.

The training is exhausting. The commander has no pity for stragglers; he demands extra effort, and weakness is forbidden. Those among us who do not meet his standards guard the base and help with the cooking. They chop wood and gather twigs for bedding.

Fighters, the commander calls us. Our training includes long runs, hurdling over obstacles, climbing ropes, advancing correctly in forested areas and swamps, carrying heavy loads. More than once, I collapsed, and had it not been for friends who supported me, I doubt I would have met all the demands.

I look in the water, and to my surprise I don't recognize myself. My face has filled out and reddened, and my shoulders are broader. In a sheepskin coat I look more like a young farmer than a *gymnasium* student. My hands are rougher, too. I've lost my previous quickness; a different quickness guides my steps. I can bend scraps of tin and iron, break poles, dig a trench in minutes. I doubt my parents would recognize me, and if they did, I wonder how they'd react. Deep in my heart, my transformation makes me happy. Every success in training, every compliment, makes me swell with pride, and I feel that on the battlefield, face-to-face with the enemy, I will perform to my commanders' satisfaction.

THE WETLANDS. Is this home base or the start of the journey? We press on through the thick foliage, where the darkness is greater than the light. Progress sometimes means strenuous chopping of trees, all hands clearing the path. I do not complain; I accept the difficulties as a duty and atonement for sin. The training exercises and ambushes do not weaken me. I assume that when the time comes, not far off, we will become forest creatures, and the trees and bushes will wrap us in a warm, wide mantle.

There's no point wasting time with fantasies; better to clean the weapon, fix what's left of my shoes. The soles are torn, and I tie them with string. That's how it is for nearly all of us. Were it not for the cold nights, it would be easier, but the cold and wet are unrelenting. Thank God for the whispering coals that keep our clothes a little dry.

3

A t first the commander planned to move the camp the very night we crossed over, but given our fatigue of the past few days, it was best to stay here another night, refresh ourselves, study the territory, and only then push onward.

It was a sleep I had not known since I left home: soft, downy, filled with bright visions. I saw my parents dressed in white summer clothes, standing at the bank of the River Prut, like every summer. I wanted to ask them where they are now, but the question got stuck in my mouth.

When we awaken, we are greeted with coffee and sliced bread slathered with jam. There is nothing like a cup of coffee and a slice of bread to banish nocturnal dreams and hunker down to reality. After a cup of coffee, the morning seems young and sharp. You're ready to march, carry heavy gear, overcome obstacles of water and foliage. Before going out on a mission, the fighters need something more: a glass of vodka. There were days when everyone drank vodka, but now the supply has dwindled, and it is reserved for the fighters. No problem; this is not discrimination; all of us here depend on one another.

Once, when the child Milio fell ill with typhus, the fighters raided the home of the village pharmacist and took all the medicines he had on hand. This was a bold action: the pharmacist lived in the middle of the village, and there was a risk that the village youth would fight back. The raid passed without mishap, and we've had medicine and bandages ever since.

OUR COMMANDER, Kamil, is not like other people; he is head and shoulders taller: six feet four inches. He graduated with high honors from the architecture academy, and everyone predicted a brilliant career. But the war, and who knows what else, turned him into a daring commander.

It should be stated at the outset: Kamil is prone to mood swings. Sometimes he will retire to his tent for hours and leave the command to his deputy, Felix. This isn't regarded as neglect but seclusion for the purpose of rethinking. Our war is complicated, and each day brings new dangers. Our enemy is filled with guile and tries to outflank and surprise us. Kamil is an artist in the warfare of the few against the many. Apparently the strain is not easy on him.

His face reflects his ascetic nature, and it's clear that he takes a long view of our war. Sometimes he sits and lays out his thinking for us: not day-to-day needs but matters of the spirit. In his opinion, our war will not easily be won, and therefore, alongside the intensive military training, our spirit must be nourished as well.

Kamil did not earn his authority overnight. In the past, several of the best fighters had their doubts and suspicions. It was claimed that his monastic disposition could undermine his judgment. But before long, Kamil proved that he knew not only how to lead his fighters but also how to win battles in which we were sorely outnumbered.

Moreover, he knows the territory like the palm of his hand, and more than once, we eluded hostile gendarmes because he knew the area better than they did. From a young age he loved to hike, climb, and spend hours alone in the woods. Even then, unknowingly, he was preparing himself to be a commander. With him, it's hard to distinguish between the commander training his soldiers strictly and a spiritual leader carefully weighing each word he utters.

To us, Kamil was at first an unknown quantity. He is without a doubt a mysterious person, but little by little we learned to appreciate his hidden powers. And once, in a moment of great darkness, he cried out, "Get rid of your sadness! A damaged people cannot afford such luxuries." Back then we saw how he could lift the defeated camp in both of his hands and set it on its feet.

We became aware of Kamil's unique strength during one of our daring raids. He stood in front of the fighters and read from the Book of Psalms. He read the psalm slowly, emphasizing each word. He was not a fluent reader of Hebrew, but he tried his best to capture the essence of the words. No one imagined that this tall man, planted in reality, who knew how to handle every obstacle and setback, would enlist the words of an ancient poem to accompany the fighters into battle. That's Kamil: unpredictable.

His deputy, Felix, is very different: short and broad-shouldered, he walks with small steps but firmly holds his ground. His solid stance sometimes makes it seem that he carries more gear than the rest of us.

Felix is a superb fighter but never served in an army. He's an engineer whose buildings resemble him, low and sturdy. I once heard him say, "A house without a garden is not a house." He says little and explains little; it's hard to get a complete sentence out of him. As opposed to Kamil, Felix inspires silence; he walks in the lead, and we all follow him with confidence. More than once, we were taken by surprise and found ourselves at a disadvantage. Felix is an expert in stressful situations. His ability to stand firm under fire, to execute an orderly retreat, are wonderful to behold. He does everything quietly, with sealed lips, never getting angry or casting blame. It's not easy to follow his example, but the moment you obey his orders, you feel sure of yourself.

In the past there were differences of opinion between these two great commanders. Kamil tried to instill some of his beliefs in his deputy. Felix dislikes being preached to. He doesn't talk about his views and beliefs. But one time he couldn't contain himself, broke his silence, and declared, "In my opinion one must not mix matters of the spirit with deeds. A fighting organization cannot afford to deal with beliefs and opinions; these should be left until after the war." Kamil, of course, disagrees with this way of thinking. Felix resigned his position, and Kamil realized that without Felix he could not lead us in battle. In the end they compromised, and it was decided that in matters of belief and opinion each person would abide by his own principles.

But don't be misled by the differences between them. As I said, Felix also has opinions, perhaps not as fully formed as Kamil's, but he, too, is sensitive to words and phrases. When he hears a false or exaggerated word, he winces. He seems to have derived his feelings from music. He began playing the cello as a boy, and once in a while we hear him quietly singing a Bach cantata. Felix is sometimes perceived as one-dimensional, which is a mistake. True, he can be silent for an entire day, but when he does express an opinion, you come to realize that he is precise and succinct, and no sight or sound escapes his attention.

4

———

I've gotten ahead of myself.

The first team to escape from the ghetto set for itself the goal of rescuing as many people as possible. In the first wave they were able to bring out another five, plus a boy of about two whom they found outside the ghetto, not far from the fences.

Kamil claimed the child would be the good luck charm who would inspire the group to perform wonders. The ghetto had not yet been destroyed, and the team led by Kamil and Felix tried to dig a tunnel into it. But, unfortunately, the watchtowers were manned day and night, and searchlights scanned every square foot. They were nevertheless able to smuggle out a few people who went out to work and a few who were standing at the train station. I, too, by luck or a miracle, joined them.

We are now forty-four in number. We are fighting for our lives, but we fear most of all for the child. After every drill or action, we gather around him, not as a child who doesn't speak but as someone who can bless us when we go out and when we return. His very existence is a miracle. Most of the day his eyes are wide open; he never cries or asks for anything, but when you touch him, his shoulders recoil.

At first we called him "boy," but one of the fighters happened to call him Milio, and now that's what everyone calls him. I think the name fits him. Milio doesn't ask questions; his eyes say, *I have no words to tell you what I see and hear; don't ask me.* But the comrades ignore his mute request, though they can see that questions pain him.

Once, one of the fighters got down on his knees and innocently asked, "How do you feel, Milio?" Milio hunched his shoulders and covered his eyes with both hands. For a moment it seemed like he would burst into tears. We were wrong. He pursed his lips.

Most of the day he sits in his tent. Now and then he gets up and goes outside. He's a strange, mute little creature, incapable of clear expression, whose every tiny gesture makes us happy. In truth, he does nothing but merely watches.

When we aren't training or going on an ambush, Danzig carries Milio close to his chest in a big farmer's kerchief. Danzig is our giant. He is about six feet six inches tall, and who knows how wide his shoulders are. Sometimes Danzig tries to make Milio laugh, but Milio is cautious and wary of trusting people.

What happened to him, how he lost his parents and landed outside the ghetto walls is hard to know. Danzig believes we need to be patient. He senses that Milio will eventually reveal his secrets, but we mustn't pressure him.

In the evening we sit around him. If he would cry or express unhappiness, his existence would be more comprehensible. His serene silence is a riddle that grows day by day. Not long ago we still expected that one morning he would surprise us by speaking a word. The days have gone by, and Milio's muteness endures in his every pore.

One day he suddenly fell ill with typhus. For two weeks he burned with fever. Danzig did not budge from the tent where he lay, and we were all on alert.

After his fever went down, Milio opened his eyes and looked at us. It was hard to know if he recognized us or if he was searching for his lost parents. Danzig spoke to him and said, "Thank God, the fever went down, and now you'll feel much better."

From day to day Milio's face brightened. Danzig was as happy as a child and fed him semolina porridge. Most of the day Milio was curled up, sleeping. The sleep was good for him. After about two weeks of sleep, he got up and looked around with a fresh gaze, and we knew that he was a perceptive child.

Danzig feels that Milio has a different sort of understanding.

"How can you tell?" asked one of the fighters.

"It's hard to explain."

Milio sometimes seems like a creature who has survived by miraculous means. The miracle was so powerful that it muted the few sounds he'd been able to make.

Danzig believes that Milio is hiding a secret. It's hard to argue with a giant like Danzig.

We love Milio's sleep. A fine, milky mist hovers over his sleep, meaning he is still tied to his mother.

When Milio wakes up, Danzig declares "Milio is awake," as if the miracle had returned and was revealed anew. Danzig himself has changed since he adopted Milio. The silent wonder of the child is reflected in his face and makes him a man who glows with an inner light.

WE'VE BEEN TOGETHER only a few months, but it sometimes seems as though we've been wandering for years on this uncharted land with an unknown future. Kamil does not instill false hope. Indeed, he increasingly demands exact compliance with his orders, but he goes easy on the weaker people. At times it appears that the purpose of our lives now is to protect those who cannot protect themselves.

5

Our daily schedule begins with exercise and running. Breakfast at seven. Tsila, our cook, prepares the meals with the help of older people who are not fighters. The morning menu: semolina or corn porridge, a slice of bread with jam, coffee or tea. Our menu is modest yet filling.

At eight o'clock we go out to train. Kamil insists on a neat appearance and clean weapons. It wasn't easy to get the first rifles. We now have ten rifles, twelve pistols, and grenades. These weapons are insufficient for directly confronting hostile patrols, so we lie in ambush and sometimes manage to surprise them. A while ago we surprised a patrol. Two of them were killed, and the rest ran away, leaving behind six rifles and many cartridges. Our arsenal thus grew all at once, and in honor of the victory and the booty, we celebrated that night.

Once or sometimes twice a week we raid the houses of farmers. Truth be told, this is not pleasant work. In the summer we would raid fields and orchards and bring fruits and vegetables to the base. But in this season the fields are barren and gray. There is nothing to be found. With no alternative, we raid houses, plunder the food and clothing, and look forward to days when more fighters will join us and we can raid military camps.

Meanwhile, our shared lives, the drills and the raids, have forged us into a unit. If not for Kamil, who insists on sharp performance, our days would slip into blind routine. Kamil is not religious in the common meaning of the word but an enthusiast in every sense: sometimes it's a plant or flower that inspires him, sometimes a word. When Kamil reads from the Book of Psalms, it gives you goose bumps. His orders are simple and clear, but at times he utters a rhythmic sentence that seems transmitted from the distant past.

Kamil wanted to organize evenings of study, but it's hard to do so without texts. For years books were our mainstay, and suddenly we were cut off from them. It was odd how we got accustomed, in so short a time, to living without them. Sometimes, mostly in late afternoon, I imagine that I have a book in my hands. I look around and remember that at this hour I would hold a book and read. I read *Crime and Punishment* before it was assigned for school. Its sentences swept me away like rushing waters. Now we lived without books and notebooks, pencils and pens, as if stripped of our insides. If not for one small volume of psalms, brought by one fighter, we would have no physical claim on a world we lived in yesterday.

Books, books, where are they? *As if they never were*, I sometimes hear, not a lone voice but a collective moan arising from within. Books, in truth, are what separate our lives then from our lives now. One of the fighters, a sensitive young man, delivered his opinion with subtle, tight-lipped irony: "We have returned to nature. In two or three months we'll be like cavemen. We won't talk; we'll howl, laugh, and bark, and maybe that's better."

Kamil heard this and reacted immediately. "We have not come here for that. We will maintain our humanity even here, and we will not let evil deface us. The study evenings will take place at first without texts, but don't worry; we will find books somehow."

6

Kamil had prophesied without knowing it. Loaded with supplies on the way back to the base after a tough raid, we saw at a crossroads a Jewish home that had been broken into. When we went inside, a great surprise awaited us. The house was bare of any furniture, any dish or bedsheet, but in two alcoves, arranged on shelves, were many books. Kamil immediately ordered us each to take at least ten books. And so we lucked upon a Hebrew Bible, a Bible in the poet Yehoash's Yiddish translation, and another one in Luther's German translation, an elegant Hebrew prayer book, a very old High Holiday mahzor, and many other rare books. The books were damp and mildewed but complete.

ON EVERY RAID we pass an abandoned Jewish home in the countryside. These are now mostly occupied by Ruthenians who remodeled them, but sometimes the abandoned house remains in its original form. The new residents wear the clothes of the former residents, and for a moment their appearance is deceptive.

On one of the raids, Salo discovered the house of his Uncle Herzig: a big house with many lamps. This was before dawn, and we were on our way to the base. Salo, who was shaken by what he saw, asked Felix for permission to go inside to see what was left.

The new residents, startled by the raid, were ordered to sit on the ground. Felix immediately announced that we were partisans and requested that they contribute to the war effort.

"We have nothing," said the father of the family.

"The house is full of fine furniture, expensive lamps, and you say you have nothing."

"Take a piece of furniture if you want," he said with a snicker.

"We do not need furniture. We are looking for necessities, warm clothes, blankets. By the way, whose house is this?"

"Mine."

"You inherited it?"

"That's right."

"And if we tell you this is a Jewish house and you took it over, what would you say?"

"I would say that's not true."

Felix did not continue to argue. He ordered a search.

The house was full of city clothes, blankets, and down quilts, and in the dining room there were elegant utensils—candlesticks, a spice box—and a charity box from the Jewish National Fund.

It had been a long time since we'd seen clothes that Jews wore. There was still an odor of camphor in the closets.

Salo trembled. He used to come here during the Passover holiday to study for semester exams and spend time with his cousins. Those had been splendid days of heart-to-heart conversation, of hikes by the river, and of tastes and smells of Jewishness.

We filled four sacks with clothes and blankets, and we also took the candlesticks, the spice box, and the charity box from the Jewish National Fund.

"Why are you taking our clothes?" the father on the ground asked anxiously.

"They are not your clothes."

"They *are* mine."

"If you keep lying we will punish you. Do not forget. We are partisans fighting for our lives, and anyone who opposes us risks his life. And where are the books?" said Felix.

"I have no books."

"If you don't show us right now where you threw the books, we'll burn down the house."

"Have mercy on me and my children."

"We'll have mercy if you show us where you threw the books. There were many books here."

"I burned them."

"Why did you burn them?"

"I didn't know what to do with them."

"Where did you burn them?"

"Behind the stable."

"Damn you. Show us where you burned them," Felix persisted.

"Don't kill me. I have five children."

Two fighters went with him behind the barn. In the pile of ashes a few unburned pages remained. Salo took a half-burned page with the words of the morning prayer *Modeh Ani:* I give thanks to God for restoring my soul.

We retreated according to standard procedure, and it was good that we were cautious. We were no more than two or three hundred feet from the house when the farmer and his older sons came out of the house and, joined by neighbors, began to shoot at us. Felix ordered us to put down our supplies and attack them. Which is what we did. Within minutes the shooting stopped. This was not enough for Felix. He ordered us to set the house on fire. And that is what we did.

7

We went on our way loaded with books and supplies. We hadn't touched a book for a long time. Our inching across the hills and the exhausting search for food had distanced us from ourselves. Among the books we carried off was Dostoevsky's *Crime and Punishment,* reminding me that I did not complete my matriculation exams and would have to be tested when the war was over. Oddly, this familiar book did not move me. Life in the unit, the training, the raids fill me to the brim. At night I drop to the ground and sleep without dreams.

Kamil was emotional and said, "A great treasure has fallen into our hands. Let us try to be worthy of it. Life without books is a crippled life. Now we will replace what is missing."

That same night we drank the wine we took in the raid and sang our hearts out. No wonder the guards didn't get up on time for duty. Kamil complained but did not get angry.

That same week we were introduced to the religious teachings of the Ba'al Shem Tov in the book edited by Martin Buber. Kamil told us that the Besht, as he was known, the founder of Hasidism, walked these very hills, where he meditated and conceived his teachings. "What a privilege for us," he said.

Even this excitement did not escape criticism. Every word out of Kamil's mouth is examined under a magnifying glass: Why is he using the word "privilege"?

Kamil, like most of us, is not an expert in Jewish texts, but his curiosity about all things Jewish makes him a man filled with wonder. On one evening, one of our rationalists said, not without sorrow, that Judaism was beyond our reach. It's an ancient, complex culture, and if one is not exposed to it from childhood, its iron gates refuse to open. You read one book and another book, and you understand how far you are from understanding.

Kamil disagreed. Martin Buber, he argued, is the guide for the perplexed of our generation. His books *I and Thou* and *Tales of the Hasidim,* which we brought from that wondrous house, can illuminate the soul. There were those among us who argued that Buber beautified Judaism, put cosmetics on its face in order to find favor with German Jews, but let's put that aside for now.

SHORTLY THEREAFTER we were discovered by a patrol of Ukrainian collaborators who opened fire on us. Two of our comrades were wounded. Luckily, one of our own patrols was coming back at the same time and quickly joined us, and we returned fire. The hostile patrol was forced to retreat, leaving behind one dead and an automatic rifle.

The enemy does not relent: the next day we again encountered a hostile patrol, but we were ready for it and fought back. So it was, every few days. The Germans are stubborn and fight us fiercely. With good reason, Kamil decided that we had to leave the hills and advance into the wetlands.

But now it's different: we have books. Hermann Cohen, a short man with a sunny disposition, is in charge of equipment and lends each comrade a book. A thorough survey indicated that most of the books have to do with Judaism. Apparently the owner of that library was a man of broad horizons who chose his books carefully. It's hard to know if he was religiously observant. I imagine him to be a tall, good-natured man who stands in the doorway of his home as evening falls and looks at the trees and their falling leaves. The big leaves, red and yellow, refuse to wilt, their colors growing stronger by the hour. This pleases him, and he decides to go into his big house and turn on the lights.

It's strange what a bundle of books can do. Our temporary base, every canvas tent a sign of impermanence, has suddenly changed, as if distant visions, quiet and calm, have arrived as our guests.

You pick up a book and you are at home, with your parents. The lamp is lit, and you are completely immersed in the book. Papa, a lawyer who represents the famous Singer sewing machine company among others, has just received a new catalogue and is studying it excitedly.

Mama is fixing a late afternoon snack. Dostoevsky's book fascinates me so much that I don't hear her voice calling me to come and taste what she's made. When I finally pry myself away from the book, I want to say, *Why did you pluck me away from these amazing scenes?*, but I restrain myself so she won't feel bad.

Salo, our chief medic, who saw his uncle's stolen home with his own eyes, doesn't talk about what he saw. His every gesture says, *I am doing what I have to do at this time. I must not succumb to grief.* One of the wounded, whose bandage Salo changed in the middle of the night, called him "a lover of mankind." Salo quickly shrugged off that label. "I do my duty. It's not exceptional." Once I heard him say, "My uncle Herzig is a hearty man, just like his name, and his house was not only full of lamps but filled with inner light. Now he is a prisoner in one of the camps and who knows if I'll see him again."

KAMIL HAS ESTABLISHED a new routine, evenings of study. We are in the land of the Ba'al Shem Tov and his followers. Here he walked, meditated, searched for God, and through his students conveyed his Torah teachings to us, and this is a perfect moment to get to know them.

Once a week we make time for Torah. This new arrangement is not acceptable to everyone. Some have reservations or even object. "If there is a purpose to our being here," Kamil explains, "it is to become aware of ourselves, of parents and grandparents and their faith. Hopefully we can shake free of fixed opinions and prejudices and open our eyes to see not only what we usually see but also what we are prevented from seeing."

8

The rains have ended, and it's possible to sit silently or read a book. Kamil insists on this quiet time. Truth to tell, there's no reason to insist. People are thirsty for a little quiet and introspection. Danzig, after reading for about an hour, sat up and said, "I used to love to read Stefan Zweig."

"And now?" wondered Hermann Cohen.

"Now he seems naïve."

"We've grown wiser?"

"We've changed, apparently."

"How so?"

"I have no idea."

Hermann Cohen is a man of action, and his practicality is obvious in his every move, but he, too, sits in his corner sometimes and reads. Having these books has changed our lives. Even before you dip into one, you feel as though you are in an armchair or in the garden of your home, together with your family or just by yourself.

Danzig didn't pursue an academic career after graduating from university but went to a provincial town and opened a bookstore. Jews and not only Jews would come to buy or borrow a book, to read the daily paper, or to purchase a periodical. Alongside the shop, he had a room where people would sit and read. It wasn't a very big store, but it hummed with life. Sometimes arguments broke out, but Danzig's pleasant manner was enough to calm the atmosphere.

Danzig loved provincial life and the Jews who came to his shop. The older generation were displeased that the young people would congregate there. They feared that their sons and daughters would be attracted to foreign culture.

Now, like everyone, Danzig is disconnected from his family and lives temporarily in these mountains, in the hope that the war will not last long and life will resume as before. Milio will return to his parents, and Danzig to his family. Danzig is so busy raising Milio and training and raiding that he can't afford to get close to what once was his. I often hear him say, "and nevertheless," a kind of answer to all those who indulge their despair in private.

Owing to his height and broad shoulders, Danzig is known as "the pillar of the platoon." During raids, he carries a double load on his shoulders. When we relocate from place to place, he moves most of the equipment. The old people are happy for his help, but his gentle manner is most evident when he carries Milio in his arms, feeds him, and tells him a story.

9

Kamil keeps reminding us that if there's a rationale for why we fight, it's to protect the weak who've been entrusted to our care. At times we go on raids, but guarding the base is continuous, day and night. To maintain this vigilance, only one squad or, in special cases, two squads go out at a time on raids. We eagerly wait for new fighters to join us, but for now they have yet to arrive.

"We must find the streams to our forgotten reservoir," Kamil reminds us. This is harder to fulfill than his other commands. The sayings of the Besht, as retold by Martin Buber, undeniably stir the heart, but make no mistake, they are anchored in prayer and the observance of religious law.

"These texts are a regression to dark days," declares Big Karl, one of the best-loved fighters, who was named for Karl Marx. "We left the ghetto not only to save ourselves but also to break away once and for all from an irrational tradition and to live as free men."

"Do we also want to cut ourselves off from our parents and grandparents?" demands another fighter.

"From their beliefs, yes."

Karl is a superior squad leader. A squad under his command feels his power, and it's easy to follow him. When he speaks of his beliefs, you can feel the inner engine that governs his existence. He's a second-generation communist, a true believer. Not by chance did Kamil choose him as a fellow commander.

Kamil, to his credit, is very tolerant. He knows that some of the fighters are loyal communists, and some are active in the leftist Bund and Shomer Hatza'ir. Their time in the ghetto and the forests has changed them but not their beliefs. To satisfy those who disagree with him, we read poems by Heine or Rilke, or chapters from Dostoevsky's *Crime and Punishment*.

THE RAIN, DAMPNESS, and cold have worsened. Several sacks of flour have grown moldy, a serious setback. At one time Kamil planned to raid military camps scattered in the foothills and to liberate and absorb the thousands of prisoners who remain in the work camps. Kamil believes that five thousand fighters could change the course of the war. The wetlands are ideal territory for partisan warfare. Fighters from here could undermine the self-confidence of an entire army.

For now nothing has come of all these plans. We are increasingly engaged with day-to-day existence: reinforcing the tents, struggling against wetness and hostile patrols. The fear that a long stay in the mountains would diminish our resolve was unfounded.

The unit is consolidated, the fighters devoted to the weaker members. Differences of opinion have not led to a rift. Moreover, our daily routine is strictly organized. Everyone agrees that without mental work the unit can become demoralized. Depression is one of our toughest enemies. A person thinks of his father and mother, his brothers and sisters, how they were snatched in sudden *aktions*—such a memory strikes like a bolt of lightning.

At first he doesn't feel the pain, but slowly the images penetrate his body, and depression soon blackens his vision. The fighter, who only an hour earlier was ready and willing, collapses as if an unbearable load has been placed on his shoulders.

When a person falls into depression, the others cautiously try to talk to him, heart to heart. Sometimes the right word revives him, but usually words are unable to free him from the snare of despair.

One of the fighters once sank into a depression so deep it seemed he was finished. All attempts to speak to him failed. His face grew grayer by the hour, and he was on the edge of collapse. Finally, one of the fighters approached and, in a voice not his own, said to him, "In the name of your mother and father, I ask you to get out of the darkness you've plunged into; we cannot permit ourselves such a loss. Your father and mother ask us to protect the widows and orphans. Depression is the invention of the devil, who tugs us away from the truth and seeks to defeat us from within." Miraculously, the words that this fighter mined from his soul took the man out of his depression, and he stood on his feet.

But success does not always smile on us. There are two fighters in our unit who suffer from prolonged depression. We keep a very close eye on them, never leaving them alone, and when we go on raids they are never in the rear.

Kamil, who is himself prone to moodiness, speaks from time to time about foul humors and depression, which impede decisive action. One must shake them off, defy them, and thwart the schemes of Satan.

"We have a great mission at this hour, to rescue the Jews from the talons of the foe and ourselves from despair. The world is filled with evil and wickedness and anarchy, but we, thank God, have not fallen into that trap. We will do everything that God has called upon us to do. The Ten Commandments are engraved in our hearts to guide us." It's scary to be around Kamil when he talks about our mission in this world. His eyes blaze, he grows taller, and he looks like one of the giants of generations past.

10

The rains limit our movement, but we're not just sitting around. Patrols and ambushes continue every night. Progress into the forest is slow but at a steady pace. If, as it now appears, we'll be staying here for the winter, we'll have to build bunkers. The winter here is fierce and merciless.

Our meals are regular: morning, noon, and evening. The food is limited but tasty, and on Friday nights we sit up late and sing: folk songs and songs of the Bund and youth movements.

Ever since we brought the books and candlesticks, the spice box and Jewish National Fund box, these Sabbath evenings are different. We see our homes in a new light. True, in most cases Sabbath candles were not lit, but when we visited our grandparents, we saw how bound they were to the God of their ancestors.

As one of the fighters has remarked, we appear to need distance in order to see what we had not seen. Karl is willing to admit that the Sabbath is an excellent Jewish invention. Sabbath removes us from capitalist slavery, and that's good enough. Any mystical component only damages this noble idea.

It now becomes increasingly clear that the controversies that raged on the Jewish street only a year ago had missed the point. No one imagined what lay in wait for us at every turn. Everyone was certain in his opinion, but no one, apart from a few pessimists, saw what was obvious. One comrade has warned us: "Don't bring any ideas from there. This territory will not tolerate them. Let's stick to what we now see and hear."

THERE'S NO DOUBT that music is good for us. Music, as opposed to speech, elevates the purest part of ourselves, does not sharpen differences but heals them. Folk songs and workers' songs blend together and instill the sense that life is not arbitrary, indifferent, or evil. Melody lifts you on its wings and takes you back to child-hood. This sweetness revives the body, but one mustn't become addicted. The enemy lies in wait for the opportune moment; he is wily and patient and will not let a single one of us get away.

Not long ago we saw from a distance a unit of Ukrainian gen-darmes chasing after a Jewish child who had escaped. The boy was quick and managed to dart into a cornfield and hide there. The German commander did not give up. He brought in more Ukrainian gendarmes, who surrounded the cornfield completely.

In the end, they caught the boy and dragged him off by his arms like a hunted animal.

When Jews are involved, even elderly gendarmes turn into fighters. We stood helplessly, shaking with fury; we were too few to come to the boy's rescue.

IT HAPPENS SOMETIMES that after a night of singing someone will stand up and speak exactly as his parents did, with the same words and intonation, as if again being the son of his father and mother.

Melodies lead to mysteries. And so, as I said, one must not become addicted. It's better to chop down trees, reinforce the tent walls, clean the weapons. Activity is preferable to introspection. After an active day, a person drops onto his pallet of twigs and falls asleep.

In the past, my dreams were often full of color. Now I throw myself onto the twigs and I sleep, disconnected from everything that was once mine. When my shift comes, they wake me and I go on guard duty or patrol.

In Kamil's tent a lamp is always burning. When he doesn't go on a raid, he sleeps with the squad that's on call. Truth to tell, he almost never sleeps. Sometimes he naps for an hour or two. He'll allow himself this only if Felix is nearby.

After a night of action without casualties, everyone is happy, especially Salo. But the medical equipment is running low. We boil the bandages for repeated use, but the iodine and other disinfectants are almost gone. There is a pharmacy in one of the big villages, about ten miles from here, that had belonged to Jews. If it turns out that this pharmacy is active, we won't hesitate to raid it, Kamil promises. One of the patrols has come very near that village but was unable to ascertain whether the pharmacy was manned and functioning. The village grocery is open, the coal depot is still in business, and there's also a flour mill that is inoperative during the fall. All of these had been owned by Jews.

Kamil and Felix have mulled this over more than once, but not enough information has been collected yet about the village, its defenders, and their weapons; Kamil would like to capture one of the farmers so he can tell us about the village and the Germans. But as of now that idea has not been carried out.

Our unit has a great treasure: Grandma Tsirl. She's ninety-three years old and weighs about as much as a ten-year-old girl, but her memory is as long as her life. The fighters constructed a sedan chair to carry her from place to place. She knows things that no one else in the group knows: the laws of Sabbath and the festivals, the laws between man and man, the laws between man and God, and of course the prayers. Moreover, she remembers the ancestors of each one of us.

Tsirl does not intervene in our activities, but if someone comes with a question, she will answer—not at length, but as necessary. She revealed to Kamil things he did not know: His grandfather's pharmacy was open on the Sabbath and festivals. He did not observe religious law and did not go to the synagogue. But in matters of charity he was scrupulous. The poor got medicine from him for free, and if a poor person needed a medical specialist, he would take him to Vienna or Prague. He was well-off but not wealthy. The poor, especially the sick ones, were welcome guests at the pharmacy. He himself, not his assistants, took care of them. When he died, there was no funeral, since he had instructed that his body be cremated outside the city. The poor and the sick came to that dreadful ceremony and stood crying for hours.

Kamil was astounded. He had never been told about the cremation. Tsirl, who generally does not interpret things, said, "Don't be shocked, my son; your grandfather wished to replace all the commandments with one commandment, which he observed with enormous devotion. One must not cast blame."

Kamil treats Grandma Tsirl with respect. When he takes time off from his many activities, he comes to sit with her. Everyone feels that she is connected to worlds we have no access to.

"My sons and daughters were gathered unto their forefathers, and I was left as a survivor. It got all mixed up; they are in the World to Come, and I'm in this world." Grandma Tsirl states this fact but does not complain. Sometimes she's sorry to be burdening us and depriving young people of food. The boy Michael also likes to sit with her. She tells him about her childhood in the village, about her parents who were farmers and strictly tithed their crop. Emperor Franz Josef would sometimes ride through town in his carriage, and Jews and non-Jews would stand at the roadside and wave.

Michael once asked her if she can see his parents.

"Why do you ask, my dear?"

"I miss them."

"If you miss them, it means they are thinking about you and will surely appear to you soon."

Most people dream; Grandma Tsirl has waking visions. Not everything she sees is uplifting. About a month ago, in the middle of the night, she asked to wake up Kamil and told him that she had just seen the wicked ones, as she called our enemies, drawing nearer to us.

Kamil did not doubt or hesitate. In a matter of minutes the camp split into three and prepared to counterattack. In under an hour their patrol was caught in a trap we had set for them. Two of them were killed, leaving us a fine haul: two automatic rifles, grenades, and many bullets.

When Kamil came to thank Grandma Tsirl, she said to him, "I'm not the one to thank. I'm nothing. What God shows me, I see."

Although everyone loves Grandma Tsirl, not everyone believes her visions. They say she has a telepathic sense, but that one mustn't rely on what she imagines. We have to know the facts, weigh them, and draw conclusions. Anyone who relies on telepathy makes blindness into a guide.

Grandma Tsirl knows that not everyone relies on her visions, and more than once she's been heard to say, "Why does God show me visions that I don't know how to convey to others?"

Most of the day she sits in her sedan chair and looks around, or naps, or blesses the wonders that surround her. If she sees visions that offer hope or a moral lesson, she tells us. About the bad ones she says, "Dreams mean nothing."

We look at her and connect with the lives we left behind. She calls me "my boy." Once she told me that in her youth my mother had been beautiful and all the male students wanted her, but she chose my father because he was quiet and not pompous. "Don't worry, my boy; your good forefathers are watching over you." Ever since she told me that, I see my grandfather Meir Yosef at night.

Once Michael asked Grandma Tsirl if she is angry with us.

"Why angry? Anger is indecent. We are commanded to love and not be angry."

"But we do not say the blessings or pray."

"The ways of the Torah are peaceful ways. He who protects widows, old people, and children observes all the laws of the entire Torah."

She's easygoing with adults and warmly welcomes children but is hard on herself. Two days a week, on Monday and Thursday, she fasts. Salo lost his temper and warned her that a woman of her age, under our trying conditions, must eat. Fasting is dangerous for her.

Grandma Tsirl took his hand in hers and said, "I have been fasting for many years and nothing happened. Fasting is like prayer."

Salo was amazed by her strong will and let her be.

Danzig brought Milio to her and asked her the meaning of his muteness. Grandma Tsirl looked at him and said, "His eyes show that he sees sights and hears sounds. It can be assumed that he saves the words and sights in his heart and won't let them go to waste. Whose child is he?"

"We found him."

"Our lawgiver Moses was also a foundling."

Danzig bowed his head, and his large body fell silent.

"Be wary of silent children; they are destined to reveal the mysteries of the earth," she said and smiled.

"What should I do?" asked Danzig quietly.

"Read him a chapter from the Book of Psalms every day."

"He doesn't understand Hebrew."

"Prayer does not require understanding, my dear."

Grandma Tsirl keeps surprising us with astonishing statements.

Ever since Grandma Tsirl told him what to do, Danzig reads Milio a psalm every day and sings him a Yiddish lullaby about a little goat. Milio pays attention to Danzig's facial expressions, and sometimes a smile crosses his lips. Now and then, to encourage him, Danzig jumps up, claps his hands, and softly sings, "Milio is a big boy; soon he will speak and sing and everyone will say, 'See how Milio speaks and sings.'"

12

The rains are devastating. The canvas tents are no defense against the wetness, but someone is watching over us. One of our patrols discovered a ruin with a roof a mile from our encampment. Kamil and Felix checked it and determined that the ceiling should be reinforced with supporting beams. But, all in all, we could find shelter there.

It appeared to be the abandoned summer home of the landlord of the forest. Some faded paintings still hung on the walls, and there was a stove in the corner. We labored all day to clean it up, and by the evening we were sitting alongside it, enjoying the warmth.

This change improved our mood. The fighters and the children sat around the stove and sang happily, and though the house was a ruin, it reminded us of the city and of the homes we left behind.

Usually we sing softly, almost in a whisper, to be on the safe side. This time our voices were stronger, and the songs were drenched in nostalgia. Grandma Tsirl told us about her childhood in the village, when heaven and earth were connected and God could be felt in every bush and tree, when a Jew stood in the midst of the field and prayed before God as a child stands before his father.

"When did the children grow distant from their father in heaven?" one of the fighters asked Grandma Tsirl.

"They didn't grow distant, my dear; they serve him in a different way. It is possible to serve God in different ways. Each generation has its own way. We must pray that God will plant thoughts in us that awaken the heart and bring us close to other people."

That same night Kamil spoke to us candidly and said, "The soldiers and gendarmes are showing no signs of fatigue, and we can assume they will keep trying to surprise us, but we will calculate our every move. We conquered the wetlands on foot, and now we know every hiding place. If they dare to come near us, we'll demolish them."

There is a quiet certainty in Kamil's voice. He gives us faith that the protectors of widows and children are superior in every way to those who seek to eliminate us. We may be few in number, but we are ready to sacrifice our lives. One's life is dear and important and must be preserved but not at any price. If women are being assaulted, one should be prepared to give up his life and not stand idly by; so, too, if the elderly are being abused. And one should sacrifice himself to prevent the murder of children. The world is enveloped in deep darkness, and we will do whatever we can to minimize that darkness.

This way of thinking is not shared by all. There are pessimists among us who see no way out. "They will not give up on killing us. The death of the Jews is their credo; they will not stop until the last Jew has disappeared."

Even though he is an introverted man who suppresses dark thoughts, Kamil does not hide from us that the enemy is determined and monstrous. But there's a good chance that we will survive, on one condition: that we know how to triumph over dark thoughts. Such thoughts must not take root in us. We have seen evil incarnate, and God has appointed us to lead the battle against it.

There are many faces to Kamil. When he speaks about evil and the war we've declared against it, he resembles a man who was silent for many years and suddenly awoke and understood what he must do. Recently we heard him tell a patrol, "You are going out tonight to combat evil. Know that you are messengers of the great Jewish faith, which from time immemorial has honored the good and despised evil. Evil is the enemy of humanity, and you are going out tonight to defeat it."

With Kamil, no deed is important or unimportant. Every deed has great significance. It's no surprise that many of us wonder where this mysterious man is leading us.

After our comrade Koba fell, there was great despair and depression among us. One of the young fighters wept and banged his head against a tree. Kamil went to him and said, "Remember what I am telling you, death is not the end."

Every time a fighter falls, our lives are diminished. As of now, three comrades have fallen. We laid them to rest, and they are buried not far from here. Only we know where. The graves are marked on Kamil's field map, and whenever we happen by the burial place, we leave wildflowers on the graves. In this silent moment we again see their young faces.

THE WETLANDS HAVE many dangers, among them forgetfulness. To overcome this, each Saturday night we hold a memorial for one fighter, or for his parents or grandparents. At first we remembered the hundreds who were taken from the ghetto and ordered to dig burial pits for themselves. Then one comrade remarked that we must not lump so many people together. Better for us to reflect on the memory of a single fighter—talk about what he did in his life or, more correctly, what he managed to accomplish—and to bond with him and his parents. Since then, every Saturday night we bond with our city and one fighter, and with his father and mother. If we forget one or two details, Grandma Tsirl helps us. Nothing escapes her memory.

Most days, and sometimes even on Saturday nights, we stick firmly to our schedule: patrols, ambushes, and raids. A raid that passes without injuries is a victory and holiday.

Usually we raid one of the outlying houses of a village. More than once, we've found armed robbers holed up in these houses, or gendarmes waiting in ambush. Having been stung in the past, we now post a lookout and collect information. Without information, we won't raid even a storeroom.

I don't want to mislead: Yes, our lives hang by a thread, but we aren't miserable. Even a small success makes us happy. Yes, there are days of setbacks, overwhelming problems, blinding despair. These have taken a heavy toll but do not undermine our will to overcome the enemy. We focus fully on our foe. In order to defeat him we are ready to grit our teeth, conquer our pain, and steel our souls for peril.

There are also miracles. Once, while on our way to raid one of the small farms, we came upon a midsize building about a mile from the farm. We broke in, and before our eyes was a breathtaking sight: sacks filled with potatoes, cabbage, and onions, and beside them sacks filled with apples, pears, prunes, and sunflower seeds.

We didn't know where to begin, how to transport this load to the base, and it was good that quiet, restrained Felix was leading the operation. He immediately ordered us to move the sacks in stages; some of us would stand guard and some would do the moving. That way, taking turns, we would take out as many sacks as possible and move them to the base.

Every return to the base is a celebration, a joyful relief. Kamil stood at the entrance and hugged every one of us. For the first time we filled Hermann Cohen's storage room to the brim with fresh produce. There were of course a few complainers who did not fail to remind us that we were engaging in theft and looting and not warfare, and that the time had come to fight those who persecute us. Yes, they say, we need supplies in order to exist, but we must not confuse existence with duty. Our duty is to fight. Every day that we don't fight is submission and acceptance. And worse: we are enabling the murders to continue. Kamil does not dismiss these claims, but he believes that for now we should patiently accumulate weapons and ammunition, entrench ourselves, and bring in more people. We must prepare for war but not commit suicide.

13

We are in the middle of the wetlands and the middle of autumn. The sky is dark even during the day. Every few feet there is a stream or bog, and a lake not far away. The ruin we'd hoped would shelter us turned out to be dangerous, and we went back to living in tents.

It's strange how this much water and the smells of the damp forest can affect you. At first you don't feel a thing; only after a few weeks do you feel the heaviness. You lean on a tree or lie down on a mat of twigs. Before long, the head grows dizzy. This isn't the dizziness of hunger or weakness: it's the start of the wetlands delirium.

A few days ago one of the fighters approached Salo and said, "I need to go home."

"Why?"

"I saw my father today, and he is very ill."

"We have no home, dear fellow. This is our home."

"Salo," said the fighter, "you're wrong. I saw my father very clearly, lying in bed, very ill. I can tell the difference between imagination and reality."

When he heard this assertion, Salo lowered his head, then raised his eyes and said, "Dear fellow—I won't keep it from you—you've got the wetlands delirium. We've all got it, to some degree. You need to tell yourself: *The base is my home. These are my friends. We are fighting together for our existence and to eradicate the evil.*"

"And I won't be able to go back home?"

"After the war, all of us will."

"And what will happen with my father?"

"The people near him will help him. We are obligated to help one another, here and there."

The fighter smiled, as if he understood something he hadn't grasped before. It was a different smile, the smile of someone with wetlands delirium.

After the conversation, the man lay down and fell asleep.

Salo saw him sleeping and said, "The wetlands delirium has hit him hard, but sleep, I assume, will calm him."

Without a doubt, the water and dampness affect us powerfully. First they attack your body, and then they play tricks with your mind, show you things you cannot change. Kamil warns us not to let the delusions drive us mad; they are as lethal as drunkenness. We must fortify the heart with simple things.

When Kamil speaks of strength and a joyful heart, you get the feeling he isn't the commander of fighters who have lost their families but a prophet training us to reach a new spiritual level.

Kamil used to say that fear is a parasitic emotion and must be erased completely. Back then his voice had a mysterious sound. But later on he became thin, his face grew hard and bony, and his eyes sank deep into their sockets. He sleeps very little. It's amazing that he keeps on going. Another man would surely collapse, lose hope, frighten his soldiers.

Kamil is not like other people. His external appearance is sometimes deceptive. He can seem distracted or lost in thought, but those who know him know he is extremely down to earth. Yes, his pragmatism has an air of mystery, but he's as solid as a rock.

He doesn't deny that a long bumpy road lies before us, but if we will learn to conquer despair, to stay fixed on our goal, and to understand that being a Jew is no small matter, we will live to see the downfall of the enemy.

Where does this clear conviction come from, people ask themselves. Once, in a burst of euphoria, he exclaimed, "Our war is not merely to stay alive. If we do not come out of these forests as complete Jews, we will not have learned a thing." It's hard to get to the bottom of his thinking. It sometimes seems that he, too, is trapped in the wetlands delirium, yet his words sound lucid, purified by experience, and the separation of body and spirit does not apply to him.

When Kamil is excitedly delving inside and striving to uplift us, Felix is curled up, asleep. His day is clearly divided: after his activities, he rests his head on a pile of twigs and falls asleep. Kamil sometimes watches him, marveling.

A true fighter needs to sleep. It cleanses his body of accumulated rubbish. Only after sleep are the legs faithful and the mind focused. This is Felix's credo in a nutshell, and he fulfills it in practice. He always exudes patience and quiet and a hint of indifference. Compared with him, we seem in constant panic. When he wakes up, he goes to the kitchen, pours himself a glass of tea, and sits down. Sometimes he lights a cigarette. He's not a compulsive smoker, unlike many of us. It's immediately apparent that sleep has renewed him.

14

A squad has raided one of the small farms about four miles from the wetlands. It was a difficult raid but without injuries. The men came back with a big haul, including several bottles of vodka, fresh bread, sugar, salt, and many other staples. We wanted to celebrate and thank them, but the fighters were exhausted and collapsed in their wet clothes.

Toward evening they finally recovered and told us that they had gotten lost on the way to the farm, got stuck in a swamp and got out with great difficulty, but once they were out, they were not far from the farm. They woke the farmers and asked them to contribute what they could out of goodwill. The farmers opened their cupboards and pantries, and it looked like they were ready to cooperate. But suddenly one of them pulled a gun from his belt and began shooting. There was no choice but to eliminate him.

Every raid is an encounter with death and with miracles, and there were raids that left us with a horror that we feel to this day. So far, I have participated in only three raids. Kamil feels that I am still young, and my place for now is with the ambushes and patrols. He's wrong; I've gotten stronger in recent months, and I have subdued the fears that troubled me. Now I am trained and quick, and I can do everything my comrades in the raiding squads do, with the same effectiveness.

I'm planning to speak to Kamil soon and ask him to include

me in all missions. Kamil knew my father and mother, and sometimes he mentions them. I hope this acquaintance will not prevent him from sending me on daring missions. Without actual raids, I will come out of this war in a state of depression. Kamil needs to understand that.

ONE OF THE RAIDERS appeared to have lost his mind—a tall, handsome guy named Sontag. At first he seemed pleased with the success of the raid, downed two glasses of vodka, and joked about the farmers who tried to outwit the squad. All that was fine, but suddenly he got up and declared, "Long live the People of Israel! No power on earth can defeat them. Moses and Aaron will lead them as they led the Children of Israel in the desert." From then on he spoke garbled sentences in various languages, recited from memory poems by Heine and Rilke, and blamed his brothers in the ghetto for not heeding his warnings and joining him. Finally, he shouted at Kamil, "Let us avenge our spilled blood!" There was a certain grandeur to his cry, as if he had freed himself from handcuffs that bound him.

Salo got down on his knees, spoke to Sontag gently, and promised him that Kamil would do everything to lead us to victory— meanwhile putting a spoonful of sedative syrup to his lips. Sontag opened his mouth like an agreeable child and swallowed the bitter liquid. He soon lay down and fell asleep.

In the end, there are no raids without injuries. For this reason the joy is incomplete. Tsila tries to overcome the sadness; she works morning, noon, and night. The pots are on the fire, and food and drink are always available. She's a first-rate cook who makes delicacies out of nothing. It's no wonder that everyone is nice to her and gladly does what she asks. She gives bigger portions to fighters, and when they go out on raids, she makes them sandwiches and fills their canteens with sweetened water.

For children and old people she prepares a special menu. Danzig brings Milio to her, and she makes him a puree of apple or pear.

Milio has been with us for several months. His face has filled out and his eyes are alert, but his mouth is still mute. Danzig reports that now and then he utters a sound, a syllable, and sometimes even a word of sorts. Many agree with Danzig that the child seems to possess special abilities that the rest of us lack. For example, Milio is only two, but he throws and catches a ball with ease and plays jacks.

"What do you mean by 'special abilities'?" asks one of the fighters.

Danzig is a bit embarrassed by the question but overcomes his embarrassment and says, "Look into his eyes, and you'll see that he comprehends more than you and I do."

"Maybe so," says the man and falls silent.

When Danzig goes on a mission, he leaves Milio with Tsila. Hermann Cohen set up a secure cradle for him between two trees, and Tsila doesn't take her eyes off him. When Danzig gets back, she says, "I'm returning your deposit."

That's how our life goes here. But there are also moments of great emotion. Last night in a waking dream I saw my father as I had not seen him for a long time: sitting at the table on the balcony, a Singer company brochure open before him. But he's not looking at it. He's looking at the garden.

Our garden isn't big, but it's full of miracles. Mama takes care of it. It has two cherry trees, an apple tree, and a pear tree. The trees are no longer young, but they blossom every year and bear fruit. The vegetables grow in two rows beside the trees: cucumbers, peas, tomatoes, onions. Every vegetable gets its own special treatment from Mama. Once she placed a basketful of cherries on the table and said, "Enjoy, children." I was momentarily surprised that she called us both children. She sat beside us and said, in a voice I hadn't heard before, "Shouldn't we make a blessing over this beautiful fruit that grew in our garden?"

Our garden makes Mama into a wondrous creature. It fills her with silence and awe, and in the evening, when she serves dinner, her eyes go wide, as if seeing us in a new light.

As Papa sits alone on the balcony and looks at the garden, he concentrates fully, seeking to absorb Mama's handiwork. The longer he sits, the more focused his gaze.

And then he suddenly pulls away, looks around, and seems to understand that Mama's world is beyond his reach, his attempt to fathom it futile. His face slowly relaxes, and a thin smile graces his lips; he's like a man who tried to penetrate a world not his own and came up with nothing. He stays at the table a long time. The smile grows smaller but doesn't disappear.

15

Time in the wetlands is a stream of thick and humid darkness. We trudge through it half blind and sometimes ask, "Where are we? What have we done till now, and what lies in store?" My father and mother, having been suddenly revealed to me, no longer show themselves. Now and then I think that our life from now on will only intensify: the darkness will deepen, the rains will turn into a torrent, and movement from place to place will be more difficult. Sometimes I have the growing feeling that, all in all, we are marching toward inevitable defeat.

The formidable army deployed along the roads and mountain ridges will not let us alone. One of these days they will decide to surround us and simply crush us. Escaping to this place is an illusion; it's self-deception. An empire that decides to destroy a people will destroy it. The empire is patient. It will let us squirm in this mud for another month, two months. Wetness and cold, not to mention disease, will put an end to us, and when the Germans arrive, they won't find human beings, just human shadows. It's too bad that we were seduced by Kamil's fantasies. It would have been better to go with all the others and not prolong the agony. The ambushes and patrols are basically childish games. The moment the army decides to destroy us, we will have nowhere to run.

One can assume that such dark thoughts occur not only to me, but no one talks about them. Kamil will not let depression gain a foothold. That's a luxury, he argues. Our fight must be unwavering and without weakness.

Do dark thoughts visit Kamil, too? He most likely secludes himself not only to read maps and plan routes of advance and escape but also to calm his agitation and suppress his sorrow. It sometimes seems that he is not merely our commander but carries each of us inside him as well, and his isolation in his tent is a communion with our secret suffering. More than once I've heard him say, "We are one soul, and we must protect it."

I sometimes think that this tall man derives his inner strength from Grandma Tsirl; he visits her regularly and hears things from her that she heard from her forefathers. She is filled with teachings and sayings of the rabbis.

Salo says her existence is miraculous; not only doesn't she eat properly, she also fasts. But she believes fiercely in this world and the next. The sight of a bright morning, a setting sun, rain pouring from the sky fill her with awe and make her as happy as a child. Kamil maintains that Grandma Tsirl should be visited at least once a day. She is the essence of the tribe.

Occasionally we forget who we are, what we were bequeathed by our ancestors, and what has happened to us in recent years. These ups and downs impair our minds, and we see nothing but darkness with no exit. Grandma Tsirl, by her very existence, is a fantastic guide. She has crossed the rivers of fire and her mind has remained whole.

Sometimes I feel that if I took part in heroic raids, dark thoughts would not afflict me. Daring action ignites the will to live, and you return to the base not merely as someone who performed his duty but as someone who defeated his fears and worries. Patrols and ambushes are inherently static. When you're patrolling or waiting in ambush, you're like a rodent rushing to find a hole to hide in, but when you go out on a raid, your very presence says death does not deter me. The body grows from moment to moment and attacks with redoubled force.

I disclosed some of my thoughts to Salo. He's thirty-seven but looks older, perhaps because of his sloping right shoulder. He is always ready to listen and will always provide a pill or spoonful of medicine to alleviate pain. Salo feels that the main thing now is to persevere. A day without casualties is a blessing.

EVER SINCE Danzig's squad brought the cartons of medicine, Salo has been of greater help. He doesn't act like an ordinary medic or doctor but like a man who is driven by his dedication to other people. "Thank God we have not lost our humanity," he always says. Once he told me, "It's too bad we don't know how to appreciate what we have. We were rescued from the talons of the beast and are able to help the weak. Why don't we know how to accept what we have with joy?"

Hearing his words I was embarrassed by my thoughts; they suddenly seemed small and selfish, and I said to myself, *I hope Kamil will assign me to the raiders so I can take part in brave actions that will train me to be devoted with heart and soul, like Salo.*

"What we are doing," Salo corrects me, "is not just marking time but making progress. We have to compare our situation here with the ghetto. In the ghetto we were subject to the malicious whims of the soldiers and police. Every week they would snatch children and grandparents and send them into the unknown. Here, a bit of our fate is in our own hands."

Salo, too, is connected with each and every one of us, especially the weak and the elderly. In the ghetto they took his wife and two daughters. Since then, his life has been devoted to others. When he speaks of our lives and those who were taken away from us, you feel he has effaced his own self.

He has uprooted the word "I" from his vocabulary and uses only "you." When he speaks to me, I feel he exists entirely for me, and everyone else feels the same way. Salo has rescued more than a few people from the jaws of death and returned them to life. He refuses the title of "resurrector" and insists that his knowledge of medicine is minuscule. He did study medicine for four years, but what he learned was incomplete, and there are areas of medicine of which he knows nothing. Everything he does, he says, is guess-work and improvisation.

That's not the opinion of others. People trust him fully. Often after a fighter recuperates from his wounds, there's a party for him and Salo, and despite his protests, people say that Salo does God's work on earth.

So it is, day after day. Kamil has decided to train us to fight in built-up areas, because the day will soon come when we will have to raid the military camps set up along the main road and in the foothills. We have to establish principles of combat so that one day, when additional fighters join us, we will have a solid set of rules.

I spoke to Kamil and asked him to include me in the big raids. "I feel ready and strong," I said.

Kamil looked at me and said, "Let me think about it."

"I feel like the patrols and ambushes demoralize me."

"Banish that feeling; a patrol is also an act of self-sacrifice. Everything we do in this land is self-sacrifice. Only in due course will we know what we have accomplished."

"I'm sorry," I replied. I didn't know what else to say.

"You did nothing wrong, my boy; there's no reason to apologize. I'll think about your request."

16

The darkness of autumn grows deeper every day and threatens to engulf us. Kamil believes this foul weather works to our advantage. The army won't risk attacking us. And yet, to be on the safe side, we don't stay long in one place. Movement in the muddy ground is heavy going, but we step quickly, as we were trained to do.

The summit is our destination. The summit sits high on a cliff, and the climb is steep. On a clear day it looks like a wide cone, its walls covered with thick moss. We'll set up our base there and build bunkers. One squad went up to survey the summit and confirmed that the approach from all sides is difficult, but the panoramic view is clear and amazingly beautiful.

Kamil knows this mountaintop. In his youth he camped there with other students who dreamed of making a better world. Danzig was also supposed to join that group, but for some reason it didn't work out.

It will take time for us to reach the summit. The rain, mud, and cold deaden the soul. But in daylight the visibility is good, and you feel you are doing your duty and even a bit more.

Michael comes and sits beside me. The boy and I haven't yet had a conversation. He shows all the signs of an educated, privileged upbringing; even his tattered clothes fit well. Maxie, his tutor, doesn't stop praising him for how quickly he learns; someday he will become a famous mathematician or physicist. I love to observe his unhurried gaze. He pays attention to detail, to the colors and contours of the landscape.

Does he comprehend our situation? "Without a doubt," claims Maxie, yet Michael often says of his parents, "Immediately after the war they'll come to get me." These words always startle us and break our hearts.

Michael surprises me and asks, "What do you want to study at university?"

"I haven't yet decided," I say, though I should probably have mentioned that because of the war I hadn't finished the *gymnasium*.

"And what do you want to study?" I turn the question back to him.

"I want to be a veterinarian, like Papa," he says with delight.

"Do you have animals at home?"

"Lots of them," he quickly replies. "Papa finds them in the street and brings them home, and whoever wants to adopt them comes to us."

"And do you have a dog of your own?"

"I do. A collie; his name is Niko. I assume our neighbors are taking care of him. He's a sweet and smart dog, and everyone loves him."

"He sleeps in your room?"

"Yes, he wakes me up in the morning."

I love the way Michael stands. Every time he mentions his father, his eyes light up. He recalls his mother in a different way. "Mama reads me bedtime stories. I love stories, and Mama loves to tell stories. Papa knows how to talk to animals, but telling bedtime stories is hard for him."

"What does your mother do?"

"Mama is a teacher, and in the morning we go to school together. Mama doesn't teach my class, but I see her during recess. Sometimes I go to her."

As he speaks, I get the feeling he's still there, with his father and mother, studying or playing with the animals in his yard. When he sits by my side, I am deeply touched.

Michael doesn't speak about his parents in the past tense but like someone who went to summer camp and expects his parents to come and pick him up.

"It's boring for you here with us," I say, to goad him.

"No. Maxie teaches me arithmetic and geometry, and soon we'll start learning French."

I remember myself at Michael's age, walking with Mama to the flower market or the clothing store to be outfitted for summer. Swimming in the River Prut has already begun. A fat sun sinks over the gazebo. This memory removes me for a moment from my routine and returns me to our house and its surrounding streets.

It is clear to me that I will not be forgiven for what I did to my parents in the past year. Will I ever be able to repair what I ruined?

17

Last night Kamil attached me to one of the squads that is soon to go on a raid. He's noticed that in recent weeks I've gotten stronger. In training I'm often quicker than my friends, and my time has come to participate in a daring raid. Until now I've taken part only in patrols and ambushes and minor raids. This period of time, I must admit, prepared me for the trials ahead.

I went to Grandma Tsirl. Grandma Tsirl knew my parents personally, as well as my grandparents and even great-grandparents. She calls my mother "my little Bunya." My mother was a late-in-life child, beloved by everyone. Her sisters were pretty and smart, but my mother, Grandma Tsirl told me, was beautiful. In addition, she graduated from the *gymnasium* with honors.

When you're alongside Grandma Tsirl, it's as if you're back home, and life is not broken and arbitrary. Even our trudge through the mud is not meaningless.

"What are you doing, my son?" she asked.

"What everyone is doing."

She looked at me and said, "You will tell future generations what these despicable people did to us. Don't be caught up in details; get under the surface. Details, by their nature, confuse and conceal. Only the core endures."

I was shocked and I said, "I don't understand what you're saying, Grandma Tsirl."

"Did I say something that isn't clear?"

"All the same, I don't understand."

"I will explain: Your grandfather, of blessed memory, was a *sofer,* a religious scribe, like his father. I remember him wrapped in a prayer shawl, bent over the parchment and writing with great devotion. I would stand outside his window and watch him work. As I did so, I understood the meaning of the Hebrew words *hamavdil bein kodesh lekhol,* the One who separates the holy from the mundane. When your grandfather was writing, he was totally holy. Your father, like most of his generation, did not walk in his father's path, but the angel of poetry watched over him. He wrote poems of longing. Everyone was surprised that a prominent lawyer, who represented big companies, wrote poems of longing. I was not surprised. The soul of his holy father, your grandfather, sang within him. Those who looked at him closely could see that his eyes drifted into higher worlds, even when he worked on temporal matters. Four generations of writers have preceded you, my dear, but you have seen so much in your short life; you must tell future generations where they came from and where they are going. If one knows where from, one knows where to."

"Grandma Tsirl, writing is very hard for me. Even writing a letter is hard."

"A person doesn't know what's hidden inside him until he works at it."

"I want to be a fighter, not a writer."

"My dear, a person's fate is not always in his own hands. Forgive me for telling you about the past and guessing about the future. Believe me, had I not been shown what I see, I would lock my lips with seven locks."

I stood up.

"I see you've grown tired of my talking."

I wanted to say, "I'm not tired," but the words didn't come out of my mouth.

THAT NIGHT ONE of the fighters read a few verses from the Book of Numbers. We spoke about the purification before entering the Promised Land. The idea of purification took hold in a few hearts, perhaps because of the words of Kamil, who spoke of purifying ourselves for the life awaiting us after the war. In his opinion, we will be privileged to witness the downfall of the enemy and the final victory. The question is whether we will be worthy of this. Doubt and despair must not be allowed to infect us with their poison. We have a great obligation. We are not fighting for the body alone.

"We are what we are," remarked one of the fighters.

"We must be more than that; we have seen evil incarnate," Kamil insisted. "To be silent means standing on the side. We have come here to fight against the worst evil, and we will not give up."

One of the fighters again asked what the religious rites of ancient times had to do with us. Purification is not relevant to modern man. If a person believes in God, so be it. But as for us, faith does not dwell within us.

Kamil listened attentively. The fighter's voice was clear and understandable and inevitably exposed a few of our hidden collective thoughts. For a moment it seemed that Kamil would rise to his feet, gather his words, and shape them into a manifesto, as he occasionally does. But this time he sat hunched over, like a man gone mute.

One of the fighters, who had never expressed his opinion publicly, suddenly burst loudly into tears. His wailing shook us all. *What's happened? What's happened?* Everyone reached out to him. But the man did not respond; his whole being wept. Even Salo, whose words are always soothing, stood beside him silently. The man's weeping grew stronger, as if he had just realized what we had lost.

So it goes here from time to time. The weeping is usually pent up, but when it breaks out, it comes in great waves. One time Tsila, the strong and friendly woman who feeds us tasty food and lifts our spirits, broke down into muffled weeping and trembled all over. This happened on a day when nothing much was going on. Danzig went into the kitchen with Milio in his arms and asked for some soup. Tsila looked at Milio and said he was adorable and making progress, and that there was no reason for worry. He will speak not only in syllables but in complete sentences. Every child develops in a different way.

Suddenly, for no visible reason, Tsila burst into tears, a silent crying that shocked us. Salo and Maxie arrived at once, hugged her, and sat her down on a crate. She shook for a long time. Finally, she quieted down, opened her eyes, and asked, "What happened to me?"

And once, on the way back from a mission, one of the fighters began to cry, quietly, inaudibly. Only Felix, whose ear is alert to every sound, picked up his stifled weeping. He immediately ordered us to lay our packs and bundles on the ground, got down on his knees, and asked the fighter what happened. The man was unable to answer. It was good that Salo was with us. He took an empty medicine dropper from his pack and squeezed some air into the fighter's mouth. After a few minutes, the color returned to his face.

What would we do without Salo? His tent is open day and night, and when a mission seems especially dangerous, he is included in the squad. Grandma Tsirl says to beware of doctors. But not of Salo: the angel Raphael, the healer, lives within him.

18

We move on toward the high, dry places, to the summit. We proceed cautiously, ever on the alert, bedeviled by many problems. For good reason the wetlands are called "a land that devours its inhabitants."

Last night I took part in an attack not far from the base, on an enemy patrol that had followed us. We attacked along with a squad that covered for us, but in the end it was a limited success. The enemy patrol was able to retreat with its wounded, leaving behind a rifle and two magazines. One of our fighters was lightly wounded in his arm.

Again, it's clear: they are not letting us be. The weather and the swamps do not prevent them from tracking us. If we had considered cutting back on our patrols and ambushes and making raids far away from the base, it's becoming increasingly clear that we won't be able to do so. They will not easily give up on a handful of Jews. For good reason Kamil repeats that the war is at a climax and we must redouble our efforts.

We captured the deputy manager of the railroad station. Felix interrogated him about military deployment in the area and the movement of trains, about collaborators and the Jews remaining in the area.

He was frightened. Felix calmed him down and promised that no harm would come to him if he would tell us the truth. In reply to Felix's question, he confirmed that the army is no longer an arrogant conqueror, as in the past. The officer in command of the civilian population has lost interest in the affairs of the local government. A month ago they were still looking for Jews who were hiding among the population. Now they've stopped. As for the trains: civilian transport has been reduced; most of the trains are now filled with soldiers, weapons, and ammunition. There are still a few Jews in the work camps. The weak and sick are killed. There are no longer any Jews in the villages. Families that had hidden Jews are no longer willing to take the risk, and they hand over the Jews who had been hiding in their homes. A family man who had hidden Jews was executed in the village square.

So ended the formal part of the interrogation. The deputy station manager grew more relaxed and provided a long and convoluted answer to Felix's question about who was now living in the houses of the Jews. "Populating the abandoned homes was not handled fairly. People with connections, the ones who host officers in their homes, who throw parties and orgies, got the fancy houses. The simple houses and apartments were taken by the bullies. The fair and honest people got nothing. That's how the world has always worked."

He spoke with infuriating calm, as if he'd forgotten he was speaking about people who had been murdered and that distributing the spoils was a continuation of the killing.

"All the houses are inhabited now?" asked Felix, not raising his voice.

"All of them."

"And what will happen if the Jews come back?" Felix asked, in a different tone of voice.

"They won't come back," the man was quick to answer.

"Why?"

"Because they were murdered and buried in the forest," he said blandly.

"Damn murderers," Felix muttered, losing patience.

"It is God's will, what can you do," the deputy station manager replied sanctimoniously.

He apparently didn't realize that Felix was a Jew. Felix speaks Ruthenian like a native. His years of service to the Communist Party, of organizing and distributing propaganda in the villages, made him into a Ruthenian. The charm of it wore off just a few years ago. Since then, Felix has been a different person, say people who knew him well.

"What do you think about murdering Jews?" Felix asked coldly.

"What can I say; it's God's will."

Felix was about to let out a curse, but the commander in him would not allow it.

After a brief negotiation, the men agreed that in two weeks' time they will meet again in these woods. Felix explained that it was best to aid the freedom fighters, since the Russian Army was approaching, and whoever helped the fighters would be rewarded. At the same time he warned the deputy station manager that while the partisans are generous and would not harm honest people, traitors, informers, and collaborators would not be forgiven.

The man listened, extended his hand to Felix, and said, "I will come to this place in two weeks; you have my word."

19

Kamil and Felix prepare us for a long, arduous stay, a period that will change us. I work hard to excel in training, to get stronger and someday be a squad commander. But there are days when I feel alone, forgotten, lost in the darkness that wraps around us like a thick robe that does not keep us warm. At those times I feel that our inner journey is a process of forgetting and that soon I won't remember anything that was once mine.

But opportunities for such thoughts are limited. Last night we went on a raid a few miles from the base. It was a big and complicated raid, and I took part. At first we were able to circumvent a dangerous swamp, but later we found ourselves trapped in thick reeds that enclosed us on all sides. Squad commander Danzig, a superb navigator, maintained his wits, and we finally found a strip of land that led us to a mountain ridge and a pair of houses on which our patrols had gathered much intelligence.

The information was this: In the big, elongated house live the parents and their younger son. In the adjacent house live the older son, his wife, and his two small children.

The raid was swift and took them by surprise. We conducted a search and took what we needed from the cupboards. The mother fainted from the shock. One of us spoke to her gently and promised her that when victory comes she will merit special consideration for supporting the freedom fighters.

The woman roused herself and cried out, "Bless you, bless you, brothers, may God protect you in all your endeavors." The married son at first refused to cooperate, but in the end he did as he was ordered and showed us the way to the storeroom.

We stocked up on supplies: sugar, salt, dried fruit, dairy products, wheat flour, and corn flour. We returned to base observing all the rules of retreat: those who carried the goods walked first, and the others protected them on high alert. More than one mission has failed on the way back. Now we are extra careful.

We returned before dawn, exhausted and filthy, but I was proud of myself. It pains me that my parents aren't here to take pride in me. The booty we took was very valuable. Kamil went from fighter to fighter and hugged each one.

Afterward, we were graced by sunshine that warmed me and dried my clothes somewhat. I slept till late afternoon. In my sleep I was at home, leaning over the blue ceramic stove. Through the curtain of sleep, I heard my father wanting to know what had happened to me since he'd last seen me, but Mama didn't let him wake me up. When I woke up, the day was fading and growing cold, but the heat of the ceramic stove felt good, and I was happy that my parents, the house, and the stove were still standing.

All of a sudden, the spirit came over Kamil, and he spoke about our forefathers and the God of our forefathers, with whom we must connect. Denial had eroded our best qualities, Kamil said, and we had reached rock bottom. We couldn't believe our ears. He didn't seem like the commander who had led us through hostile forests and strangling swamps but like a spiritual leader flooded with faith.

The veteran fighters do not think as Kamil does. A thin trail of fog always accompanies his words. But there are people who interpret his states of mind as wings that propel his bold actions. Now he is talking more and more about denial, alienation, abandoning the wellsprings of life, international movements that eat us up inside. Without our forefathers and the God of our forefathers, our lives hang by a thread.

This tall and powerful man—who leads his soldiers in daring raids, who knows the map of this region like the palm of his hand—is transformed at night, when he is joined to words and phrases whose sounds frighten us.

Tonight Kamil spoke about the great Russian writers: Gogol, Dostoevsky, and Tolstoy, whose thinking was ahead of their time. They understood that there is no existence without faith. Their writing is an icon of Russian Orthodoxy. It is only we who have abandoned our beliefs, followed foreign creeds, and have thus forgotten who we are and what our place is in this world. Dostoevsky, Kamil said, should be read chapter by chapter, paragraph by paragraph, the way religious books are read.

Several fighters ran out of patience, and one shouted at him, "You want to do the impossible. The connection with the ancestral god has been broken once and for all. You can't connect what can't be connected. We've gone into the mountains not to receive new tablets but to save our lives. Protecting life is an important value, and revenge is not without value. To connect with the old beliefs that led us to the ghetto and the camps—this is an unforgivable sin. This is not a time for mystical delusions. Yes, we have been mortally wounded, and the pain is enormous, but we will not bandage the wounds with false bandages. We need iodine to disinfect the wounds, not whispered words."

Kamil did not respond. He sat leaning on his hands, hearing the accusations as if baring his back to the whip. There was no one that night lonelier than he. For a moment it seemed as though he was about to break down, lay his weapon on the ground, and say, *I can see that my faith is not to your liking. I have no desire to argue; there is no point in arguing about faith. If you lack confidence in me, it's best I leave, go on my way and to my fate, and you do what your heart tells you to do.*

Instead, he did not utter a sound.

Hermann Cohen was able to defuse the confrontation. Though he is no longer young, his mind is as quick as a young man's. He reminded the accusers that were it not for the inspiration of Kamil, who led us step by step, from hill to hill, avoiding traps, we would not be here. "Let Kamil finish the work until victory comes," he said.

Although Hermann Cohen spoke with old-fashioned moderation, his words were strangely effective. I've already learned: Strong words don't always sway the mind. It's often practical, logical, colorless language that works its way into the heart's hidden recesses.

This may be the place to mention one of our men who is neither seen nor heard—Reb Hanoch by name.

Reb Hanoch has been blind since birth, and all his life made a living by knitting and basket weaving. In his youth he married a blind young woman, and they had three intelligent children. In one of the last *aktions,* the blind were rounded up and sent in carts to the train station. Reb Hanoch fell out of his cart and lay in a ditch till nightfall. Then he got up and, luckily, was noticed by Kamil, who was looking for fugitives and brought him to us.

Reb Hanoch is one of the founders of our base. He knits stocking caps, scarves, gloves, and socks. All the fighters are pleased and praise his handiwork. There's nothing like a stocking cap to rescue the ears from the bitter cold. Reb Hanoch knows our needs and works day and night.

Sometimes he asks if there's any news from home.

"Let's hope for the best" is the answer.

"They already sent everybody off to the camps?"

"Apparently so."

"Have any letters arrived from the camps?"

"Not yet."

The men respect his blindness and don't hide the truth from him.

Every few hours Reb Hanoch stops his work, stands up, and prays. His prayers have a unique melody. Kamil goes into his tent now and then and tells him that his hats and socks save people every day. Hearing his words, Reb Hanoch says with a smile, "May we all be privileged to perform the commandments."

20

We will not forget the night Kamil spoke about the tribe and the God of the tribe. His words echo to this day. It's hard to escape the thought that the man leading us in this dangerous territory is motivated by ideas that make us uneasy, even scare us.

People still remember that at the beginning of the journey Kamil was like anyone else, without highs and lows. His moods appear to have changed during the journey. His face, in any case, has changed; more and more he resembles a Christian monk.

If doubts remained, it is now clear: Kamil wants to instill in us the feeling that it is impossible to fight a determined enemy without love of the tribe, its God, and its beliefs. These three concepts, separately and together, drive people crazy.

"Commander," one bold fighter shouted on that night, "take pity on yourself and us and get these delusions out of your head."

After that, Kamil secluded himself in his tent and handed the command to his deputy. His absence was hard for us. I sometimes feel that our opposition demoralizes him and that he prefers to be alone and see no one.

Following a few days of isolation Kamil returned to the children and the elderly and Grandma Tsirl.

DANZIG HAS INFORMED Kamil that Milio's progress in recent weeks has been surprising. "He looks at me attentively and asks me with his eyes to sing him the lullaby of the little goat."

Milio is no longer frightened when a fighter wants to hold him in his arms, and when Kamil asked to hold him, Milio smiled and agreed.

"What else does he do?" asked Kamil with curiosity.

"He watches. He can sit for hours and look at things."

That same night Kamil led a patrol to the lake to catch some fish for dinner. His determined expression was back. He checked the fighters' weapons and ordered two men to switch their heavy coats for lighter ones. Every outing with him has a fateful air but also a sense of confidence that Kamil has the power to strike fear in our enemies.

They returned with a big haul. Tsila and her friend Miriam quickly set about preparing the fish for dinner, and Hermann Cohen built two fires to roast them. We sang till late at night, and there was a feeling of togetherness, that we should not speak ill of others and must honor a commander of the caliber of Kamil, even if we do not agree with his opinions.

ON SATURDAY NIGHT we didn't go out on a mission. We sat around the campfire, and our comrade Sontag felt moved to tell us about his grandparents' village: about the long pastures that reach to the horizon, and his grandfather and grandmother sitting at dusk on the veranda, watching the light change colors. They don't speak, and their silence is uncomfortable, as if this evening was not similar to the previous evening but, instead, something they had never experienced before. They love this stretch of land in the foothills, which changes its face with every season.

"I would come there twice a year," Sontag said, "at Passover and on summer vacation. Sometimes in the winter, too, at Hanukkah. The passage from city to country, from tumult to quiet, from explicit to implicit, left me speechless. During my first years of *gymnasium*, the village seemed remote and primitive—a word we often used, not always fairly. I didn't understand their way of life. I thought their lives lacked consciousness—another word we relied on now and then.

"Only in my last year of *gymnasium* did I suddenly discover the interior and exterior rhythm of their lives, the way they merged completely with the seasons, their capacity for wonder but more than that—their capacity for gratitude. They always spoke softly, their heads lowered, eyes downcast. And suddenly my ideas and those of my friends seemed shallow. We were creatures of the intellect, without simplicity and genuine vitality.

"Once my grandma asked me if I prayed. I couldn't lie to her, and I said no. She didn't respond or ask anything more. I didn't know what else to say and foolishly added, 'In the city they don't pray.' She didn't respond to that, either.

"That was my last conversation with her. Who knows where my grandparents are now? Last night I dreamed about them and asked their forgiveness. They were surprised by my request, and Grandpa said, 'What do you mean? You always brought us joy. We couldn't wait to see you. We would look at you and ask ourselves which of our relatives you looked like, and both of us, Grandma and I, decided you looked like Uncle Efraim—the same features and facial expression.'

"I started to say to him, 'Grandpa, I'm from the city, and the turmoil of the city is in my bones,' but Grandpa ignored me and repeated, 'You look like Uncle Efraim.'

"Uncle Efraim lived in a small village, ran a small general store, and was regarded as an expert in herbal remedies. Everyone trusted his medicines and concoctions. The farm wives would bring produce to barter, but most people came and received his advice and medicines without paying a penny. Uncle Efraim never complained. Whenever he heard that the advice or medicine was effective, his eyes filled with joy and gratitude. In his village it was said of a good man that he had a soul like Efraim's. I don't know what resemblance my grandparents saw between me and Uncle Efraim. Uncle Efraim was a simple man who worshipped God with awe and happiness.

"I don't know why I told you this," said Sontag, lowering his head, close to tears.

THE NEXT DAY we left the swampy hillside and began the climb toward the summit. The climb is winding and slow, half a mile each day, sometimes less. According to the plan, if there are no storms we'll reach the top in two weeks' time.

If at the start of the journey we didn't know where Kamil would lead us, there is now a feeling that we're fighting not only for our lives but also for the others who will join us. This feeling, inspired by Kamil, gives us hope that we will witness the collapse of the kingdom of evil.

Ever since we left the swamps, Grandma Tsirl seems to speak through a veil. A few days ago she said to one of the fighters, who complained of nightmares, "You deserve innocent sleep. I assume your holy ancestors will protect you and your sleep."

Every utterance is cloaked in words that belong only to her. Her ancestors are embedded in her frail body, and they speak from her throat. More than once I've heard her say, "Indeed, they will speak; they will say it better than I do." When her ancestors speak through her, her face lights up and a subtle smile plays upon her lips.

One time she surprised me and said, "I don't know what to tell you. I will ask the forefathers and they will tell me."

Grandma Tsirl does not speak every day. Most days she is enclosed within herself and seems to be drowsing. This is merely on the surface: she is actually on the alert, and whenever she senses danger nearby or someone from the World to Come wishing to speak to her, she wakes up.

IN EARLY EVENING we reach one of the highest peaks—a stop on the way to the summit. We unload the sacks and packs, and a magnificent vista appears before us: forests upon forests and magical, silvery bodies of water. And we have the feeling that at last we have freed ourselves from the sticky mud and the prying eyes of our enemies. From now on we will control a big territory, and if they dare to come close, they'll be struck by our fire.

Kamil reminds us that here, too, we will have to live with our wits about us. The enemy does not relax, and all indications are that they take a long view. They calculate our every move. Our enemy is not like other enemies. Their great war does not let them neglect even one of us. Look at the effort they expend to catch us. How important we must be to them.

There are fighters who love the daytime Kamil: the one of training and fiery talk of the future, when more fugitives will come to join us, when the shared pain will forge a magnificent force. And there are people who love the Kamil of the night: when he is bent over a text, speaking of nuances, seeking the music, examining a sentence or a word. It seems then that it's not a military man sitting before us but a man who possesses the word, the sound of the word, in his soul. At night, even if we're exhausted, Kamil manages to arouse in us the ancient hunger for the text. At night Kamil has epiphanies that he will not voice in the light of day.

It sometimes seems that Kamil draws on Jewish sources passed down to him by Martin Buber and Franz Rosenzweig. And sometimes he seems connected with Russian literature, with Dostoevsky as his spiritual mentor.

One of the fighters approached him and said, "I apologize for what happened."

"What are you talking about?"

"The debate we got into."

"As long as I am commander, soulful speaking is free."

We were puzzled by the expression "soulful speaking," but no one asked what he meant.

I got a stocking cap from Reb Hanoch. He placed his hands on my head and blessed me. I left his tent, put on the cap, and felt the power of his blessing.

21

The boy Michael will never forget the train station lit by dozens of searchlights. A mass of people uprooted from their homes, among them his father and mother, lost in the teeming yard. Soldiers gone wild, whipping people's backs and shooting. Moans of pain and grief rose like waves from piles of humans and toppled those still standing.

Michael's father pleaded with him to run away to their servant Diana. The mother joined the plea. Suddenly, the beloved parents seemed to distance themselves.

"I'm afraid." The words flew from his lips.

"Please go to Diana." His father ignored his fears.

Michael finally tore himself away and ran to the darkened tracks. He knew the way to Diana's house, but the darkness and the terror blotted out his memory of the address. He thought he was lost and would be seized and crushed at any moment by the soldiers.

When he left the station, the fields were completely dark. He sat down and hoped for a stiff wind to lift him up and return him to his parents.

He recovered, stood up, and kept walking. It was fallow land, filled with prickly bushes. Lights flashing from afar blinded him. He was angry that his beloved father and mother had sent him away so abruptly, and therefore he thought that Diana would also not be pleased to see him.

As he stood wondering where to turn, a man came near. Certain that this was the end, he got down on his knees.

To his surprise, the tall man knelt down, too, and asked his name. Michael answered him.

"My name is Maxie," the tall man said. "Don't be afraid; come with me."

They walked for an hour, maybe two.

The base was small then and looked like the summer camp of a youth movement. A few tents, a pot hanging over a pale fire. Michael doesn't remember many details about those first days. He remembers the first slice of bread with oil that Tsila gave him. He didn't think about his parents. Their pleading with him to go to Diana had cut him off from them.

From that night onward Michael has been with Maxie. When Maxie goes out on a mission, Michael can't fall asleep. He eagerly waits for Maxie's return before dawn.

Hermann Cohen turned a crate into a table and a smaller crate into a chair. Michael sits and copies verses from the Bible and from Martin Buber's collection of Hasidic stories. At night he hands out the pages to the study group. Maxie teaches him arithmetic and geometry. Michael excels at arithmetic and will soon start to study geography and French. Maxie promises that when Michael returns to school, he will skip at least one grade.

"When will the war be over?" Michael asks every so often.

"Soon, I assume," Maxie answers casually. "Do you miss your home?"

"Yes."

"All of us do, and we want to go home, but until then we have to do our duty."

"What is my duty?" Michael asks.

"To learn."

Michael feels good here; he's everybody's child. Once in a while the fighters come upon a packet of chocolates or halvah. It is divided at once between Michael and Milio, and everyone is happy for the joy of the children.

Were it not for the nights, the vivid nightmares that come night after night, Michael's days would be quiet. In the nightmares he sees his father and mother standing in the railroad station, kneeling under the whips of the soldiers. In the first months he saw their faces; now he sees their bent-over bodies falling heavily.

Once he asked Maxie if the dreams were true.

"Do you dream a lot?" Maxie tried to avoid an immediate answer.

"Yes."

Maxie tries to speak to Michael in terms he can understand and does not talk of horrors. This time he ventured to ask, "What do you dream about?"

"About the train station."

"Is it scary?"

"Very scary. Are my parents still standing in the train station?"

"No. They left a long time ago."

"And where are they now?"

"It's hard to know. I presume they're with all the others."

"Are they working?"

"I would assume so."

These are tough questions for Maxie, but Michael doesn't relent. He wants to know what kind of work they do and when they will be freed.

But he doesn't ask so urgently every day. Most of the time he's deeply involved in arithmetic and geometry and dictation. Maxie watches him concentrate and says to himself, *Only with such diligence can a person achieve anything.*

What to reveal to Michael and what to conceal, this, too, is a subject of controversy. One of the fighters voiced his opinion that

Michael should be told that the people at the station were sent to death camps.

"To tell the whole truth?" Maxie said anxiously.

"Only the truth."

"Michael is only eight and a half."

"But wise enough to understand what is happening around him."

Maxie feels differently: he believes that the naked truth will do the child no good. Things will become clear to him eventually; why deprive him of even one day of childhood? Every day that the child lives in his own world is a blessing.

"That's the wrong approach."

"I think it's fine," Maxie insisted.

Maxie is a quick and nimble soldier but a patient man, slow to anger. He answers Michael's questions without adding "and that's the truth," or "that's the real truth," the way some fighters talk.

Michael has learned not to ask too many questions. Everyone is busy, working in the storehouse or training with his squad. Kamil is strict about the schedule, and training for the raids is a daily routine.

One of the fighters again remarks, "We've turned from people who were trained to fight an armed enemy into a bunch of bandits who live off stolen booty."

Kamil's plan that, when the time comes, we will attack the military camps around the wetlands is for now an imaginary plan. We are too few, and it's impossible to leave the weak unguarded. Only if other fighters join us will we be able to engage in direct combat.

In the meantime, we continue to raid private homes and small farms. These are disgraceful raids: We wake a family up in the middle of the night and demand that they hand over their food and clothing or face the consequences. The farmers usually understand that there's no point in arguing with an armed squad, and they give us what we ask for, but there are farmers who refuse or suddenly draw a pistol, and then we must act in self-defense.

These raids, it must be said, are not uplifting. For good reason the fighters return to the base drained and depressed. Kamil reassures them. "The action was successful, beyond expectations. The goods you brought will feed the base for a week. Our war is not for booty but to save people and smash the monster. For now we are preparing the fortress. The fighters will go out from here to destroy the enemy."

"Where will the soldiers come from?" says a doubting voice.

"The same place we came from."

It's hard to argue with Kamil's powerful beliefs. Kamil's highs, it sometimes seems, flow from his lows. We know very little about his lows. Sometimes he hands the command over to Felix and withdraws to his tent. Now and then a voice is heard from inside. It's hard to guess what he is talking about, or to whom. Even his deputy Felix, who sometimes enters the tent, doesn't know.

THERE'S A SURPLUS of mushrooms, and Tsila energetically cooks tasty dishes. It's marvelous what this tiny woman can do. The dishes remind us of home, but Tsila adds flavors of her own. Even her corn or semolina porridge has a new flavor. Kamil has said that even after the liberation we'll come to Tsila so she can treat us to her food. Who could have imagined that here, of all places, far from any home or restaurant, we would eat such delicacies. Tsila, for her part, does not boast about her handiwork, sometimes simply saying, "Just bring me the basics, and I'll make them into a meal."

There are people here who know what she has gone through, but nobody talks about it. Tsila is consumed by doing. Her hands race from pot to pot, and at first glance she does not look like a bereaved mother.

22

The days do not pass simply. Every day brings a problem or disappointment, not to mention a disaster. Kamil is as sturdy as a stone wall. The enemy may be cruel and merciless, but we have our values. If a farmer refuses to give us food willingly, we will not beat or kill him. We will take what we need without anger. Kamil's pronouncements always contain a word or phrase that stays in our heads for hours.

Ever since he escaped from the ghetto, the fighter Paul had wanted to go to the village of Holovka, to which his wife had fled with her Ukrainian lover. If she had fled alone, he would probably have uprooted her from his heart, but she ran off with his beloved daughter, and his life has not been worth living ever since.

Paul spoke privately with Kamil several times about this painful matter. Kamil did not reject his request to send a squad to Holovka to rescue his daughter. At a certain point he even trained a squad for this mission, but the information we had gathered about the village and its surroundings indicated a large supply of weapons; it was doubtful whether a squad, even two squads, could defeat an armed mob.

"Let's wait and see," Kamil said. "If conditions change and we have more fighters, I won't hesitate to send a whole platoon. Paul, your daughter is precious to us. If we succeed in rescuing her, it will be a victory to celebrate."

Kamil's clear message seemed acceptable to Paul. His pale blue eyes widened, and he said, "I appreciate your readiness, Commander, and eagerly await the moment when we'll start the mission." There was a formality in his voice that suggested a temporarily suppressed anguish, but nobody else noticed this nuance.

Paul went out on a few daring missions and won the praise of his immediate commander—and, of course, of Kamil as well. But in the interludes between missions, he would sulk alone, chain smoking. Salo would occasionally invite him for a glass of tea, but Paul didn't open up to him.

Everyone knew what was weighing on this impressive man, but no one knew how to help him. Salo gave him aspirin from time to time for his headaches. Kamil, seeing his distress, would also approach him now and then and say, "Paul, what you requested has not been forgotten. I'm waiting for more people to join us. The first major raid will be on the village of Holovka. Don't torment yourself; I have a feeling we'll be doing this soon."

More and more, Paul withdrew into himself. It sometimes seemed that he was plotting the details of a raid on that village. But most days he was busy like the rest of us with training, raids, and work at the base. On one of the study evenings, he spoke with bitter emotion about the individual who refuses to surrender to the will of the collective. "The individual ego is a big obstacle. It is gripped by alien motives and ambitions." It was clear that he was angry with himself for his inability to overcome his selfishness at this fateful moment.

Even as Paul's problem festered like an open wound, the squads went out on a series of raids. The approaching cold weather compels us to stock up on food and warm clothing. Who knows what the winter will bring. It's best to prepare in advance and be ready in time. Paul took part in all the raids.

The last one was the most successful. In the early morning the fighters returned, bearing many essentials. Everyone was happy to see them. Danzig reported on everything that had happened on their way to the target and on the way back.

After a special breakfast prepared by Tsila, they went to sleep. Paul slept deeply. When he awoke, his face was wrinkled and he looked dissatisfied. He poured himself a cup of tea, sat down, and chain smoked. Tsila offered him another sandwich, but Paul refused her with a wave of his hand.

Later he sat off to the side, lost in himself, and for a moment he seemed still fatigued from the raid and in need of sleep. That was an illusion. He approached Hermann Cohen and asked if the cheeses had arrived intact. Hermann Cohen confirmed that they had arrived well packed, were already stored in jars, and at dinner everyone would get a slice. And he quickly added, "Thank you, Paul."

"Don't thank me; it was a collective activity."

"Soon I'll go to each man and thank him," said Hermann Cohen in a fatherly tone.

In late afternoon Salo went over to Paul. Paul reported that during the action he lost his wristwatch and that from now on he'd have to get used to living without one. Salo asked for details of the mission and Paul supplied them. He concluded by saying, "The mission was successful, only I'm not so successful." He chuckled softly, exposing his front teeth.

When darkness fell and the soup pots were already set up in Tsila's kitchen, Paul stood up and faced the forest. At first it seemed as if he rose to listen to the night sounds, as he sometimes did, but then he went deep into the darkness and disappeared from my view.

I felt I should call out "Paul!" And so I shouted and shouted again, but Paul did not reply.

Without delay I ran to Kamil and told him what I had seen. Kamil immediately ordered the two squads on duty to fan out and find Paul.

We stayed awake all night. The men drank soup and finished

their rations of cigarettes. Paul's sudden disappearance hit us like lightning. We had the gnawing suspicion that he might go out on his own to the village of Holovka to rescue his daughter, but everyone had hoped that a squad commander like him would overcome his painful humiliation and not endanger himself in a hopeless mission.

Rain had fallen. The fighters returned after midnight wet and empty-handed. The riddle of Paul's disappearance grew by the hour. Kamil looked worried. This time his intuition had misled him. Paul was a superb squad commander. He introduced a new concept to our military lexicon—elegance. And, indeed, there was a quiet grandeur, barely perceptible, to his movements.

Quite often when a soldier uttered a word of army slang, Paul would grimace, as if personally offended. During raids, he was careful to take items in moderation, and never personal belongings like a watch or jewelry.

Once he told one of the farmers that we were a group of Jewish freedom fighters. The farmer was surprised and said, "You don't look Jewish."

"All the same, we are Jews."

"Jews are businessmen, not fighters."

"Wrong. They can be brave soldiers, but when it comes to the civilian population, they do not abuse them."

"From me, you took everything," said the farmer ironically.

"Not everything, sir. If you check you'll see that we took in moderation, and later on, when we are well stocked, we'll try to resupply you. This is not pillage for its own sake. We have to sustain ourselves so we'll have the strength to fight a ruthless enemy."

"I have nothing to say to you," said the farmer, rejecting his apology.

"And I promise you that the Jews will not do you any harm."

"You already looted us," he insisted.

"You must admit, it's considerate looting."

23

At dawn's first light we went out looking for Paul. It was a strange sort of search, as if he had fooled us and hidden somewhere we could not find him. The rain stopped and the visibility was sharp. We could see the slopes down to the plain, but no one was spotted in the area. Kamil, who led the squads, was taut as a bowstring.

After searching for two hours, we sat ourselves down. It seemed for a moment that Kamil was about to say something. But we were again mistaken. He, too, sat down, seeking a key to the mystery.

Finally, he spread out the map and pointed to the village of Holovka, about ten miles away, most of the area open and cultivated.

"Paul is an experienced soldier and would not risk walking in exposed fields," said one of the fighters. "He must be hiding now, or lying down, camouflaged."

These were just blind statements that groped in the dark. All we were left with was Paul's face, that of a kind, gentle man who spoke little but listened much. But beyond this exterior we didn't know a great deal about him—who his parents were, his grandparents, what he had studied.

Presumably he had graduated from *gymnasium* like the rest.

Whether he continued at university we had no idea. In any case, he didn't talk about himself.

Kamil had promised him repeatedly that if we got reinforcements, Holovka would be our first mission. Paul knew our manpower problem and assumed that the promise, made with goodwill, was ultimately unrealistic.

"His honor compelled him to take this step," said someone.

We kept scanning the area and returned at dusk exhausted and empty-handed. The squad on duty greeted us at the entrance of the camp with a silent look.

That same night we learned that Paul's wife, a well-known beauty, frivolous and egotistical, had always been attracted to non-Jews.

"How was this smart guy caught in her web?" somebody asked.

"No point in asking about witchcraft," someone else replied.

Dinner was meager. Tsila wept and brought out the plates with trembling hands. But the soup was hot and the bread fresh, and the pain of Paul's disappearance was alleviated slightly as we ate the meal.

People kept their distance from one another. Togetherness was oppressive. Paul was loved by everyone. You couldn't help but love this thin, muscular young man, whose refined way of speaking made you think of poems by Rilke. Yes, the humiliation and disgrace bruised him and marred his beauty, but not his nobility.

"And we won't see Uncle Paul anymore?" asked Michael.

"If we think about him, we'll see him," answered Maxie.

"Where is he now?"

"It's hard to know, surely not far from here."

"Is he alone?"

"I assume he is. But don't worry; Paul is an experienced soldier, and he'll come back to us one of these days."

One of the fighters heard the conversation with Michael and whispered aloud, "Tricking the boy again."

"I'm not tricking. I'm telling the truth," Maxie replied coldly.

This testy exchange, clearly audible in the darkness, was the ending to an anxious day.

The feeling was that with Paul's disappearance, the bright side of our togetherness had also vanished. From now on it would be difficult to heal the fractures.

Patrols and ambushes went out on time. Kamil saw the squads off without philosophizing. The password was *tzedakah*. Kamil made sure to explain that the root of the word was *tzedek*, justice. *Tzedakah* also means charity, kindness, generosity.

Felix, who led the fighters, was restrained as usual and did not add a word of his own.

24

The next day, with great effort, we began the climb toward the summit with all the equipment. Even on a foggy, cloudy day the visibility on the way to the top is not impaired. The ears, despite the roar of the water, are not deafened. The feeling here, it must be said, is transcendent.

Not everyone was in favor of this climb. Some argued that the haste after Paul's disappearance was immoral. We should have waited a few days to see what became of him. He might have changed his mind, and if he returned and didn't find us, he would think we were abandoning him.

"Paul knows us well and knows we would not abandon him," said Hermann Cohen in his levelheaded way.

"We must not burden a suffering man with even the tiniest doubt," someone replied.

Kamil had reasons of his own. "We cannot waste time," he said. "Autumn is coming to an end; there are already signs of winter. If we don't start building the bunkers, who knows if we'll be able to complete them. Paul will forgive us. We are going to the summit not for ourselves alone. I anticipate that the war will be a long one, and we must prepare the place for the others who will join us."

"On what do you base this prediction?" Again a skeptical voice was heard.

"On will and on justice," Kamil replied at once.

AFTER WE UNPACKED the equipment and set up the tents, we built two fires for the soup pots. Soup is the elixir that saves us not only from the cold but also from gloom. After a bowl of soup, you feel that your body is filled with vitality. Kamil jokes that an army, as Napoleon famously said, travels on its stomach, but then adds, "Napoleon never tasted Tsila's soup. If he had, he would have said, 'Tsila's soup is like fire in the bones.'"

We continue to canvass the area, searching for traces of Paul. Soon the patrols will go down to the orchards at the edge of the forests to collect information about Paul's movements. Everyone believes that he is not far away and will soon be found. We need to be patient and enable him to return to us.

Our covenant cannot be broken. We are tied together with bonds of compassion. If a comrade leaves for a while, he must not be judged harshly. We are only human, and weakness must be respected. But the main job in the coming weeks will be climbing to the summit and digging the bunkers and the trenches that connect them. For this big project Kamil enlists Hermann Cohen, our quartermaster, who once owned sawmills. He knows the secrets of wood—which type will insulate and which will absorb water, which wood for flooring, and how to build walls that will stand up to stress. As the man responsible for food and clothing, he has worked wonders. Now he will make use of the knowledge he gained over the years at the sawmills.

I should mention that Hermann Cohen graduated from the *gymnasium* with honors and had begun his studies at the university. He studied Greek and Latin for two years and planned on an academic career, but the sudden death of his father forced him to abandon his studies and devote himself to the family business. He took over his father's role and did very well. Hermann Cohen is a master at preserving our supplies. He utilizes rags and cardboard, sacks and ropes. All the while he takes care of the weak and the sick, as well as Grandma Tsirl. He sets aside specific foods that protect their health.

Based on his age, he counts as one of our old men, but he refuses to be exempt from duty. At night he sometimes takes part in patrols, and once he was even wounded. He does not get involved in matters of faith. "A man who has divorced himself from the faith of his fathers should not take sides in the argument," he says. "In my youth we were certain there was nothing greater than the *gymnasium* and the university; we strove with all our might to go there. The study of Torah, not to mention ritual observance, we regarded as empty and useless. Our denial pained our parents and grandparents, but we showed them no mercy. This was naïveté. Or, if you like, the folly of youth."

He speaks with a calm voice the rest of us lack. One of the fighters once asked him if he would act differently today. His answer was, "It is hard to fix what you have broken. If my elders were alive I would ask their forgiveness for hurting them, but I can't do as they did. I remember the prayers, but I cannot stand and pray. Every person, I assume, ruined something in his life, in my case perhaps a bit more."

"What are you studying?" Grandma Tsirl asked Michael, who had come to visit her.

"I'm studying arithmetic and geometry."

"It's also good to learn the prayers, my little bird."

"What for?"

"Because prayer brings us close to God."

"How?"

"Prayer leads our voice to him."

"Is it possible to sometimes see God?"

"Not now and not openly."

"How do we know he loves us?"

"The heart tells us."

Ever since Paul disappeared, Michael has been uneasy. He asks Maxie what he should do to bring him back to us.

"We'll think about him; maybe he'll feel how we miss him and will want to return to us," says Maxie.

"The thoughts can reach him?"

"I believe so."

"Did he run away because we hurt him?"

"We loved him, but we couldn't help him. He went to look for his lost daughter."

Michael tries to understand the dilemma, but his questions lead to a blind alley. Maxie sees his confusion and decides not to complicate his mind further. From now on he will tell him, *I don't know.*

Maxie is around forty and a pharmacist, but he has the face of a teenager. He looks at the world with a sort of perpetual amazement. He loves animals, and they are drawn to him. The birds hop onto his shoulders and peck bread crumbs from his hands. Even a stray dog clung to him and spent several weeks with us. In the end it died, suddenly.

Some say Maxie is naïve, but that's not apparent when he speaks. Salo comes from time to time to consult with him on matters of illness and medication. Maxie is expert in concocting remedies and has considerable knowledge of medicine.

I once heard Hermann Cohen say, "Be heedful of the poor, for Torah goes forth from them." He knows Maxie's family; Maxie's father worked in Hermann Cohen's sawmill. He was a poor man who could barely support his family, but he sent his five children to the best *gymnasiums,* and all of them graduated from university.

25

We completed our shift. The squads who replaced us went out on patrol and ambush, and Karl, who after a shift usually closes his eyes and falls asleep, instead drank two cups of tea and shared a few incidents from his life. He began:

"I am more accustomed to autumn and winter than to seasons of light. We communists begin activity in the fall. In spring and summer we would hide in cellars and study political doctrine and propaganda. During those months, we would pay close attention to the commissars, make maps, and plan operations.

"With all due respect to theory, we wanted action, contact with great things, and real rivals. In other words: confrontation. Young people—seventeen, eighteen—who join the Party are trained to be single-minded and violent: to break down gates and doors, to rip out window bars. Violence not only strengthens the hands; it also makes you a hero. Well-bred young people, nice people to talk to, are turned overnight into a gang. We were convinced that everything we did was for the common good. The past and present were unimportant; what was important was the future. Rabbis and merchants are enemies of mankind, and whoever abuses them brings salvation to the world.

"We would attack religious institutions, tear charity boxes from the wall, set Torah scrolls on fire. We hated religious Jews: the way they stood, what they wore, how they talked. There was nothing about them we didn't hate. Small wonder that we eagerly burned synagogues, religious courts, and ritual baths. But most of all we loved to interrogate rabbis, religious judges, and Talmud teachers.

"At night we would break into a rabbi's house and inform him we were from the Department of Education and Culture of the Communist Party and had come to investigate how he teaches and preaches his defunct religion. The questions were listed in a notebook. The first question was, 'What do you teach, and to whom?'

"'I teach what my ancestors taught me. I add nothing and subtract nothing,' the rabbi would answer right away.

"The second question was, 'You undoubtedly know that your teaching corrupts the soul of the young people?'

"'God's Torah is pure.' The rabbi would cling to that verse.

"'You don't know that times have changed?'

"'Changed?' The rabbi would be puzzled. 'Changed for the better?'

"'Science has advanced, thinking is broader, but your teachings stand in the way of progress and cause injury to mankind. You must stop at once, or our department will deal with you the way you deserve.'

"Some of the rabbis were undeterred by any threat. They would stand their ground and confuse the young investigators. Of course, there were also weak rabbis who quickly capitulated to the investigators' threats. They were ready to plead guilty as charged, to sign documents, just to be left alone. Those we hated even more.

"One night we bullied a blind rabbi. The investigator demanded that he stop teaching the young. When he heard the demand, his eyelids fluttered and a kindly smile crossed his lips. 'I'm not hearing you well, for surely a fellow Jew would never say such a thing to me.'

" 'I repeat the demand of the Party to immediately halt the teaching of Talmud,' the young investigator said, leaving no room for doubt.

" 'Good God, what harm have I done to deserve such language? My dear boy, you surely mean well, but to my ears this sounds very harsh.'

" 'The demands of the Party are always for the common good.'

" 'If so, then thank God, I have done nothing wrong.'

" 'But the study of Torah is a crime, a crime against humanity.'

"As he heard the investigator's explicit words, the blind old man's face froze, but he quickly recovered and said, 'You are surely speaking ironically.'

" 'What do you mean?' The young interrogator flinched.

" 'You are surely saying the opposite of what you mean.'

" 'I do not mean the opposite. I am speaking in simple, direct language. You must stop this teaching immediately. And if you don't, the Party will know how to deal with you.'

" 'Good God!' The old man looked imploringly toward heaven.

" 'Leave God alone and do as you are ordered,' continued the young, arrogant investigator.

" 'What is my sin, God Almighty?'

" 'You know your sins; there is no need to recite them again.'

"The old man pressed his hands to his forehead and said, 'I thank you for your words and your warnings. You are a loyal messenger, it seems. From now on I declare a fast, a ban on food and on speech. God willing, I will hear only good and worthy things.'

" 'You are not just blind,' the young investigator said with disgust.

"The rabbi's expression changed to one of incredulity. 'My blind eyes have been open for many years. Your sin will not be forgiven.'

"The interrogator continued to berate the rabbi, whose forehead furrowed in disbelief. The interrogator finally gave up, arose with contempt, and left the room. I followed him.

"I conducted investigations on my own and witnessed many others. Where we got the gall and arrogance to browbeat elderly rabbis in the middle of the night, I don't know. Yes, the commissars prepared us for these interrogations. Their policy was never to take pity on benighted people. Anyone who takes pity on them harms the beating heart of the Party. They hold captive many people who must be redeemed. There was magic in the words 'captive' and 'redemption.'"

"And you weren't afraid?" asked one of the listeners.

"No. We were certain that we were doing what was good and right."

"Who were the commissars?"

"Jewish university students."

"And who were the investigators?"

"Young Jews from the *gymnasium*."

Karl's face grew still, and for a moment it seemed that he was asking his listeners not to bother him with more questions. But there were a few more queries that embarrassed him.

"That's how it was," Karl concluded. You couldn't tell if he was referring to the sin that was hard to forgive, or if he was perhaps confessing to all charges in an indictment that he himself had composed.

Nearly every night, images and incidents that had been buried in our hearts come forth. I sometimes think that Kamil is distressed by these revelations, which take the place of the study of the texts.

26

As the rain and cold got worse and the climb to the summit slowed down, a patrol discovered three young men, starving and desperate. Three months earlier they had managed to escape from one of the last transports, and they had been hiding in the forests ever since, subsisting on berries, mushrooms, and birds' eggs. Luckily, one of them had a box of matches, which saved them from the cold.

We were happy to see them and brought them to the base.

Ever since Paul's disappearance, our base has been wallowing in depression. Our drills are conducted as usual, nighttime studies go on as before, but there's no passion. Paul's desperate act eroded our will to live.

The three young men were astounded by our base and couldn't stop murmuring, "Unbelievable, unbelievable." Tsila served them bowls of soup.

"We didn't want to escape and leave our elderly parents at the train station," one of them revealed. "But they begged us, *Run away, children*. It wasn't easy to leave the parents to their fate and escape. We were sure our fate would be no different from theirs, but by a miracle, we survived."

"What's your name?" Kamil asked him cautiously.

"My name is Isidor. I'm preparing to study at the university with the humanities faculty," he added, without being asked.

"We are a fighting unit, small but solid," said Kamil.

"Will we be allowed to join you?"

"With pleasure."

Kamil told them about the training and the nighttime raids and ambushes. "You'll need to sleep for a few nights, and after you've rested, we'll start to train you. We have rifles, hand grenades, and machine guns."

The young men woke up during the night and stood alongside their tent. Hermann Cohen noticed them and took them to the kitchen. Tsila served them corn porridge and cheese.

After they finished the meal, it seemed they were about to recite the blessings. We were mistaken. They continued to marvel. Isidor finally asked, "Where do you get the food?"

"We raid houses and farms in order to survive, but in truth we are preparing ourselves for the day when we can raid military camps," Hermann Cohen disclosed.

"We constantly ask ourselves if we were right to leave our parents," Isidor said mournfully.

"We, too, left parents and grandparents behind," Hermann Cohen quickly reassured him.

"They won't blame us when the time comes?"

"Courts will not judge us; we will judge ourselves," Hermann Cohen said, not in his usual voice.

That same night, Kamil introduced them to Danzig and Milio, and to Maxie and Michael.

"How old is Milio?" one of them inquired.

"He's two, maybe two and a half."

"Does he cry at night?"

"No. Asleep or awake, he doesn't cry. He's a marvelous child," Danzig said with obvious pride.

Kamil didn't take part in the conversation. He asked to hold Milio in his arms, and Danzig handed him over.

"Michael is eight and a half," Maxie declared. "He can copy from the Bible, he studies arithmetic, and he started geometry."

"He copies from the Bible?" The young man was puzzled.

"At night we study selected chapters from the Bible, among other things," Maxie clarified.

The questioner was amazed to find himself in such an uncanny place.

When they were brought before Grandma Tsirl, she looked at them for a long time, as if searching for familiar faces. She of course knew many things about the ancestry of the three. Of one grandfather, Itche Meir, she said, "He was a great Torah scholar, and people would come to ask his advice."

"I am named for him, but my name is Isidor."

"With your permission, I will call you Itche Meir. Your grandfather was a kind man who did not condescend to others and spoke to everyone as to a friend. His virtue will protect you and us."

"Thank you," Isidor said with embarrassment.

THE NEXT DAY the young men asked to start training, but Kamil felt they must rest, recuperate, and get stronger.

That night two squads went out to raid houses at the foot of the mountains. Before they left, Kamil talked about the three newcomers. The prediction Kamil had been making for weeks, that many people would arrive and alter our situation, was slowly coming to pass.

27

The arrival of the three young men inevitably changed our lives. In each of their faces were bits of the life we had left behind. They brought with them new feelings of disquiet, as well as questions we had stopped asking. They are thrilled by what we do and how organized we are, and by Kamil's presence. To them he seems like a spiritual leader. Salo examined them and asked Tsila to give them extra food. He also explained that Kamil is a superb commander; to go out with him on a raid is an unforgettable experience.

"But he looks like a philosopher," Isidor insisted.

"He's an intellectual, no doubt about it, but first and foremost he is a commander. He believes we must strengthen the Jewish spirit within us. Without spiritual reinforcement, we will not be able to defeat the enemy."

"He's a religious believer?" asked Isidor cautiously.

"You might say so but not in a conventional sense."

Isidor's questions had transformed Salo from a medic into a loyal disciple.

"Have you heard of Martin Buber?" Salo continued in a tone I didn't recognize.

"No."

"Martin Buber collected the teachings of the Ba'al Shem Tov.

By the way, this is the land of the Ba'al Shem Tov. Here he walked in seclusion and drew closer to God."

THAT NIGHT, Werner, our other medic, brought to our attention the verse from Leviticus, "And you shall keep My commandments, and do them; I am the Lord. And you shall not profane My holy name; and I will be hallowed among the children of Israel: I am the Lord who hallows you."

Werner, a sensitive reader, directed his listeners to the words "I will be hallowed." God is not removed and distant from human beings but wants them to be near Him and wants to be sanctified by them. People are not the submissive serfs of God, but His partners in managing the world.

Werner is a quiet man, a devoted soldier. When he goes out at night with his squad, he carries a heavier pack than the others because he is the medic. He wasn't aware that he had just walked into a minefield. The verse he quoted aroused anger. Karl, who had confessed to terrible deeds, raised his voice and shouted, "You are distorting the scriptures. You are making the deity into a humanist. The deity, if there is one, is and always was a dictator. Even in the verse you cited, the word 'I' is repeated over and over. He doesn't want man's proximity, he wants man's submission."

Werner sat there dumbfounded. Karl's voice, a powerful voice, stunned him. He had innocently thought he was offering a new interpretation and that people would relate to it. He had not anticipated such a flood of anger.

The three newcomers were shocked. The study evening, which had begun with quiet singing around the campfire, had exploded. There were several fighters who defended Werner's right to speak, but chaos reigned. Werner sat down without a word, realizing that he had offended those for whom any religious thought was anathema. A shouting match broke out, and only in Tsila's tent, by the big pots of tea, did people calm down.

THAT'S HOW OUR LIFE goes here. At calmer moments we forget that we are surrounded. The enemy is cruel, watching from afar, determined to kill us. Their patrols gather information about us. When they discover the truth about who we are, they will attack us without mercy.

But meanwhile, in the narrow space between what has been and what will be, we are alive, delighted by the forest scenery, by Milio and Michael, by Tsila's cooking, by the words that pour from Grandma Tsirl's heart: "Love and teach love; there is nothing in this fleeting world other than love. Love is a gift. The giving does not impoverish us but enlarges our soul. Only a few of us are left, and without great love we diminish God's world."

Sometimes Grandma Tsirl seems like a priestess whose tribe has been lost and who tries to pass on to the remaining few, to the embers who have been plucked from the fire, beliefs that are beyond their understanding.

28

During the last raid, we got hold of a radio receiver and some batteries. The old man whose home we invaded begged us on bended knee not to take the radio from him. "Take what you want, take a cow, but don't take my radio. I have no family, and the radio is like a mother and sister to me; I will die of loneliness."

Felix spoke to him as a friend, politely explaining that for partisans who protect the homeland this equipment is as vital as oxygen. The war will soon be over, and we will return the radio with respect and appreciation. And as a sign of gratitude, Felix removed his wristwatch and told him, "Take this as a gift from me to you." The old man was despondent; he wept and refused to part with the radio.

"If there's good news, we'll come and tell you." Felix tried to appease him as he took it.

"What good is the news without a radio," the old man wailed.

The return home did not go smoothly: we came upon a hostile patrol and attacked it. The very thought of our new radio empowered us. The patrol fled.

For months now we've been holed up in the hills. On each raid we tried to extract news of the front from farmers and landowners, but with little success. The bits of newspaper we found offered no good news.

When we returned to the base, the tents were shrouded in

darkness. The guards welcomed us as we entered, and when they heard about what we had taken, they rejoiced. Their cries of joy woke the sleepers.

Sandwiches and steaming tea awaited us in the kitchen. Everyone surrounded the mess tent and wanted to know how we had acquired such a precious device.

At first light, a Russian voice boomed from the radio, announcing that the enemy's lines had been breached at Stalingrad. The German Army has retreated in panic and is urgently calling for reinforcements. The war is at a critical phase, and all forces will be mustered to defeat the invader. We danced around the radio to the sounds of Russian military music. Happiest of all were the communists among us, and those who had mocked them were stunned by the power of their faith.

Kamil's reaction was restrained. "We must learn loyalty and devotion from the Red Army, but most of all be true to ourselves. The time has come to be what we are." The communists, of course, reject this argument. "The human being comes before the Jew," they again insisted.

In honor of the radio, Tsila prepared a festive meal. Tsila continues to work miracles. She makes meals out of nothing. Miriam helps her. Most of the time, Miriam is busy doing laundry and repairing torn clothing. In the evening she helps Tsila cook the main meal.

Miriam doesn't speak. Had Tsila not told us that her entire family had been sent to the camps, we'd have known nothing about her. She works from morning to late at night. She patched the trousers I brought from home, and I wear them on the base. During operations, I wear one of the gendarmes' uniforms that we'd taken. The uniforms are awkward and hard to walk in. Unfortunately, there's no alternative; they are made of a heavy fabric that protects us from the cold. But when it rains, they absorb water and are heavier than the loads we carry.

At one point Maxie turned to me and asked, "Edmund, what are you writing in that notebook?"

I was surprised; I hadn't realized that people noticed I was jotting things down.

"I write down the day's events so I can tell my parents when I return home."

"Good idea. I don't think at all about the future. You always shared your thoughts with your parents?"

"I shared them with my girlfriend, too," I confided.

"What happened to your girlfriend? Were you separated from each other?"

"No," I said quickly.

Maxie appeared to understand that this was a complicated and painful story. He stood up, nodded, and withdrew. I remained seated. The disturbing memories that I had buried resurfaced all at once, as if the walls containing them had cracked.

I went to the kitchen and asked Tsila for a drink. Tsila generously gave me a full glass of vodka. I drank it in one gulp. The liquid scorched my throat, and I saw what I had not seen for a long time: Anastasia, in full.

Since my escape, Anastasia had retreated from my thoughts and occupied a zone outside of me. Yes, once in a while I'd glimpse a bit of her face or one of her movements, or I'd hear a sentence she used to repeat: "You're a bit different but very sweet."

"You love me," I would venture.

"How is it possible not to love you?"

I was sensitive to her every word but not sensitive enough to hear the reservations hidden within them. She seemed perfect to me then, and one does not protest perfection.

Suddenly, Anastasia emerges from hiding: It's the end of June, summer vacation. The evening light is in shades of red as we walk along the river. The urge to embrace her is so strong that my fingers don't obey me, they tremble.

Anastasia is a child of nature, and her true self is revealed in the outdoors: the way she skips, tilts her head, speaks words that don't connect, tugs the cotton shirt that shows off her firm breasts. Suddenly, she asks, "Why don't Jews play sports?" Even the gentle teasing has its charm. She knows that I'm one of the best at long-distance running and the high jump. And some of my Jewish friends are just as good, but the old stereotype pops up nonetheless.

But when evening falls and we are pressed tightly together under a willow tree and drinking greedily of each other, all the words lose their meaning. The bodies join and are one body, and when darkness grows thicker, we strip off the rest of our clothes and dive into the black water, rising and floating and shrieking like seagulls. The fragrant waters strengthen the desire. So it goes for hours till late at night.

"Anastasia," I call out in a voice not my own.

"What?" she replies in a voice that sounds as though it's coming from underwater.

I wanted to ask something, but the question has flown out of my mind.

Nothing seems to bother Anastasia. She is wholly devoted to her pleasures; she floats and dives. My pleasures are moderate, distracted by feelings of guilt. For good reason Anastasia remarks, "Jews are always thinking and worrying."

"A person is not mineral or vegetable, and even animals apparently have thoughts, or something like thoughts," I beg to differ.

This answer triggers her laughter, wild laughter that totally dismisses what I said.

Anastasia, my water goddess, held me captive. Everything that had been between me and my mother, between me and my father, the magic of the quiet conversations and subtle understandings between us collapsed all at once and was gone. And along with it,

I lost my drive to excel in my studies and surpass those who tried to be better than me.

The *gymnasium* was an endless contest: you climb and you climb to reach the top. The parents watch with amazement, anxious yet proud, and suddenly, this desire is gone, and you are pulled away, enchanted by Anastasia, to wherever she wants to go: under the canopy of trees, into the black waters of the night, to the popular café where young workers sit after hours and let off steam, or just to wander the back streets and laugh, to smoke with affected gestures, to get crazy and spit on the ground. Suddenly, Anastasia says, spitefully, "I hate the math teacher, his bent nose, his little hands that run across the blackboard. He looks like the devil himself. Do you hate him, too?"

"Yes," I feel compelled to say.

"So together we'll defeat him, get rid of him. The world without equations is more beautiful. Why are all the math teachers Jewish?"

"Not all," I correct her.

"You're wrong."

So it goes night after night. And when I come home after midnight, my parents are still sitting at the table waiting for me.

"Why are you waiting up for me?" I ask with suppressed anger.

"It's very late," my father says quietly.

"There's no reason to sit and wait for me. I'm grown up," I say, aware that I am hurting them.

"Where have you been so late?" my father asks.

"It's not important," I answer not in my voice but in a voice I picked up in the café.

I go to my room, take off my clothes, and dive into deep sleep.

The rain has stopped, and in the air there is a whiff of snow. The climb to the summit is slow—only two or three hundred feet per day. Despite all the difficulties, we draw nearer to the goal. The last stages will be complicated; we'll need to use ropes and ladders. But Kamil and Felix are trained in engineering, and we will bring everyone to the summit with skill.

The radio is full of good news: the enemy's front lines have been breached at Stalingrad, and trainloads of wounded soldiers are making their way to the rear. The Russian broadcaster urges citizens to join the partisans and promises that victory will not be long in coming.

There's another cause for celebration: we recently found a big hoard of potatoes, and every night we carry up full sacks. Carrying them is hard, but each sack that arrives is greeted with cheers of joy and thanks. Hermann Cohen has his hands full. He takes inventory of the sacks and makes sure to put them on wooden pallets to protect them against wetness.

The radio is on at night and sometimes also before dawn, when we return from an operation. It is now our oracle, updating us on the present and foretelling the future. We stay close, glued to every word.

Kamil again warns us not to become addicted to far-reaching hopes but to prepare for immediate challenges. If the Red Army comes and liberates us, we will shout our thanks, but until then, drills and more drills, text study and more text study: what comes from within is doubly strong.

Organized study at night has halted for the time being. Fatigue and the dampness have subdued us. But Kamil won't give up. Before supper, he reads out a few verses from the weekly Torah portion or a chapter from the Book of Psalms. Before we set out on an operation, he reads the psalm that begins "The Lord is my shepherd."

"What's the point of reading verses we don't understand?" ask those who don't agree with him.

"Because our ancestors depended on these verses day and night."

"This isn't rational, it's hocus-pocus," someone says.

Every statement by Kamil that touches on tribal faith remains provocative. At times he seems unable to respond. Because of the many objections, his thoughts aren't as well phrased as they should be. More than once, the words have been stuck in his mouth, and one time, as he tried to overcome these obstacles, he began to stammer. But when Kamil goes out at night, his orders are clear-cut, and he marches like a young man. And on top of that, when one of us becomes short of breath, Kamil props him up and doesn't leave him until he gets his wind back.

THE PERSON WHO has brought a new spirit to the base is Isidor, one of the three young men who recently joined us. Isidor has a pleasant voice, and he knows prayers and Hasidic melodies. When he was a child, his grandfather took him to a Hasidic synagogue, and there he heard the Sabbath, festival, and daily prayers.

His parents were not pleased that he went to synagogue, but Isidor loved his grandfather and the prayers. When he was small, his grandfather would wrap him in his prayer shawl and show him the words in the prayer book. When he was older, he would stand beside his grandfather and pray with him.

At night we are greatly fatigued, but when Isidor sings some prayers, his clear, pure voice enchants us and we follow it, like a magic flute.

"Do you observe the commandments?" Danzig asked him.

"No, but when I pray, I see vivid images, and my heart yearns for my parents and grandfather."

"Do you pray every day?"

"No."

"Did your father pray?"

"No."

Everyone was surprised by these blunt questions, which forced Isidor to bare his soul. Danzig—who takes care not to hurt those under his authority, in particular Milio, whom he protects like a parent—he of all people was carried away by curiosity.

One evening Isidor announced, "Tonight I will not sing."

"Why?" everyone wondered.

"The melodies ran away from me."

"They'll surely come back."

"I hope so."

Isidor looked surprised, as if he were speaking not of himself but of someone else who was confused or troubled.

I have learned: everyone here carries an inner secret, or a bitter disappointment that's hard to speak about. It's no wonder that our conversation is mostly restrained. Isidor, too, who had appeared to pray so fluently, turns out to have restraints of his own.

This odd reticence makes us very uneasy. Kamil senses that Isidor's problem is no trivial matter. The few nights when he prayed had filled us with longing for parents and grandparents, and suddenly that melody was extinguished.

Ever since Isidor stopped praying, he is unable to rest. He

works at odd jobs at the base and is always asking, "When will we go out on a mission?"

Grandma Tsirl tells him, "Itche Meir, you have nothing to worry about: Prayer will come back to you. Your grandfather, who lives inside of you, will open your mouth."

"And what should I do until then?" Isidor asks cautiously.

"Nothing, it will happen by itself, when you least expect it."

There is a calm in Grandma Tsirl's voice that immediately relaxes him. "Did you know my grandfather personally?" he inquires.

"I knew him well; we were neighbors. And I remember you, too, little bird. On the Sabbath and on holidays you would go with your grandfather to the synagogue, always nicely dressed."

"Why were my parents displeased that I went to synagogue?"

"Every generation goes its own way; they also meant well. Your parents bought a record player and liked to listen to classical music. They would sit for hours on the glassed-in porch and listen. While they listened to music, you sat with your grandfather in the little synagogue of the Vizhnitz Hasidim. The praying of the Vizhnitz Hasidim is very sweet. You tasted more than a little of it and it lodged inside of you."

AT NIGHT SOME of the fighters get gloves from Reb Hanoch. Reb Hanoch dresses them in stocking caps, gloves, and vests, and although we don't talk about him much, his presence is felt and seen. Not a day passes without his gifts. He knits day and night, and every item he makes is nice and warm. It's too bad we don't know how to thank him as we should.

30

Kamil has hatched a new idea: learning Hebrew. "Every day we'll learn a word and use it as a password," he says. Fortunately, one of the books we brought from that abandoned house was a German-Hebrew dictionary. "It's impossible to be a Jew without the original Hebrew language, where all the ancient spiritual treasures are hidden. Every day we'll learn a word, and it will revive us."

The communists and Bundists object. If we study, they say, we should study Yiddish, not Hebrew. Yiddish is the language of the people, and it should be cherished. Hebrew is the language of the religious rituals that clouded the minds of the masses. Hebrew belongs to prehistory and not to history. We must study Yiddish, the language of the tormented people who were deported to the camps. Hebrew will lead us far away from ourselves, into the primeval darkness.

There are many more strong objections. Kamil makes the decision. "Whoever wants to learn Hebrew will learn it, and whoever wants to learn Yiddish, that's fine, too. Both are holy languages. The first Hebrew word we will learn is *avodah*. *Avodah* means work but also *avodat kodesh*, holy work. This describes our situation here. Let's repeat: *avodah*."

This gesture of goodwill is also met with objections. Fortunately, Tsila has prepared a dessert of compote from dried fruit that the fighters have brought. The compote bridged the differences of opinion and improved the mood.

ISIDOR AND HIS TWO COMPANIONS have completed their personal training and in two days will begin to drill with a squad. For their first mission, Kamil added them to Felix's expanded squad, which went to catch fish in the lake, not far from the base.

The three have gotten stronger and no longer walk like raw recruits. In a short time they have learned the various ways of walking and are pleased with their first assignment.

We spread out the net and waited for about an hour. When we lifted it, we found, to our surprise, five big fish and about ten small ones. We would have tried again, but a sudden rain came down and drenched us. We put the catch in sacks and returned to the base.

Kamil saw the fish and called out, "Marvelous! What a wonderful meal Tsila will make us." Kamil gets excited about things that make everyone happy. His excitement brings out the boy in him. The fighters hurried to help Tsila and Miriam prepare the fish and cook them on the coals.

It was a meal fit for a king. We sang Russian marches till late at night.

Kamil had a few drinks and announced: "Today we rescued from oblivion the Hebrew word *avodah*. The word *avodah*, unlike its cousin *melakhah*, which means labor, also has the connotation of holiness. The opposite of *avodat kodesh* is *avodah ẓarah*, idolatry, and there is also *avodah shebalev*, work of the heart—prayer. Every Hebrew word we acquire is a gift. It holds within it so much of our spiritual property. Do not forget, we are the last guardians of these treasures."

Kamil was not drunk, but his spirits were high and he was clearly connected to worlds beyond our reach. Tears eventually came to his eyes. He tried to stop them, but he was overcome with weeping and slipped away into the darkness.

31

We conserve our batteries and listen to the radio only at night. Ever since we've had a radio, our lives have changed. At exactly seven in the evening, if there's no alarm or sudden alert, we huddle around the receiver and eagerly listen to the news. In Kamil's opinion we are overly wedded to expectations from elsewhere. Training our hearts is more important.

When Kamil speaks, we have the feeling he is not speaking to our handful, but to the many people who are on their way to us.

For now, only three have arrived, and we held a party to mark the conclusion of their training. Tsila and Miriam baked cookies filled with plum jam. A few days ago Hermann Cohen, with the help of two fighters, set up a field oven, which has now proved its ability.

We all respect Kamil, but it's hard to accept his insistence that holing up in the mountains is a journey into ourselves and to the God of our fathers. There is a strong light in this mysterious man that pulls us toward him but is scary and intimidating at the same time.

His deputy Felix is closer to us in all respects. Felix may be a silent man who will rarely utter a complete sentence, but his broad, steady body inspires peace and quiet. Raids with him are not wrapped in weighty thoughts, like raids with Kamil. His whole being says, *Act and don't talk and don't interpret.* Whoever wants to talk and debate should do so at night by the campfire. Too many thoughts undermine concentration. One has to focus on the mission. The mission is the main thing, and the rest is unimportant. It's best to sleep after the mission and not end the nights with arguments. A person who talks depletes his spirit for nothing. Sleep makes us ready for difficult struggles; it not only refreshes our energies but also cleans out the debris within us. So says Felix, without uttering a word.

I sometimes think we harm Kamil, and ourselves, when we argue. But what can you do, the arguments arise spontaneously. It's good that on recent nights Isidor has been telling us about the last days in the ghetto. There's a melody to his words. He chooses them carefully so that each word and phrase paints a picture.

In the final days before the last deportation, Isidor told us, the people stood at the high fences and pleaded with the Ruthenian women, "Take one child; we'll pay you for every day." The farm women waved their hands in refusal. More maddening still were their gestures toward the heavens, as if to say, it's God's doing, not ours.

Isidor's two friends are still in a state of shock. The three train all day, they saw wooden beams, and they help in the kitchen. They've gone out on small raids, but the two of them don't talk. When they train and work, they resemble us, but when they sit, eating or gazing, they seem stupefied. *What happened to us?*, their eyes say. *How did we get here; was it all by chance?*

Even in the midst of a fireside conversation, their puzzled look remains the same. I sometimes think it's not bewilderment but dread about what the future holds for us.

SINCE THE ARRIVAL of the three young men, I again see Anastasia's face clearly. When the war broke out, I was certain that the dangers would only strengthen our relationship.

Once, on our way home, smitten and saturated with love, Anastasia asked, "Why do people hate the Jews?"

"It's prejudice; Jews are no different from other people."

"I know," she said, her lips pursed in an alluring smile. She had the grace and beauty of a girl who grew up outside the city, with fresh air and a big garden, and a stable and cowshed beside the house.

Within the *gymnasium* her manner was reserved and she spoke little. She was a good student yet didn't excel in any subject. She did her homework, paid attention in class but didn't ask questions. She always looked wary, as if she didn't belong. But outside of school her movements were free, her speech unrestrained, and by the river and at the park she would laugh loudly. Every little thing would make her laugh. Once, when I told her I wanted to learn to ride horses, she let out a rather scornful chuckle. When I asked why, she said, "I was already riding when I was seven."

In those besotted days I didn't look at the details but at the whole, and the whole was Anastasia—a kind of living miracle who keeps amazing you: the magnificent neck, the head bobbing like a young bird's, and the body sculpted like a statue. I was sure she'd be with me forever and we would always be young.

When I was with Anastasia, talk seemed superfluous. To hug, to kiss, and to laugh seemed the right things to do. To write, do homework, excel, take part in a debate—they seemed to me unnecessary, artificial, and pointless.

Not surprisingly, my schoolwork deteriorated. Classmates were jealous of me, and I was once kicked by a bully who yelled, "Stick to your own kind and don't bother our girls." I hit him back twice as hard. In truth, I wasn't looking for confrontation at that time. I was overflowing with happiness.

My parents' world darkened as my studies suffered. At first they said nothing and sat sullenly at the table. But after they were called to the school for a meeting, they cried out in pain, "What's happened to you, Edmund?" They looked at me as if I'd been struck by a hidden illness.

"Nothing; soon it'll all be back to normal," I said, knowing I was keeping the truth from them.

Disaster followed disaster. First I was expelled from school along with my Jewish friends, and right after my expulsion, my mother's illness got worse.

I would occasionally bring Anastasia home, to show off her beauty. My mother didn't say a word. My father would joke with her. Her beauty apparently impressed him, too.

We were still allowed to walk on certain streets. But then walls were erected around the Jewish area. Money ran out and food was lacking. People stood alongside their homes and sold clothes and household goods. But I ignored the turmoil around me. Even my mother's illness. She would sometimes turn to me and ask, "What has happened?" She didn't realize I'd been swept into a whirlwind.

The meetings with Anastasia had become dangerous, and she hinted that we should keep them to a minimum. I wasn't afraid. I was smitten with Anastasia and I said, "We'll always be together. Fate will not separate us, cannot separate us." Anastasia responded with a thin smile that I took as agreement. In those days I saw only what I wanted to see.

And then came that fateful Tuesday. We had made a date to meet at seven o'clock at Lilac Lane. I waited a full hour and Anastasia didn't appear.

I was about to go to her house but held back. Her father with his peasant's face didn't much like me, and one time he'd said to me, "We don't stay long at parties. An honest person goes to bed early." I knew this was a warning, and I avoided going to her house.

That same week we were banished to the ghetto. I was sure that in the evening I would see Anastasia at the fence. I looked for her among the farm women who came to sell bread and vegetables, and I gave one of them, a woman who used to work at our house, a short letter and asked her to give it to Anastasia. "I'll wait for you by the fence at five o'clock," I wrote to her. "Love always, Edmund."

That entire time I was certain her father had locked her up at home, and this was why she didn't come. I imagined her sitting by a barred window, her eyes filled with yearning.

I planned to slip out of the ghetto, come to her house, and rescue her. But all my attempts to mix in with the workers going out to their jobs nearly ended in disaster. I was stubborn. Day after day I went back to the fence, surveying the people strolling on the sidewalk, looking intently for Anastasia.

As I stood waiting by the fence, I saw from afar a young girl coming out of Lilac Lane, a tennis racquet in her hand: Anastasia. She was headed for the tennis club. I couldn't believe what I saw and became very emotional: my eyes filled with tears.

Only the next day did I realize: Anastasia's daily schedule had not changed. Tuesday afternoons she goes to the tennis club. The next morning, I saw her walking to the *gymnasium*, schoolbag on her back, surrounded by our classmates, joking and jostling. I couldn't hear her voice from far away, but all her movements said: *What was, was. Life goes on and let's enjoy it.*

For months we were imprisoned in the ghetto; every day we saw the face of death. A man was shot because he went too close to the fence, and people were removed from their homes and sent by truck to unknown places. Someone who tried to escape was punished by being hung in the square.

Dangers lurked everywhere, and eventually we also began to starve. But for some reason I was sure that in another day or two Anastasia would appear and show me a breach in the fence through which I would squeeze my way out to her.

On our way back to the base from one of the raids we returned to the same abandoned house where we had found the books. We took whatever we could; every book on those shelves was valuable. Again we saw in our mind's eye the remarkable people who had lived in this house, far from any Jewish community, in the heart of a tranquil, wide-open landscape. Every time we come here, their images appear before us. Dear Jews, Kamil calls them, who left us this great treasure. Were it not for them, this green wilderness would be the end of us.

I am reading Heinrich Graetz's magnificent *History of the Jews*. It's still hard for me to see the whole picture, but I am eagerly reliving the conquest of the Land by the Tribes of Israel, their first exile, and their wondrous return to the homeland. And then their second, terrible expulsion and their dispersion among the nations. As I read, I can share Kamil's sense of awe.

I've already noticed that I've picked up Kamil's rhythms of speech. I can't presume to resemble him or emulate him, but the tempo of his speech comes out involuntarily whenever I utter a sentence or just think. Ever since I've been going with him on raids, his voice whispers in my head—and apparently not only in mine.

Manfred, one of the fighters, believes that Kamil has a hypnotic power, and one must not get trapped in his net. Every sentence of his should be examined. He is only a man, and like all of us he makes mistakes and misleads, or tries to pull us toward what he thinks is right. It's best to keep your distance from such a hypnotic influence and preserve your independence.

I told Manfred about my reading of Graetz and my amazement at the ongoing existence of the Jews. From earlier conversations with him, I should have known that a word like "amazement" is not part of his vocabulary.

"Why is that amazing?" bristled Manfred. "Every creature wants for whatever reason to live and multiply, from amoebas to human beings. Admittedly, the Jews have done this with skill and guile. All through their exile, they have not confronted their enemies face-to-face. They learned to evade and escape, not always elegantly, until they got to where they got. No miracle here; it's biology or, in other words, the instinct to survive."

With that, he stripped away my amazement and left me naked.

Manfred often quotes Darwin. "You should go back and read Darwin, and you won't talk so optimistically about mankind," he says. Kamil stays away from Manfred and doesn't speak to him directly, only through Felix.

Manfred has no one among us to talk with. The communists do listen to him, but he doesn't like them. Their practical agenda, he argues, is brutal. He says that Darwin opened a window into the understanding of nature, but the communists adopted Darwinism as a way of life. The militant proletariat is the zenith of their aspirations.

IT SHOULD BE MENTIONED that we now number forty-seven souls, each with his unique countenance and destiny. Truth be told, togetherness is strong and tight here. Whoever goes on a raid with his squad hands over part of himself to the squad, and the squad gives him something of its unified essence. And when you return in the early morning to the base, you are not the same person who went out at night.

But at the same time everyone here carries within him the burden of his own life. We are wary of confessing to one another. Even the fighters who go out on missions with me—such as Werner, Manfred, Karl, and Danzig, not to mention Paul, who was lost to us—what do I really know about them? Kamil and Felix are also enigmas wrapped in mystery. We escaped from a place where we should have stayed to help and support others, and we have been haunted by guilt ever since.

Kamil says that God in His mercy has brought us to this place and given us the books of the forefathers; alas, we don't have the time to study them in depth. Without the books, we are orphans. For Kamil, each movement and action acquires an added significance. I have often heard him shout in the middle of an operation, "We are not alone; there is something higher than the highest!" On one of the raids there was a surprise attack on us by police who are collaborating with the enemy. There were many of them, and we retreated under heavy fire. Kamil suddenly raised his voice and cried out, "Do not fear, the Lord of Hosts is with us."

LAST NIGHT I witnessed the following conversation. Michael went to Grandma Tsirl and asked, "How do we know that God is in the world?"

Grandma Tsirl looked at him with wide-open eyes and said, "Every tree and animal and person testify that the world has a Creator."

"Why don't I see him?"

"Because you have to train your eyes, so they will see the miracles the Creator performs at every moment."

"How will I train my eyes?"

"You have to say what is written in the prayer: 'God of Abraham, God of Isaac, God of Jacob,' and then add, 'show Your face also to me.' "

"How many times a day should I say this prayer?"

"Three times a day."

"If God is everywhere, is he also in me?"

"Of course, my little bird."

"Why don't I feel him?"

"You, my little bird, are a wise boy, and when the time comes, God will shine His face on you."

"Thank you, Grandma Tsirl."

"For such a thing you don't need to thank me, my dear."

"And, Grandma, are geometry exercises his miracles, too?"

"Everything is His miracle. He is in all places and all acts, even in the places most hidden."

"From now on I will start to train my eyes, Grandma Tsirl."

"May God protect you and all of us."

MICHAEL IS LOVED not only by Maxie; he is dear to all of us. He is a child who brings our hearts back to our homes and to ourselves at his age. He does everything thoroughly and precisely, but at the same time he is a child who likes to look around, play jacks, and laugh.

"He has an excellent head," says Maxie. "Arithmetic comes easily to him, yet who knows what other hidden talents he may have. I sometimes think he has a gift for language. He speaks very little about his home, but his whole manner shows that he was loved by his parents, aunts and uncles, and grandparents. I have the feeling that nothing escapes his notice. He once asked me if after the war we will live together, as we do here. I told him, 'Each of us will go back to his family.' 'Why can't we live in a commune, like here?' he asked. I didn't know what to say, so I said, 'Let's wait and see.' "

33

We are deep into routines—ambushes, patrols, and raids—and we're glad that the big assault on us, which Kamil speaks of endlessly, hasn't yet happened. While we secretly hoped that the Red Army would reach us before the attack, there arrived, as if borne by the wind, a medium-sized dog, which sniffed around, located Maxie, and sprang toward him.

"Edward!" Maxie cried out in shock and joy. "What a surprise! How did you find me?"

This was our first, tangible greeting from home. Maxie had adopted Edward as a puppy, and all through university the dog was at his side. After he married, he and his wife, Magda, shared their love for him. They had no children, but this did not mar their love. They took good care of their home and worked together in the pharmacy.

"How did you get here? How did you find me?" Maxie got down on his knees. The entire base was excited. A dog that makes a journey of more than fifty miles in search of his master is no small thing.

After the great excitement, Edward sat at Maxie's feet and looked around alertly, as if to say, "I did it. Even I don't believe that I did it. I got lost many times, but I finally found the way and got here."

Edward is not a purebred dog; those dogs are spoiled, self-absorbed, and want only to be pampered. Edward is a simple dog who loves his master more than himself. Because of this loyalty, he was able to get all the way here.

Maxie, like all of us here, doesn't tell much. He did reveal to Michael that he had a dog named Edward, but nobody except Michael knew he existed. Maxie does not glorify Edward. He keeps saying that he's a levelheaded dog who is willing to put himself in danger. Thieves once broke into his house, and Edward attacked them. He was badly injured but didn't let up until the thieves ran away. Maxie cared for him for weeks, and there were days when it seemed that Edward would succumb to his wounds, but he rallied, and since then, his loyalty to his master has grown sevenfold.

Magda, Maxie's wife, was caught up in one of the first transports. After Magda disappeared, Maxie didn't budge from Edward, but his life without Magda lost its meaning. He would talk a lot to Edward, torment himself, and wish he were dead, but fate desired otherwise. Kamil came to him and said that he and Felix had decided that when they returned that evening from work, they would slip away and escape to the forest. Maxie didn't hesitate; it seemed to him the right way to end his life. He was going to leave Edward in the hands of his Ukrainian neighbor but then realized the man would likely turn him in. Maxie went to work the next morning without saying goodbye to Edward. Kamil and Felix carried out their plan, and the three of them found themselves in an open field.

FOR A MOMENT it seemed that Maxie was about to speak to Edward and tell him everything that had happened since he left home that morning and ask his forgiveness for abandoning him. That was a wrong impression. Maxie sat motionless, caught up in his thoughts, without saying a word. His initial happiness waned, and sadness swept over him. Fortunately, his friend Salo approached him and said, "Let's show Edward to Grandma Tsirl. She'll surely take an interest in him and say something worth hearing." Maxie cast his eyes downward, took Edward in his arms, and followed Salo silently.

34

The melodies have come back to Isidor, and he has resumed praying at night. His voice is pure and soft. Most of us do not understand the words of the prayer, but the melodies stir the heart and arouse our yearning for home.

Admittedly, the nighttime studies are sometimes filled with quarrel and strife. People argue over every word and every comma. Toughest of all are the communists, who insist that our involvement with the Bible and Hasidism is a retreat to the Dark Ages, and who find Isidor's prayers distasteful. One of them said, "If Isidor takes off his cap while he prays, we'll know he doesn't plan to drug us with his enchantments."

Many of us feel that Isidor is leading us to mysteries hidden within us. More than once, after an hour of prayers, someone bursts into tears. Or blurts out words of accusation.

Last night, after the prayers, Miriam fainted, and Salo took her to the clinic. For hours she didn't utter a sound, but when she awoke, she began sputtering words at a rapid pace. Finally, she stopped her mumbling and sank into sleep.

After spending the day in the clinic, she went back to her work. Salo wanted to keep her another day, but Miriam refused. She's always reserved and silent, but now her silence is more absolute. The people who bring clothes to be mended don't dare open their mouths when they stand before her.

Only Tsila, our big sister, speaks to her. I once heard Tsila say to her, "My dear Miriam, don't forget that many people rely on us. We mustn't disappoint them."

Miriam lifted her head and looked at her, as if to say, *Nothing depends on me. I have no control over my body or my thoughts.*

Tsila knows Miriam's pain. It's not easy to be a twig rescued from the fire. You keep burning but, defiantly, you are not consumed.

It's easier for us fighters. We go to war almost every night. We return exhausted and sleep without dreams, but for Miriam, who launders and patches clothes, each garment leads her back home, to her father and mother, her husband and children.

By the way, Tsila is not afraid of Hermann Cohen; she serves the fighters full bowls of soup and thick slices of bread. When Hermann said she should be more frugal, she told him that a full ladle of soup and a thicker slice of bread won't make that much of a difference. But for fighters, it's like the air they breathe.

To Miriam she said, "My dear, don't be afraid of him. We're not able to do much; what little we can do, we'll do wholeheartedly. Soup without a decent piece of bread is a mockery. After a night of walking with a heavy load on their backs, the fighters must be served a full bowl of thick soup; they are hungry and thirsty. With all due respect to Hermann Cohen, we must not skimp at the expense of the fighters. If he says something to me, I won't stay silent."

Miriam heard this and didn't respond.

This, among other things, is how the days wear us down.

SALO NOTICED THAT from time to time I ask Tsila for a glass of vodka. He came over and asked me if I needed help. I said, "It's a very personal issue, and I'm sure I'll get over it soon. Thanks for your interest."

"I just wanted to ask," Salo apologized.

"Thank you."

One night I happened to sit with Werner, who told me that the days in the ghetto were relatively good days for him. He read the French classics, book after book. It turned out that he had a solid basis in French from the *gymnasium*, and the constant reading later on in the ghetto had deepened his knowledge.

"It was odd," he said. "I was buried within myself. I wasn't part of the suffering that surrounded me. My parents and brother fought desperately for every loaf of bread, but I obsessively clung to my books.

"Later, when I went out to work, I would hide a book in my coat pocket and read during breaks. I was enchanted by Maupassant and Flaubert, and later on, when I got hold of the first volume of Marcel Proust's *In Search of Lost Time*, my happiness knew no bounds.

"My father and mother didn't comment on this addiction of mine. Sometimes they looked at me with wonder. My big brother once said to me that at this fateful time it was wrong to escape into books. This remark did not prevent me from buying more and more books from people who were about to be sent to the camps. Because of this addiction, I didn't see my father and mother and brother during our last days at home. Of course no one knew those were the last days. In my heart of hearts I deluded myself that it would soon be clear that the Germans' cruelty to us was a mistake. They would apologize and recruit the Jews to the war effort."

"And how did you spend your time in the ghetto?" Werner suddenly asked me.

"I was also addicted," I said, without elaborating.

From then on, we've been chatting every once in a while.

35

The arduous final climb to the summit has begun. Luckily for us, the snow has ended and a big winter sun has scattered its silvery light. Everyone has been enlisted in the effort. First the gear and food are taken up and next the children and the elderly. Even at this demanding hour, security is not neglected: an emergency squad is on alert.

The summit is spread out over a broad area and includes the remnants of two forts from Turkish times.

The operation is carried out with precision. We again pitch the canvas tents. We set up the tripods for the pots. Hermann Cohen arranges wooden boards to hold the food. Tsila makes lunch. The new place, perhaps because of the sudden sunshine, seems different from all our previous encampments.

The new home gives us the feeling that they won't surprise us easily. The bunkers, explains Kamil, will be built of two layers of wood as insulation from wetness and cold. We have blankets and an ample quantity of sheepskins to cover the walls and floor.

The view from the summit laid bare the whole area: the roads and railroad tracks, the buildings and military camps. Kamil again pointed out the river and the village of Holovka on the map. Paul is a wound that refuses to heal. More than once, I've heard Kamil say, "We should not have left him alone on the battlefield."

It's been more than a month since he went off, and it's hard to talk about him. He stands before me, alive.

Time is short. We dig and lay foundations for the bunkers. The bunkers will be connected by trenches. Hermann Cohen not only gives advice; he also saws and planes wood and prepares for construction. The vigorous activity fills me with new life in a way I can't quite describe.

I sometimes think that our lives from now on will be more settled. I'll be able to play chess and study for my final exams. There are educated people here; in fact, everyone here is educated. I can turn to them for help, and when the war is over, I'll take my tests. I ask Maxie if he could help me.

"Gladly," says Maxie with a smile. No need to worry, the war will continue for a long time. In the past we would think logically, putting two and two together. In the ghetto, we learned there's no point in calculating, you only get confused. Reality looks different every day.

I dreamed that we were dug into our warm, lighted bunkers, playing chess. Suddenly a stiff wind lifted the cover of the bunker, and cold air blew inside. We tried to replace the cover, but the wind was fierce and stubborn. Hermann Cohen held out his hand and with the ease of a magician put it back in place.

Building the bunkers proceeds slowly but thoroughly. The patrols and ambushes and raids are also on schedule. No wonder that at the end of their shifts the fighters collapse like sacks.

EVER SINCE WE REACHED the summit, the mood has changed. The comrades have begun to discuss things they experienced and saw that till now they didn't dare talk about. It's strange that here of all places, where the cold is unrelenting, a person connects with his soul.

I see my father and mother standing together at the train station. Mama is very pale. She has just had an operation, and the short hospital stay hasn't restored the color to her face. Papa, too, looks shaken. Now he is unable to do anything except stand by Mama's side.

"Sit on the rucksack," Papa says softly.

"I'll stand," says Mama. "It's easier for me to stand. We'll be getting into the railroad cars soon."

They stand frozen in their long coats. Everyone else runs around as if knowing what is in store. Were it not for me, their concern that I escape, my parents would surely sit down.

"Run away, my son," Papa urges over and over. There is a certain distance in his voice that chills me. Mama grips my hand and says, "Run away, my child, escape. There is no future here for young people." She lets go of my hand, and I escape between the railroad cars.

IN HONOR OF REACHING the summit, Tsila and Miriam prepared a festive meal: fish roasted with mountain herbs and potatoes, and two full pots of tea fragrantly steaming on their tripods.

Kamil praised the squads that worked with care and coordination, Hermann Cohen for his work behind the scenes, and Tsila and Miriam, who make us food fit for a king. Kamil called the summit "the very heart of Besht country." Here the Ba'al Shem Tov sought ways to come near to God. Witnesses have reported that when he walked the hills in solitude, he was of average height. When he came down, he was taller than other men.

Isidor was asked to say a prayer. Isidor doesn't talk about feelings or faith or the prayers that he says. The prayers simply pour out of him, as if they have been inside him forever. Someone said that he is a vessel, and because he is a vessel, the prayers are unblemished, not too lofty or ornate.

How does one pray without believing the words of the prayer?, asked the know-it-alls. Isidor did not reply. His face momentarily widened with wonderment, ultimate proof that he, too, had no answer.

36

The cold grows more intense. We insulate the bunkers with mats and sheepskins. First we will shelter the older people, the women, and the children, and then, if there's room, the fighters.

We've lately gotten hold of a large quantity of weapons and ammunition. Kamil decided to build a weapons depot beside the bunkers. A few fighters wanted to have a party to celebrate the bounty. Kamil asked them to postpone the celebration until the first refugees arrive.

Kamil's faith is unwavering and has a solid basis: The Russian radio station broadcasts optimistic news, and not only from Stalingrad. The German station is not as belligerent as before. It reports victories in the East and West but does not promise a rout.

In the last raid Kamil interrogated one of the farmers about the war situation. The man disclosed that the occupier is not concerned with local affairs but is busy conscripting people for work in the factories. Trains filled with soldiers are rushing to the front and returning with the sick and wounded.

Everyone here reads the map of the battles differently. Kamil's opinion has not changed in any fundamental way: we must train our hearts to be fighters and to be Jews. There is no contradiction.

ONE OF OUR FIGHTERS has suddenly plunged into depression. He sits in his regular spot, but the light has gone out of his eyes. Only last night he enjoyed the delicious corn porridge that Tsila made. He, perhaps more than others, appreciates her cooking and often thanks her; now he sits listlessly, filled with doubt and despair.

"Where does this lead?" he asks.

"To ourselves," Kamil answers him, "and from there to victory and light."

"We are few and they are many, and they are determined to destroy us."

"We were always few, but we did not despair. Despair is not a quality worth having."

The fighter's empty gaze does not change. Yesterday he sat listening to the radio, figuring out the distances and calculating the odds with us, and his forecast was no different from that of the optimists; now he had fallen, for no apparent reason, into a black hole.

Kamil is called to the command post, and Salo takes his place.

"What are you afraid of?" Salo asks the man gently.

"Of the tremendous German Army, of their incredible discipline, their network of trains, their terrifying air force. There has never been such a power in the world." He clearly has more to say but shuts his mouth.

"This is why we climbed to the summit. From the summit we can not only defend ourselves but also fight back," says Salo, aware that his words are a weak reply to the gloomy fighter.

"But there are so many of them, and they're so well trained," the fighter responds softly, as if he had not been understood.

"Not everything is measured by power. Sometimes justice and the determination of the few triumph over great power. The Hasmoneans were also few in number," says Salo, emphasizing every word.

"Excuse my ignorance, but who were the Hasmoneans?" asks the fighter.

"Jewish fighters."

"I haven't heard of them."

"They were few and fought against the Greek empire."

"And they succeeded?"

"Very much so."

Hearing these words, the fighter gestures with his head as if to say, *It sounds like a myth.* We see clearly that the faith we've been cultivating for months has faded within him. Salo wants to speak to him from the heart but can't find the way. Finally, he says, "One must not despair," and immediately regrets his superficial words.

Then he tries another approach. "Look at our success," he says. "We're almost finished building the bunkers. We have plenty of guns and ammunition. If the refugees reach us, and they will, we can stop the trains, attack military camps, and ambush them at every turn. We have enough fury inside us to strike them hard. I agree with you: logic often leads to despair, but there is something higher than logic."

"What is that higher thing?" The fighter looks Salo in the eye.

"Faith," says Salo, pronouncing the word cautiously.

"I am empty of faith," the fighter replies blankly.

You must overcome this mental block, Salo wants to tell him but decides not to.

"I have no faith," he continues. "I wonder about people who talk about faith as something to be taken for granted. I don't know what they're talking about," he declares.

"You doubt the justice of our cause?" Salo tries another approach, blunter this time.

"I don't doubt our justice. I doubt our chances of escape from the jaws of the enemy. The enemy is huge and monstrous. The monster's thundering hooves grow louder every day. All people surrender to it and do its bidding. Anyone who saw the railroad cars sucking up thousands like a gigantic vacuum cleaner knows its massive power. The world has never seen such a monster."

As the moments pass, the fighter is consumed by this horrific image that threatens to devour him entirely. Salo puts a hand on his shoulder, takes him to the infirmary tent, asks him to sit on a crate, and says, "I'll give you something good; you'll feel better right away."

The fighter does not refuse. He opens his mouth and drinks the liquid like a pacified child.

Salo keeps talking to him in a soothing, rhythmic voice, as if telling him a fairy tale. The fighter closes his eyes and falls asleep while seated. Soon, with Danzig's help, Salo will move him to the pallet of twigs.

MICHAEL COPIED OUT a song that Rabbi Levi Yitzhak of Berditchev used to sing to himself. At night, after distributing the pages to the study group, he was asked to read it. Michael was self-conscious, but Maxie, who stood beside him, encouraged him, and he read:

> *Wherever I go—you.*
> *Wherever I stand—you.*
> *Only you, again you, always you.*
> *If I feel good—you.*
> *If I feel bad—you.*
> *Only you, again you, always you.*
> *Sky—you,*
> *Earth—you,*
> *Up—you,*
> *Down—you.*

I look thus, I see this.
Only you, again you, always you.
You, you, you.

Coming from Michael's lips, the poem sounded as if it were written for him. The sharper minds among us who were about to pounce and dissect it fell silent at once, and all were filled with wonder and emotion. With every passing minute it became harder to hold back our tears.

37

We are motivated by the increased number of trains. The patrols collected data showing twice as much rail traffic in recent days. In between the trains rushing to the front are trains taking Jews to the camps. All the testimonies we've taken indicate that these are death camps, with smoke pouring from their chimneys day and night.

"We can no longer stand aside. Our mission at this hour is to stop these infernal deportations," Kamil says, gritting his teeth.

Kamil is alone in his tent, bent over a large map. He is planning the operation to the last detail. From time to time he calls in squad leaders to hear their opinions. We know the area well, but we need to prepare for surprises: bad weather, hostile patrols.

Meanwhile, the cold gets worse, and thick, silent snow falls without a break; this is a sign that from now on our lives will change, will grow more intense. We are running out of time.

Kamil doesn't improvise. He is now training two squads for this mission. In Hermann Cohen's storehouse, fighters are trying on shoes and clothing suitable for the operation. "Better to suffer from cold than from clumsiness," repeats Kamil.

We moved Grandma Tsirl into a bunker. The move was lovingly performed. Grandma Tsirl was cross about the excessive attention. "I should have gone already to rest in the World to Come and not be a burden here," she said.

Kamil came out of his tent to greet her. Grandma Tsirl does not pay attention to the radio but rather to voices she hears and visions she sees. Her ancestors are her guides again at this critical time. She often says, "That's what my ancestors did and that's how I try to act." She's not afraid of contradictions, misunderstandings, or embarrassing questions. For the most part she answers questions clearly and simply. When she has no answer, she says, "If God puts words in my mouth, I will know how to answer. If he doesn't, it is a sign that I am not worthy." She speaks simply about God, a God who is close to human beings, who bestows His grace and goodness on them. One must accept the good and the bad and not complain. She never tires of saying this. The statements that Grandma Tsirl keeps repeating drive the communists crazy, and not only them. One of them raised his voice and fumed, "This is wrongheaded foolishness, and fraud to boot."

Everything here is hard; we are rattled and moody. I sometimes think that not only did the Germans and the local population declare total war on us, so did nature. A few days ago we were attacked by a pack of wolves. They were hungry and ready to tear us apart. Felix threw a grenade and wiped them out.

Killing them didn't make us happy. We saw the wolves' bodies quivering in the snow and remembered the ghetto: the soldiers fired indiscriminately, and human body parts were strewn on the ground, red and exposed.

Kamil has issued a special order: "We are nearing the day when we'll be forced to fight the enemy face-to-face. It's no secret that the enemy is determined to kill us all. Thank God we are free, well trained, and ready to fight.

"We are few, but even the few can derail trains that take Jews to their death. We have among us officers and fighters who are opposed to taking such action, but Felix and I take full responsibility upon ourselves. No doubt this is a risk, but our courage led us to escape from the ghetto and come to these mountains. And this courage will be our guide when we go down to wreak havoc on those who run and guard the trains. It's a risk but a necessary and holy one. Life is important and precious, but when the enemy is wild and vicious, we cannot stand idly by. 'He who comes to kill you, kill him first.' That is what we are called upon to do at this hour. Your commander, Kamil."

38

Amid all this, one of our patrols came upon a Ukrainian who immediately raised his hands and asked for asylum with us. He was taken to our command post and under no pressure revealed his secret: "A few days ago the last Jews working in the quarry were brought in chains, ordered to go into the river, and were shot there. Since then, I have not been able to live. The screams are stuck in my head. I don't eat and I don't sleep. Take me; do what you want with me. I can no longer live in my village."

Kamil questioned him about his village and surrounding villages, and about what became of their Jews.

"They killed them all. They were forced to dig pits near the forest, and when they finished digging, they were shot in the back and fell in. Other Jews were brought, and they covered the pits. After that, they dug pits for themselves. This was day after day. Now in the whole area not one Jew is left. The Jews brought from the quarry were the last ones. I cannot live in such a place." His whole body trembled.

"How many days did you look for us?" Kamil asked quietly.

"Two days."

"Do they know about us down there?"

"They know."

Salo took him to the kitchen, and Tsila served him soup. He gulped the soup but continued to tremble.

That same night Kamil interrogated him about the trains and the army bases scattered along the main roads. He calmed down as he confirmed that in recent days train traffic had doubled. Civilian transport had been suspended. Of the trains carrying Jews, he said, "The screams reach to the heavens."

"What do you want to do?" Kamil asked him in a friendly tone.

"To be with you," he said, and he burst into tears.

DANZIG REJOICES: Milio has called him Papa.

"How many times?"

"Just once."

"You're sure?"

"Yes."

Everyone is happy for Danzig, as if forgetting for the moment the dangerous missions ahead.

"Milio is not mute, I knew it," Danzig murmurs over and over in a monotone, out of character for a huge man and squad commander.

"If he said 'Papa,'" Salo weighs in, "it's a sign that his speech has awakened and he will soon start talking."

Milio is our perpetual mystery. His wide-open eyes are with us always. It's hard to ignore him, even if you want to. His silence is stronger than any talk, but it's hard to decipher this muteness.

He appears to understand very well everything that goes on around him. But at times his appearance suddenly changes, and he looks as though he feels sad for himself and for Danzig: *Today we are together, but who knows where we will be tomorrow. Once I had parents, and they are gone,* his eyes seem to say. *Now I am afraid that Danzig will go away and not come back.*

The word "Papa" emerging from Milio's sealed lips has completely transformed Danzig. When Danzig is happy, his face changes and he stares into space like a child. Everyone who goes out with him on a mission knows how dedicated he is to each of us. Sometimes it seems as though he's going to sit his squad down under a tree, and he alone will continue the mission.

Grandma Tsirl has said, "We should learn to be happy from Danzig. He knows how to empty himself of everything unconnected to joy and happiness." When Danzig goes to visit Grandma Tsirl, she declares, "I'm happy you came; it's not every day such a giant comes to see me."

39

Maxie, Michael's mentor, served as a demolition expert in the previous world war. He knows all about the use of explosives and is being attached to the squads that will go deep into enemy territory.

This time the preparations were a bit different. Perhaps this was because a few fighters wrote letters and left them with friends at our base camp, perhaps because of the thick layer of snow that covered wide areas, or perhaps because of the heightened anticipation for this unprecedented mission.

Kamil spread out the map and pointed to the route and the obstacles. In recent days the squads practiced fighting under heavy fire and in populated areas, and of course the setting of explosives. Clearly, this action would prepare us for others to follow. Later, we would derail only trains carrying Jews.

Michael did not leave Maxie's side. He didn't pester him with questions; he just studied his movements and the loads he was going to carry on his back. Earlier, Michael had promised Maxie that he would complete all the geometry exercises Maxie had assigned to him, and if he had time left over, he would help Tsila in the kitchen. Danzig, who entrusted Milio to Tsila, couldn't hold back and kept murmuring, "Milio has made great progress in recent weeks. If he asks about me, tell him I'll be back soon."

Kamil announced that the password for this mission would be

simcha, joy. "The Ba'al Shem Tov, in whose land we now live, asked his people to rejoice in everything they did—even in days of despair—because joy expands the heart and the mind. Happiness is the opposite of sadness, which degrades us. We must cling to happiness, which brings us close to other people and to God. And so our password today, do not forget, is *simcha*."

Grandma Tsirl blessed the fighters in a whisper. Kamil read the psalm "The Lord is my shepherd" in a subdued voice, handed the Bible over to his deputy Felix, and took his place at the head of the squad. I was sorry that I was left behind to guard the base. I stood and watched them as they grew distant, and part of me went with the fighters.

That night Isidor chanted prayers of the High Holidays. Grandma Tsirl could hear Isidor's pure voice and praised him: "Itche Meir carries within him the melodies of the Vizhnitz Hasidim."

There was a sense of Yom Kippur, our Day of Judgment.

I remembered. In our house Yom Kippur was gloomy because we shuttered the windows. Papa and Mama fasted but didn't go to the synagogue. They read books they had selected in advance. Last Yom Kippur they read Marcel Proust's *In Search of Lost Time*. Mama read me a few passages, and I was enchanted by the melodious prose, the serenity of household objects, the soft, melancholy light of summer. I felt a connection to Mama's voice and to the words of Proust. Papa was completely immersed in reading and wasn't ready to share his impressions. Only when the holiday was over did he open up and enthuse about a sentence of Proust, marveling at its magic.

WHEN ISIDOR'S PRAYERS fell silent, it was nearly one o'clock in the morning. We knew the squads were still an hour away from the target. At two o'clock, according to our information, the train was supposed to pass by, and if the explosives went off as expected, the locomotive and carriages would be derailed, the guards would run away in all directions, and our squads would open fire and pursue the fleeing soldiers.

We stood at the entrance to the bunkers, listening for the sound of the explosion, but it was delayed. At 2:05 a huge blast was heard, and we knew that Kamil's meticulous preparations had been accurate, as always.

We remained silent. We were familiar with raids and skirmishes, but we had never before undertaken a military operation. Twelve fighters are too few for a mission like this, even if they are well trained. I could see Maxie and Danzig, with the explosives on their backs, and the other fighters swallowed up into the darkness. I was distressed as I envisioned them going down into the abyss; I felt that we had abandoned them.

Isidor asked if the operation was dangerous. I didn't know what to tell him, so I said, "The fighters are well trained."

Isidor walks among us like an enigma. He prays, but we have not heard such prayer before; it is Isidor's alone. He seems bound to it on many levels. Outwardly he resembles us; were it not for his nightly praying, we wouldn't have believed him capable of it.

For a moment, I wanted to ask him if he practices for the nighttime prayers, but I quickly realized this was a foolish question. Isidor sensed what I was about to ask and said, "The minute I close my eyes and open my mouth, prayer rises within me. Grandpa taught me the letters and the words, but the melodies filled me up without my knowing they were inside me."

"What is prayer, my friend?" I wasn't sure why I asked him in quite that way.

"Desire," he said, and a little smile crossed his lips.

40

W e spent the rest of the night in the kitchen; we drank tea and didn't talk. I suddenly sensed the same dread we had felt at home in the last weeks before our deportation. My mother's face bore signs of illness. My father ran from hospitals to private clinics. There were doctors who thought an operation was urgent and should be done immediately, and others who advised us to postpone it until we were settled in the new place.

"Who knows what will be in the new place?" Papa said, and he decided the operation should be performed by the renowned surgeon Dr. Orenstein.

I was still a student at the *gymnasium* and didn't accompany my father on the day of my mother's surgery. I was studying for the comprehensive exam in German, but my soul was consumed by Anastasia. Dark rumors rustled everywhere, but I continued to meet her every evening.

We promised each other loyalty and everlasting love. A smile I didn't recognize appeared in Anastasia's eyes. I asked her if she regretted the promise. She laughed out loud at my question, as if I didn't understand her. I apologized.

It's hard to describe how blind I was, but it was more than blindness. I saw my parents' agony, but their agony didn't touch me. My contact with them had shrunk to a quick hello in the morning and evening. As soon as I left the house, I pictured Anastasia. I ran to meet her on Lilac Lane.

Meanwhile, my mother underwent the surgery. Papa didn't budge from her bedside. When I came and went, Mama looked at me with compassion. I knew what I should tell her, but I didn't say it.

I was an only child and meant everything to my parents. They saw me growing distant from them but let me do so. They didn't want to disrupt my happiness. Who knows what they thought of me in those days at the edge of the abyss.

The ghetto opened my eyes but not wide enough. I kept telling myself: it's a mistake, a misunderstanding. I would stand by the fence for hours waiting for Anastasia. I was certain that she, too, was a captive in her home and unable to come to me. Her father had once said to me, "Edmund, don't be like the Jews." It sounded like a joke. Only later did I realize it was a warning that meant, *Don't go too far with my daughter. Our girls, unlike the Jewish girls, protect their chastity until the wedding.*

Later on, at the train station, surrounded by dozens of soldiers, I kept looking for Anastasia among the people who walked freely a short distance from the fence.

Several young people escaped from the station. I, too, wanted to escape, but the sense of obligation I had belatedly come to feel held me back. Were it not for Papa and Mama, who began to whisper urgently, "Run away!," I might not have escaped.

ISIDOR CAME OVER and put his hand on my shoulder, which snapped me out of my reverie. He was focused on the fighters who had gone out that night on the dangerous mission. I was ashamed that at this fateful hour my thoughts were not with those who went down the mountain to risk their lives.

"Isidor," I said to him, "your prayers are not only moving, they also show us our parents and grandparents in a light we hadn't known."

"I don't know what to tell you," Isidor said, lowering his eyes.

"My parents kept their distance from collective ritual," I said, "but their hearts were attuned to the mysteries of nature and art. Their ongoing love for Bach connected them with God."

My words must have confused Isidor, and he closed his eyes.

It occurred to me that Isidor is not a cantor but an artist of prayer. Like an artist, he doesn't know exactly what he is doing or what he makes happen.

I didn't want to further confuse him, and so I kept quiet.

"It's too bad they didn't include me with the fighters," Isidor mumbled.

Time inched along slowly, tensely. Tsila and Miriam made sandwiches for the fighters' return.

One of the fighters waiting with us, whose voice I hadn't heard till now, tried to explain his worldview to another fighter who sat beside him. "A person must reject Darwinism and not be part of the struggle for existence. We have an inner world that guides us."

The other fighter listened and said, "When you say 'inner world,' I assume you mean a moral world."

"Correct."

"Who is the ruler of this inner world?"

"How do you mean? The individual 'I' of each of us."

"But isn't the 'I' likely to fall into error and become addicted to itself, or to some corrupt ideology? Man's heart is evil from his youth."

"The self cannot be damaged or corrupted; it is good, it is moral."

This conversation seemed to have been uprooted from elsewhere and brought here. The fighter who began the conversation appeared to forget where we were and what was happening to us. Perhaps in order to distract himself, he returned to a place he loved—the philosophy department at the *gymnasium*.

I went outside with Isidor. The snow didn't stop and lit up the darkness with its falling flakes. I've loved to watch this magic since childhood.

"Did you graduate from the *gymnasium*?" I asked Isidor.

"A year ago."

"I was about to graduate, but I didn't. How is it that I never met you there?"

"There were so many of us, running down the long corridors, everyone to his classes and examinations."

"Many things happened in my parents' house in the last weeks before the deportation, but they didn't affect me. Not even my mother's illness," I found myself saying.

41

Felix entered the kitchen with Victor, the Ukrainian who surrendered to us. Tsila served Victor a sandwich and a cup of tea, and he was invited to sit on a crate. For the first time we got a good look at him.

After Victor finished his meal, Felix asked him in a businesslike manner, "Tell all of us, please, what you told the commander and me."

Victor raised his head, looked Felix straight in the eye, and said, to everyone's surprise, "It is hard for me to talk at this moment." His tone implied a request for patience.

"What's the problem?" Felix did not consider his request.

"When I speak, I see the pits and the soldiers shooting people in the back of the neck, and the horror silences me."

"The fighters need to know the reason why they are risking their lives," continued Felix in his emotionless voice.

Victor hesitated and then surprised us again. "I pray to God to put the right words into my mouth and that I will not be afraid to tell you exactly what I saw. You know better than I do how hard it is to convey to another person what you have seen, especially atrocities. It's very easy to be inexact, to be vague, to justify yourself and appear blameless.

"I will confess right away, I'm no different from other people in my village. I, too, stood by the side indifferently while the Jews in my village were murdered. I, too, slept in my cozy bed after the slaughter of the Jews, but something inside me—call it fear—robbed me of my sleep and showed me the horrors of their death. I wanted to ignore those images. I went to the river, walked into the mountains. Everywhere they stood before my eyes, as if waiting for me.

"For many weeks these visions tortured me. I didn't know what to do with myself. I feared that if I told my family how I felt they would ridicule me, denounce me. Even worse, they would say I had gone crazy. I kept quiet, and my silence strangled me.

"Forgive me for getting ahead of myself; I want to say more, if I may. I was born in Holovka, a small village. My father owns a farm, and the whole family works there; some do manual labor and others tend the sheep or bring the fruits and vegetables to the market.

"At the age of eighteen I was conscripted into the emperor's army, did my basic training, and was sent to guard storehouses. Unluckily for me there was an explosion in one of the depots, and I was wounded in my right leg. I was discharged from the army and went home. My brothers and sisters had moved on, and I was left behind: assistant bookkeeper for the farm. The wound, which left a scar, made me different from my brothers and sisters. A person with a scar like mine doesn't sleep well; he's worried with good reason and also without—he's afraid of people. A woman I was close to from my youth, who loved me and I loved her, the minute she discovered the scar on my leg she wanted to end our engagement with the excuse that she had never seen anything so hideous in her life. I admit, a scar like mine is not an uplifting sight, but I would say she exaggerated. Women do tend to exaggerate.

"Why am I telling you all this? Are these trivial details important, compared with the events that follow? Why do I dwell on them? Because were it not for the scar, I think my life would have been different. I would have done well at the farm or set up my own, and the death of the Jews would not have concerned me. But what can I say, a man's fate in not in his own hands. The scar, in any event, made me a different creature but by no means righteous.

"When the Germans invaded the village, we felt they were more polite than our police and behaved fairly. Yes, a few of their officers were condescending, but this is normal for a conqueror, so said the old people of our village, who had seen other conquerors in their day.

"In the village there were five Jewish families, and they were treated differently. They were taken from their homes and lined up in threes, old people, women, and children included, and made to march through the length of the village. Whoever could not march was forced to crawl, but beyond this humiliation there was no further abuse. In the evening they went back to their homes.

"In the village, confusion was mixed with satisfaction. The bizarre parade was seen as amusing mistreatment, nothing more. 'It's good to remind the Jews to act humbly and honestly and not get rich at the workers' expense,' my father declared.

"The attitude toward the Jews of the village was always distant. Be wary of them, our fathers taught us. In public school I studied alongside Jewish children. Most of them wanted to excel, but there were also two dimwitted ones who were ridiculed. I was intrigued by the Jewish children, but I didn't really like them. Their strangeness attracted my attention. I liked to ask them questions and hear their answers. They filled my dreams—sometimes as creatures who performed miracles with their magical powers, and sometimes as little monsters, slithering and grabbing hold of people.

"I come back to the main story. Again they took the Jews from their homes and again marched them in threes through the village, but this time the women and men were ordered to dance and kiss each other. This sight was funnier. Everyone laughed, even the blind and deaf. The entertainment lasted about two hours, and they were finally ordered to return home.

"Every day the commander came up with a new abuse. One time a pig was brought to the square, and the marchers were ordered to dance around it, then to bend down and kiss it. Everyone exploded with laughter and looked forward to the next show.

"It went on this way for about three weeks, maybe more. Two old people died, unable to endure the marching, and a young man named Max, who had been my classmate, committed suicide. One woman went insane, cursed the soldiers and called them storm troopers, and was shot in the belly.

"Then the commander went away, and his deputy left the Jews in their homes. The Jews reopened their shops, and it seemed like the abuses had passed and life was back to what it had been before.

"As it turned out, this was merely a lull.

"The commander returned and the following day ordered the Jews to assemble in the village square, dressed in holiday clothes. This time they were marched to the river and ordered to go into it. Anyone who didn't go in was pushed in. The Donets River isn't wide but it is deep. The old people and children drowned quickly, and those who tried to swim were shot. The clear river water turned red. The screaming stopped very quickly.

"That was how the Jews of Holovka perished. In the nearby villages the Jews were also abused, but their death was different: They were taken to the forest, they dug themselves pits, and when they were done, they were shot at the edge. Their fellow Jews who came after them covered the pits and dug other pits for themselves.

"That's how the killing was carried out. Life in the village continued as normal. The farmers worked the fields, stored vegetables and fruits. People broke into the homes of those who were killed and took whatever they wanted.

"My father summed it up: 'They brought it on themselves.'

And I think everyone agreed with him. Don't get the wrong idea; I'm no saint. If it weren't for the scar on my leg, I assume the sights that I saw would have vanished from my head, and I would have gone back to work. But what can I say? The sights gave me no rest. I felt a rope tightening around my neck, and if I didn't run away from that place, I would have choked. And so here I am before you."

Felix asked him very politely, "Maybe you know of a fellow named Paul, who disappeared from here about a month ago? We don't know what happened to him."

"No," he replied, then took his head in his hands and said, "but in a hut outside the village lived a strange couple with a daughter, newcomers. He worked as a day laborer and she at home. One night a man broke into their house, shot them dead, and kidnapped the daughter. There had been rumors about the couple in the village. The next day they were buried in a plot outside the cemetery, and the matter was dropped."

Felix leaned toward him. "And what else was said?" he asked.

"That's what they said."

We knew it was Paul. We shuddered.

Victor sat for a while on the crate without moving. The things that he said hovered in the empty darkness. We had known abuse in the ghetto, but the horrors that Victor described were more raw and more terrible.

42

It was five o'clock. At this hour the fighters usually return from their raid; people come out of the tents, light cigarettes, and anxiously wait for them. But we were still gripped by the horrors described by Victor, and our fears for the returning men grew.

"The snow must be delaying them," said Felix, who emerged from the kitchen and held out his hands to feel the snowflakes.

We stood and stamped our feet.

Michael, who had fallen asleep for a while, woke up and stood with everyone. We envisioned our patrol walking the way Kamil had taught us. Because of their heavy clothes, they looked short and low to the ground, and for a moment it seemed that if a shot rang out, they would not lie flat on the ground but simply sink.

Another hour went by. Victor sat in his place and didn't come out. Felix returned to the kitchen and asked him for details about the couple and their daughter. Victor confessed that in those days he was flooded with scenes of death, always on edge, and uninterested in what went on in the village. Felix told him that Paul, a brave fighter and loving person, had gone out to rescue his kidnapped daughter and then disappeared.

Michael, who saw the tension, asked me if everything was all right.

"I assume so," I told him. That's the answer that Maxie, his foster father, usually gives him.

"How is this raid different from the earlier raids?" he asked, surprising me with his question. For a moment I was struck by his maturity, and I didn't know how to reply. I decided I must not lie and said, "This time the fighters went to derail the train."

"I know," he said, surprising me again. "My question is, is this operation more dangerous?"

Michael has matured during the months he has been with us. His mind races and his thoughts are coherent and well formulated. It's for good reason that Maxie says that Michael will surprise us in the future.

AS THE DAWN SKY grew pink, Felix spotted our fighters on the slope, and we immediately ran toward them. The snow that had piled up made their climb difficult, but the fighters moved quickly, helping one another, Kamil in the lead.

When they reached the summit, we instantly saw that Danzig's arm was bandaged. It was Danzig, but it wasn't really him: his shoulders had narrowed and he looked shorter. Salo, who had cared for him the entire way, now led Danzig to the infirmary tent. He asked me to remove his shoes, and together we laid him down on the mat of twigs.

Danzig didn't complain, just bit his lip, and we could see he was in acute pain. Salo injected him with a painkiller and asked for bags of ice.

Because of Danzig's injury, there was no proper welcome for the fighters. In the kitchen they were served sandwiches and cups of tea. They were hungry but also overcome by fatigue, and most of them fell asleep with the cups in their hands.

Milio was brought to Danzig. Danzig, feeling a bit less pain after the injection, opened his eyes and softly called, "Milio."

Milio looked at him without making a sound.

"How are you, my child? Don't you recognize me? I missed you."

Hearing these words, Milio raised both his hands, lowered them, and uttered a few syllables.

"He's happy I've come back," Danzig said, his face brightening.

In the evening Kamil told us about the operation. "The two squads acted in exemplary fashion," he began. "We arrived on schedule and fanned out. Salo and Danzig carried the explosives to the tracks. Everything went like clockwork: the explosives were detonated, three cars were thrown from the tracks, and the soldiers panicked. They ran around, desperately looking for cover. We fired at them and killed many. Do not rejoice in the death of your enemy, our Scripture warns us, but we couldn't help but be happy that they had fallen. Were it not for one German soldier who shot wildly and wounded his own comrades as well as Danzig, the operation would have ended perfectly.

"This is just the beginning; from now on caution and alertness are vital. The reprisal will not be long in coming, I would guess. An army cannot tolerate such a humiliating defeat. We must prepare. From now on we're in a state of total readiness, day and night. But we must not forget our main purpose: to derail the trains taking Jews to the camps. Let us not deceive ourselves; there will be casualties, but every Jew we save from the jaws of the beast is cause for celebration."

Silence. No one took issue with his words. Kamil looked that night like a man with a great responsibility on his shoulders.

Then he abruptly asked us to pray for Danzig's well-being.

"What should we say?" asked one of the fighters.

"Very simple, 'God, heal our beloved Danzig.' That's all," he said with a chuckle, as if he'd overcome a mental block.

THE PATROLS AND AMBUSHES continued to go out. The guards of the base took their positions, and the rest of us gathered in the big tent with a sense of togetherness. Differences of opinion that had sometimes wrecked our evenings seemed to vanish. The thought that in upcoming actions we would save our brethren trapped in the boxcars lifted our spirits.

I closed my eyes and recalled the summer vacation with my parents in Dismora: the park and forests that surrounded the small family hotel.

I am almost eight years old and enveloped in love. The hotel owner enjoys chatting with Papa about politics and society and playing chess with him. The headwaiter makes sure that our meals are varied and delicious and served with perfection.

The days go by slowly; we hike in the woods and around the lake and finally arrive at the river. The River Prut is calm at this time of year. Its water is clear, and small fish swim close to the bottom. Papa and Mama swim. My strokes in the water are improving, and I can float.

Suddenly, in the midst of this happiness, I am shaken by a fear that darkens the sunny day. I think that a creature in human form is staring at us. And he's not alone—there are others hiding in the trees, lying in wait for us. There is no sound anywhere, just the quiet flow of the Prut and the whisper of the wind. Papa and Mama are focused on their swimming, and when they come out of the river, there are droplets of water on their faces and necks. They look so pleased that I hate to puncture their happiness, and I tell them nothing. And wonder of wonders, I look around again, and the ambushers have vanished. I'm glad I didn't alarm my parents. But what can I do; such fears pounce on me sometimes— when we walk in the woods or in the park, or when we sit in the pretty garden of the hotel.

These are illusions, I tell myself, happy to have thought of that word, and I say nothing to Mama. But Mama is sensitive. "What are you daydreaming about, Edmund?" she asks me.

"Will we always be together?" I ask, immediately regretting my question.

"I would think so," she replies. "Why do you ask, my darling?"

"I was thinking that one day someone will separate us."

"Who would dare to do that?"

"I have no idea."

"Of course," Mama says, "you'll grow up, graduate from the *gymnasium*, study at the university, get married, and have children of your own. But we'll always be together, and we'll love your wife and your children the way we love you."

"I apologize," I say.

When we return from a day of sun and water, a lavish meal awaits us. The summer days are long, and we sit by the window and watch the slow sunset as it changes colors. Nighttime is still far off.

Dinner is elegantly served; this time it's fish from the river, new potatoes, and fragrant peas. The food here is tastier than the food at home, perhaps because of our appetite and our overall feeling of contentment.

After dinner, we sit in the park and inhale the evening fragrance. The fear that gripped me in the morning, by the water, has returned, but now it's for real: a local drunk, his knees wobbling, pukes and curses. "The Jews should be thrown out of this holy land; they defile it," he growls.

When we hear this curse, we get up and return to the hotel.

I think for a moment that Papa will lodge a complaint that this evil man has disturbed our peace. But Papa doesn't say anything. We sit in the lobby. Papa and Mama are served tea and strawberry cakes with cream, and I get a cup of cocoa and chocolate cake. The pleasant, delicate lighting erases the fear and the face of the drunkard for me but not for Mama. "There seem to be devils everywhere," she says, "even in peaceful Dismora." Papa reacts differently. He lights a cigarette and says, "You call them devils?"

"What would you call them?"

"In high school, 'devils' and 'evil spirits' were considered epithets that shouldn't be used."

"I consider them to be accurate."

"I assume you're right, as always."

"Again you're teasing me; I forgive you," Mama says with a smile.

THOSE WERE the last words I understood on that long, light-filled evening. We went up to our room and sat on the balcony, but I didn't comprehend anything that was said or left unsaid.

Papa moved me to my bed and I dozed off, with my mother's hands stroking my forehead; within minutes I was sailing in the depths of sleep.

43

The snowfall is heavier from day to day. The women, the children, and the elderly huddle in the bunkers. The fighters, the emergency squads, Kamil, and Felix all sleep in the tents. Drills and exercise are strictly performed. Soon we will go on a raid; supplies are low, and we must replenish them.

Russian radio is jubilant: the Stalingrad front has been completely broken. The German Army, despite its reinforcements, is in retreat. The excited radio announcer leaves no room for doubt. We want to celebrate, but Danzig's injury and the decline in Grandma Tsirl's health undercut our happiness. Kamil had thought of sending two squads to capture a surgeon to treat Danzig but concluded that the risks were great and the chances of success were minimal.

Victor reminds us that the camps to which the Jews are taken are death camps. There are fighters who are skeptical of his testimony, but Kamil and Felix trust him and hope that in the upcoming mission we will succeed in derailing a train that is taking Jews to their death.

Amid the enormous tension there are nights when Michael hands out pages in his neat handwriting with biblical verses or an anecdote from Martin Buber's Hasidic tales. Studying by the campfire takes us back to the days when we had a home, parents, and grandparents, when we would sit by the stove and read till late at night. There's nothing like long winter nights for reading and silence.

I REMEMBER: When I was in the first grade, Mama would take me to school every day and come to pick me up when classes were over. Our home wasn't far from the school, but it seemed distant to me, farther than I could walk alone. Also, I loved walking with Mama, looking at people and birds, and asking a lot of questions. More than once, Mama told me, *Run along, darling. I'll catch up with you.* But I refused, held her hand, and wouldn't let go.

Most of the children came to school without their mothers. I noticed that only a few made their mothers take them to the front gate. For this we were teased. The other children would shout to us, "You're still little babies; you need Mommy's breast!"

They were rude and they cursed like grown-ups.

Mama would say, "Don't pay attention to them; they're uncivilized." I couldn't ignore their mocking. Only later at the *gymnasium*, in the physical education class, did I develop muscles and learn how to hit and take a beating.

GRANDMA TSIRL'S HEALTH has gotten worse. Salo and Maxie took her out of the bunker and moved her to the infirmary tent. Grandma Tsirl does not complain; she keeps saying that the time has come to remove the barriers between this world and the World to Come, and then it will become clear that death is an illusion. "Salo, my dear, save the medicines for the fighters and don't feed them to me. I can manage without them."

"Grandma Tsirl, don't rush to leave us. We need you," said

Kamil, who came to visit her. "We need you now more than ever."

"How can I help you, my dear, I'm so weak. Every little movement makes me dizzy."

"Soon we'll go down to derail a train, and we'll ask for your blessing before we go."

"They have already told me, my dear, that in the coming days they will come to take me."

"And you won't be with us on the day of victory?"

"Don't worry, my dear. I'm sure that this whole devoted community will see wonders and miracles."

Kamil bowed his head and left her.

Later on some of us went to see her. She immediately recognized me and said, "Don't worry. Your mother, Bunya, is watching over you."

"Where is she now, Grandma?"

"In a place that God assigned her to be."

"Will I see her again?"

"If God wishes it."

She also recognized Isidor and called to him. "Itche Meir, take good care of the prayers. You are lucky; your grandfather Itche Meir planted the prayers in you, and they speak from inside of you. You are the pillar of fire of our camp," she said and closed her eyes. It was clear that talking had exhausted her.

The same night, the winds raged and took Reb Hanoch and his tent. When we got up in the morning, there was nothing in his place but white snow.

Kamil ordered the emergency squads to surround the summit and search for Reb Hanoch. Later another squad joined them. No sign or trace was found, and everyone was in shock. No one spoke; it was as if our lives had again been dealt an unfathomable blow.

The winds continued to howl, and we stood frozen in place, not seeking shelter. Only now did we grasp what Reb Hanoch had given us. What would we have done without the stocking caps, the gloves, and the vests. We had taken his gifts for granted.

Kamil did not give up; he ordered us to descend from the summit to continue the search.

44

The next day two squads went on a raid. Supplies are dwindling, and there's no alternative other than a raid to provide food for the people we will rescue.

Before we went out, Kamil took us to Grandma Tsirl to receive her blessing. Grandma Tsirl covered her face with her hands and spoke in a whisper. When she finished the blessing, she said, "God will protect you."

Grandma Tsirl's miraculous existence is now a part of us. We think about her, and we see her not only when we are on alert or in training. Her face, her hands, even the scarf around her neck often appear before our eyes. "There is no need for worry," she has promised us several times. "We will always be together. Barriers are temporary. What seems impossible to us is simple and possible. Doubts and contradictions are illusions."

We went out into the night, quiet and disciplined, with a sense that we were capable of changing the course of our lives.

Ever since we escaped from the ghetto, our hearts pound with the desire to change and be changed, and every mission, as Kamil says, is an act of soul-searching. No wonder that after a successful operation the fighters sometimes burst into tears.

We were on the road for two hours. The information gathered by the patrols was accurate. We attacked the farm and surprised its inhabitants, and had it not been for the two small children who awoke and screamed, all would have worked out for the best.

The family elder, the grandfather, looked at Felix and said, "See what you've done." He was apparently referring to the children who woke up in a panic and screamed. Felix answered him very politely, "We are partisans, defending the homeland and justice. We are not robbers; we are fulfilling a mission. We need food, clothes, blankets. We hope you will give these things to us willingly. If you don't comply with our request, we'll take them anyway."

"Take what you want, I don't care," said the grandfather scornfully. His two grown sons stood by their father without saying a word. They watched tensely, suppressing their anger. We are used to such encounters, and our weapons are ready for whatever happens.

"Who are you?" the grandfather suddenly asked Felix.

"Partisans. Can't you see that we are partisans fighting for justice?"

"I think you are Jews."

"So what?"

"One doesn't expect Jews to be fighters."

"The time has come to correct your prejudice."

"I'm not giving my food to Jews!" he shouted.

"If you don't give it, we'll take it ourselves."

"Damn you!" the old man hoarsely cried.

Felix didn't hesitate and called out, "Men, tie him up."

We quickly moved to tie up the grandfather and his sons. The children and women continued to scream. We had no choice but to silence them; Felix fired a round into the ceiling, and everyone fell silent.

We took what we could carry and withdrew in an orderly fashion.

When we were a mile away, we heard the men cursing. They wished death for the Jews, every last one of them.

The operation was a success, but it left us with a murky feeling. The grandfather's boldness and the sons' hostile looks continued to hurt us even as we neared our base.

Some of the fighters thought we had handled them too gently; the time had come to hit them hard. Felix said nothing, and his silence was powerful, as always. Salo, who had not gone with us this time, made sure to inform us right away that Danzig's condition had improved slightly; he felt less pain. Milio slept by his side and raised his spirits.

Grandma's Tsirl's health had not improved, but she was fully conscious; her memory was active, and she was happy to see everyone who came to visit.

I decided to go to the infirmary tent and visit her. Grandma Tsirl sat leaning on pillows and when she saw me called out, "Bunya's son is here to visit me. I'm ashamed I don't remember his name."

"My name is Edmund," I said.

"I assume your Jewish name is hidden in your foreign name. I once knew how to peel the names and find their Jewish seed; now my memory is weaker, and this is another sign that the time has come to pass into the World of Truth."

"I left my father and mother at the train station, and I ran away. What can I do to atone for this sin, Grandma Tsirl?" I could hardly breathe.

"Everything that you do now, my son, is charity. And as we know, charity saves a person from an unnatural death. All the more so from sin. God in heaven knows you well and knows that you did not do what you did out of malice."

"What more should I do, Grandma?"

"You are doing more than enough. All of us need to regret, but thoughts of regret must not damage the desire to act righteously.

You have just returned from a mission with a sack of provisions on your back. What you brought is not for yourself but quarry for us all, as it was called in the past. He who is devoted to others, as you are, is protected by angels."

"Will I find my father and mother?"

"Your father and mother are with you always, and it makes no difference where they are now. You are their only child."

"Thank you, Grandma Tsirl," I said, knowing that thanks were not called for.

"Don't worry. God in heaven knows the heart of His children."

THAT NIGHT, Felix summed up the operation: "The mission was a success, but every operation leaves a muddy residue that is not always our fault."

Kamil, next to speak, informed us that, according to our best intelligence, most of the trains were carrying soldiers and armaments. But after midnight on Tuesday, a train would pass by that the station managers called a "special train," filled with Jews on their way to the camps. "This is the one we want to derail," Kamil said. "This will be our great test."

That same night, Michael chanted the Yom Kippur prayer *Hineni*, "Here I am, poor of deeds," his pure voice filled with devotion. People hid their faces and cried. Even Felix, usually solid as a rock, shed a tear.

Kamil had not given up. He asked the patrol that went down the hill to call out, "Hanoch, Hanoch."

45

Grandma Tsirl announced that she was going to die the next day and would like to see us. The first to enter the tent was Kamil. He sat with her for a long time, and it was not known what she said to him and what he asked of her. He came out of the tent with his head bowed.

Next to go in was Felix. It's hard to imagine Felix speaking and asking questions. Probably Grandma Tsirl spoke and Felix listened. He sat with her for a short time, and when he came out, he wore a look of amazement. This self-controlled and decisive man seemed lost in thought, as if things he had never contemplated had been revealed to him.

After them, the fighters went in. Grandma Tsirl sat in her sedan chair, reclining on two pillows. Her face appeared unchanged, apart from a hint of happiness at the thought of rejoining her sons and daughters, whom she had not seen for a long time.

"There is one thing I want to tell you again, my darlings," she began. "The partition between this world and the next is very thin. Death is an illusion. Tomorrow at this time I will be with my loved ones. Do not mourn for me more than necessary. Our togetherness in these magnificent mountains, every minute of it, was filled with devotion. We overcame despair and did not allow its poison to seep inside us. Despair is our greatest enemy. Despair blocks our sight and seals off the soul. We must not give it a foothold within us.

"We have seen much grief in this world, more than former generations, and it's no wonder that it did not purify us. Great sorrow darkens and does not illuminate. But we thank God for bringing us to these mountains that made us stand tall and that connected us with ourselves; now each one of you is a messenger of God in this world. Earlier generations saw God everywhere, even in the lowliest mosses; in our generation there is great blindness, and people see only what the physical eye can see. In our generation God has entered into us. My darlings, let God dwell within you, let God direct your inner life. Love and increase love, have mercy and increase mercy. Don't look for God outside. The outside is controlled by evil, and no one knows how long this will go on. Open your eyes and look inside. God is within you." And so she concluded.

We stood for a long time without moving. I doubt we absorbed everything she told us, but the feeling was that from now on we would not be as we had been. Suddenly one of the fighters cried out, "Don't leave us, Grandma Tsirl," and we were shaken by the force of his words.

Grandma Tsirl was not frightened by the shout. She quietly said, "Listen to what an old daughter of Israel is telling you: We will always be together. These mountains have taught us to be together, and if you do not see me tomorrow in my usual place, paint a picture of me in your heart, seated in the World to Come. There are no partitions, as we wrongly imagine. Torah and love bind us together here and there. The doors and gates are imaginary; they are inventions of Satan. Whoever saw the voices and heard the lightning at Mount Sinai is a part of the Lord on high."

46

Grandma Tsirl finished speaking, and we didn't know that these were her final breaths. Salo approached the sedan chair and sat on the ground. We didn't dare look at her silent face, and as we stood there we realized that Grandma Tsirl was an angel of God who had come to us at a time when our world lay in ruins. It hadn't been easy to accept her. There were days when her words sounded absurd, but there were other days when we felt that she spoke from within our hidden hearts.

We couldn't bear the overwhelming silence, and we went outside. Oddly, no one cried. The cigarettes we took from our pockets and lit were the most genuine expressions of the moment. What can you say about an angel of God that we had all seen, and what can you say when it has suddenly folded its wings?

We stood outside. Everything appeared as usual and yet different. The tents, the stoves, the tripods with their big pots, all the equipment we had struggled to collect in order to keep ourselves warm and fed—all these were material things. One could touch them, and yet they seemed to have arrived all of a sudden, and who knew if they would stay.

Isidor asked me for a cigarette. He lit it, cupping his hands. His movements, too, which looked real, seemed to say: *What is the meaning of this life; where is it going? Will we soon go down from here to meet our loved ones, or will we stay here until disease and freezing weather finish us off?*

Even the communists, who openly or privately opposed her words, were touched by Grandma Tsirl's passing. Karl said, "I didn't understand much of what she said, and what I did understand, I disagreed with. But I loved her. It's hard to explain this contradiction."

Salo rescued us from confusion. He took a piece of paper from his coat pocket and read the will that Grandma Tsirl had dictated to him on the day before she died: " 'Don't fuss too much over me; bury me right after I die, together with my sedan chair, which has become part of me. Itche Meir will say Kaddish, and you will answer Amen. Don't mourn for me. This is not a time to mourn an individual, but for a great moaning of the heart over what the sons of Satan have done to us.

" 'On the night that I leave, you will be going on a big and dangerous operation; I will pray from my new dwelling place that you will save many Jews. I don't know if I will be able to send you a sign from there, but you can be sure that I am with you and will never stop telling the heavenly hosts about everything the evildoers have done. But as for you: see the good and only the good that is in each and every one of you.' "

Salo folded the paper. His hands shook, and he was obviously standing at the edge of the abyss. He hugged Michael, who trembled and said to him, "Don't worry. Grandma Tsirl died peacefully and is on her way to heaven."

"And we won't see her again?"

"I don't think so."

It was fiercely cold outside, and several fighters went to dig a grave in the ice. We were close to Grandma Tsirl, and we loved her, but we didn't know how to express that love in words. The wounded Danzig, who was brought to the tent, hoarsely cried,

"We will no longer be able to ask Grandma Tsirl what is happening to us!"

The fighters who had dug the grave carried the sedan chair. Grandma Tsirl's face was covered with the scarf she often wore. Before they lowered the chair into the pit, they covered it with wooden boards. The sedan chair lost its old shape and now resembled a plain coffin.

Isidor recited the Kaddish and *El Maleh Rahamim*, stressing every word. He suddenly appeared older than his years, as if he were the embodiment of his grandfather.

The fighters who dug the grave covered it with dirt mixed with snow. Miriam fainted and Salo tended to her. People didn't move from the site.

Heavy snow began to fall. Those who expected Kamil to speak didn't understand his silence, but people who did not look forward to a sermon appreciated his reticence at this time. Felix moaned to himself as if to say, *What can one say?*

We sat and drank tea for a long while, and there was a feeling that with the death of Grandma Tsirl, the pillars of our togetherness had begun to collapse. From now on we would carry out the commanders' orders, but everyone would be bound up in himself. Kamil would not try to take the place of Grandma Tsirl. He might repeat some of her sayings. He's a great commander, but he does not possess the power of the ancients.

About an hour before midnight, we could hear Kamil's clear voice. "The fighters are requested to dress in appropriate clothes, clean their weapons, and securely tie their leggings, eat supper, and stand ready for departure at midnight sharp." The explicit words instantly cut through the silence we had wrapped around us.

Someone said, "Maybe we'll meet Reb Hanoch on the way."

47

I was glad they included me this time. We slowly made our way downhill, and with each step I felt Grandma Tsirl's death alongside me. *What had Grandma Tsirl hidden inside of us?*, I momentarily wondered. While she was alive, we knew she was not like other people, but now her presence seemed more intense.

The night before Grandma Tsirl died, I saw her in a dream talking to my mother, and I was happy that Mama looked healthy, discussing everyday topics. I wanted to approach them but didn't dare. They were connected to one another, like sisters who had awaited each other for a long time.

Grandma Tsirl finally noticed me and motioned for me to join her. I went over and was sure Mama would be happy to see me. Mama looked at me and asked, "Who is this young man?"

"Don't you recognize him?" asked Grandma Tsirl with a smile.

"He looks like my son, Edmund, but it's not him."

"He *is* your son! He *is* your son! Be happy!" exclaimed Grandma Tsirl joyfully.

It occurred to me that this is how it is in Grandma Tsirl's world. People who are alive and people who are gone exist together. Sometimes they don't recognize one another, but in the end they meet, weeping with the thrill of recognition.

WE WALKED WITH ENERGY and due caution. Kamil and the men who carried the explosives were in the lead and we followed. The thought that the fighters would soon plant the dynamite on the tracks, that the train would be derailed, and that we would greet the prisoners and shout, "You are free! Run quickly after us!" made us all walk faster, and we arrived a bit ahead of time.

We dug in and waited. Isidor, lying beside me, asked in a whisper if my toes also felt frozen. I told him I had a pair of socks in my pocket for emergencies, and I would give them to him.

Isidor thanked me and said, "If I were a believer, I would say a blessing for all that has happened to me in the last few months."

"A person who prays *is* a believer, isn't that so?"

"Prayer is inside me but not faith," he confessed to me, even at this critical hour.

"We'll talk about it later," I replied, knowing I had nothing to say.

"Ever since I've gone on missions, I've changed," Isidor said. "The death I feared in the past still frightens me, but I've learned to conquer it before it conquers me. What do you do to overcome it?" he asked.

"I say to myself that my parents, who were sent to the camps, are surely suffering more than I am." I was shocked by my words.

I suddenly understood that each of us carries within him not only painful experiences that could unnerve him at a dark hour but also strong words to toughen his resolve. This is the case for Kamil, for Grandma Tsirl, for Hermann Cohen, and for Karl; the rest of us try to follow their example. Now Isidor has joined us.

The appointed hour drew near. The men with the explosives walked toward the tracks, and the squads were ordered to ready their weapons. I remembered: Sometimes, in the first pink light of dawn, on the way back to the base, Kamil would halt us and say, "Look for a moment at the sky—what splendor, what purity. Nature is not sentimental; it always speaks with full strength.

Thank God that we are not indifferent in the face of miracles." That's Kamil; it's easy to love and follow him, even when he says things we don't understand.

And once, in a moment of exhilaration, he said, "I love all of you equally; the world is sustained by each of you. We are not bandits or looters but protectors of God's image in this world."

48

The hour approached.

We knew: the trains—and not only military ones—run on time. The Germans are devoted to precision. We've learned from experience that a German patrol is unlike a Ukrainian patrol. The Germans are ready to fight with clenched teeth and fierce determination.

And the train did indeed arrive. This time, too, the explosives did their job; the locomotive and front cars were blown off the tracks. But the soldiers guarding the train leaped off and fired their guns in all directions. We attacked them. They cursed us and kept shooting, even as they lay wounded on the ground. Fortunately, there were not many of them, and we finished them off.

Kamil handled the evacuation skillfully. First we moved out the children, then the women and the elderly, and then the men. Salo and Maxie tended to the wounded. We were forced to decide whom we would take and whom we would leave behind.

The retreat into the forest began at once. We split the refugees into three groups. Each of our squads led a group, and we started on our way. The fear that reinforcements would soon arrive and attack us never left us, even when we were deep in the woods.

Reinforcements didn't arrive, but the winds howled, heavy snow fell, and our progress was slow. The refugees were weak, and we weren't able to give them even a slice of bread.

Among the rescued was a man who recognized Maxie. A classmate from the university, he embraced Maxie and cried out, "You are angels. We never imagined we would survive." Maxie, stunned by the encounter, said, "You have nothing to fear; we know the area like the palm of our hand, and soon we will be home."

The new day began with bright sunshine, and Kamil, carrying a child in his arms, urged us to push on, for we were getting close to the base where we would be with our own. Just us. We have tents, food, and water.

49

The trek was slow. We carried those who were exhausted, the elderly and the children, and at every stop we lit campfires to warm them as best we could. Kamil told the refugees about the area—its security advantages and spiritual qualities—and especially about the summit, a fortress that could be defended. The refugees were physically drained, and it was doubtful that they absorbed what he said.

Felix, who spotted us from afar, sent us some sliced bread, cheese, and a pot of tea. But the survivors were so weak they could barely sip the tepid tea.

Only at dusk, when we brought them to the summit, did the situation become clear: There were three starving children who could barely stand; four women, their eyes swollen and legs wobbling; and twenty-one men of various ages, emaciated and ravaged by hunger. These are the ones we managed to save. The others had scattered and fled or had been shot and left for dead on the ground.

We were now faced with enormous, hideous suffering. It was for good reason that Kamil had asked us to see only the human suffering and not its ugliness. We must not forget: ugliness is only the exterior of suffering; a soul resides within everyone who suffers.

Everyone mobilized to serve the refugees the tea, cake, and

cookies that Tsila and Miriam had prepared for them. Salo and Maxie took care of the wounded, and suddenly our base looked different. This was not how we had imagined the rescue. We assumed the refugees would be weak, wounded, and in pain but not people whose exhaustion had shut down their souls. We had forgotten what the ghetto had wrought, what the work camps and the death train had done. A person is flesh and blood, not made of iron. Kamil explicitly said, "From now on we must be not only fighters but also caregivers and medics and nurses for all those in pain."

Our test began at once. The legs of a few of the men were so thin they seemed to be eaten away from the inside. The legs of two of the women were swollen to a frightening degree. I could hear what Grandma Tsirl had told us in her final moments: "Love and increase love, have mercy and increase mercy." She must have had this test in mind.

One of the refugees, a middle-aged man, said they had been locked in the boxcars for five days and that many had died from thirst and lack of air. That was all he had the strength to say. His voice was choked with loud weeping. The others sat silently on the twigs in the big tent that the fighters had set up. The stove spread light and warmth and illuminated the faces of the survivors.

Kamil addressed the fighters who took part in the operation. "We are privileged to have saved a precious handful," he said, "a holy handful, from the talons of the beast. We battled the ultimate evil, and this is only the beginning. We will care for our brethren until they can stand on their feet.

"I wish to tell you something more: Human suffering is holy. We will care for these survivors with generosity and love, and we will thank God who enabled us to care for them."

I felt sorry for this tall man, that such redoubled responsibility had now fallen on his shoulders. Yes, there were some fighters who cast doubt on the rescue operation and wondered if we were pointlessly prolonging the suffering of those we had rescued. How could we heal them, feed them, and keep their tents warm in such bitter cold? Kamil's view was clear-cut: life is precious, life is holy, and we must devote ourselves to these people.

That night it was decided we would act on Salo and Maxie's suggestion: to go down and abduct a doctor to treat the sick and wounded. Meanwhile, we brought them blankets and sheepskins and an additional stove. Tsila and Miriam prepared semolina porridge, and we got down on our knees and fed them. Now, for the first time, we saw gratitude in the eyes of a few of them. But they were exceedingly weak. They collapsed, and we covered them with blankets and sheepskins. In Salo's opinion, they needed to stay in the tents for now, and only when they got a bit stronger could we move some of them to the bunkers.

Two squads, led by Felix, went down to capture the doctor. Before the operation, Felix consulted with Victor about the open roads and dead ends in the village. Victor drew him a map. It was clear: the mission was complicated and dangerous; the doctor lived in the center of the village, and presumably his screams would rouse the local residents.

Felix sat and planned the operation in detail. Victor, who knew the doctor's house, made a sketch of the front entrance, the back door, and the yard.

We sent the squads off with great trepidation. Kamil may have been the most anxious of all. He repeated that our obligation was to relieve the suffering of those we had rescued. Recent days had left their mark on him: his face was pale, and his right hand, which held a cigarette, trembled.

Ever since the decision was made to go down and rescue people from the trains, the disputes among us ended. Now the fighters submit to Kamil's authority without a word. Perhaps they finally understand that he is one of a kind and must be defended.

One of the communists, a quiet fighter whose voice I had rarely heard, spoke up and said, "This is all thanks to the revolution, to the Red Army. He who denies communism is wicked or incompetent. Soon we will see the liberating army, and all those who slandered Lenin and Stalin will ask their forgiveness. One thing is clear: the old beliefs are gone from the world. The new dawn is coming soon, the days of justice: from each according to his abilities to each according to his needs."

Oddly, the fighter did not look happy or victorious. His mouth and his heart seemed to speak in different tones. His mouth continued to voice the old slogans, but his heart knew: there were too few of us left to be happy.

50

Again tonight we haven't slept a wink. Salo and Maxie have their hands full with work: they bandage the wounded and care for the weak. The snow outside has not stopped falling, and the concern for our comrades who went on the mission grows by the hour.

Kamil gets down on his knees and tries talking to the children, but they are too tired and feeble to say a word.

Our previous life here, filled with deeds and ideas, is suddenly overrun by a wave of human suffering. Kamil reminds us that until now we have looked out for ourselves; now comes the real test—to help those we are able to help.

The food is running out. Kamil promises Hermann Cohen that the pantry will be soon be refilled. The main concern is for the survivors: for five days they were caged in the boxcars.

Danzig has recovered but lacks the strength to carry Milio in his arms. He is up on his feet, however, and helps Tsila and Miriam make porridge. The survivors aren't able to digest solid food, just porridge and hot tea. One of them beckons to me to come over. I think he is about to ask me for a cup of tea. I am wrong.

"Where are you from?" he whispers.

I tell him.

"What is your family name?"

I tell him.

"I knew your father and mother."

"Maybe you've seen them?" The words just come out.

"No."

"I abandoned them at the train station," I confess.

"Every one of us did something terrible," he says and closes his eyes.

We reinforce the tents, tighten the canvas, strengthen the pegs. The survivors' pains do not subside. Danzig, who has himself known great pain in recent weeks, tries to assist the medical staff. His height and pleasant voice are reassuring. He even manages to make a child laugh.

One of the children asks if there are punishments here. Danzig answers right away. "Here there's only love. This is the land of love, and punishments are forbidden. Our dear Tsila cooks day and night. Uncle Hermann Cohen is a very sweet man; he has food in his pantry, also clothes and tools, and when you get better, you'll be able to see all his tools," he says, pointing to Hermann Cohen.

"And we won't be taken back to the train?"

"Absolutely not. This land is ours. Here the food is divided up equally. The older people work at the base, and the younger ones go out to defend this place, bring back supplies, and sometimes bring Jews from the trains. In another week or two there will be a lot more Jews here. Until now we had only two children, so there aren't any toys, but soon we'll have a lot of children, and we'll make sure there are toys."

"And when will the parents come?"

"We'll do all we can to bring them. We'll knock the trains off their tracks and bring the people in them here to be with us."

"And what about those who were shot?"

"They will go up to heaven, dear fellow. They will rest there. Everything there is quiet and peaceful."

"And when will we go there, too?"

"When we are old and won't want to stay in this world anymore."

The boy falls silent. Danzig stands up and says, "I have a child here named Milio who is two and a half, a very sweet child; his eyes speak more than his lips. When you get well, you can play with him."

There are no more questions, but moans are everywhere. Salo hands out pain pills and promises relief.

Karl once again declares that for the time being it's hard to change the world, but in this little corner there will be justice. Everyone will be entitled to attention and help. Two squads have gone to fetch a doctor and medicine. True, the world is full of wickedness, the cruel murderers are plotting to destroy us, but we will not lose our humanity. We will protect it. He speaks clearly and firmly. The survivors probably understand only a fragment of what he says; they are so ill and so weak that they can barely swallow a spoonful of porridge.

51

The squads return before dawn, with the abducted doctor, a man named Krinitski, in their hands. Werner, a fighter I didn't know well, was wounded in this action. He occasionally takes part in the study evenings. Like the rest of us, his knowledge of things Jewish is limited, but he is greatly sensitive to the text, to words and their intonation. A reticent man, he examines the words meticulously. He had been an excellent student in high school. He didn't complete his second year at university because of the war. He had been studying French literature. Sometimes he cites a French proverb or saying with perfect pronunciation.

I like to watch the way Werner sits, smoking a cigarette and sipping tea. In our evening debates each side tries to enlist him. Werner is not a creature of ideology. Words do not come easily to him. He would rather observe than speak. Whenever he hears something worthwhile, his eyes smile.

THERE WERE SURPRISES during this operation, but the squads led by Felix were highly alert. They returned fire at the right moment and killed the attackers. Werner was wounded in his stomach. He was quickly given first aid and placed on a stretcher and was closely supervised the whole way home.

Kamil stood at the entrance to the camp, hugged each one of

the fighters, and thanked them for the successful action. Werner lay on the stretcher, his eyes half open. When Kamil asked if he was in pain, he nodded. Salo immediately admitted him to the infirmary. The captured doctor was ordered to see to the wounded man. He examined Werner and said, "Without a hospital, his chances of recovery are very slim." Salo and Maxie did not accept the doctor's opinion and continued to care for Werner.

The squads, the captured doctor, and Kamil went into the kitchen tent. Tsila, Miriam, and Hermann Cohen served everyone a sandwich and cup of coffee. The fighters were thirsty and hungry and ate silently.

When they finished the sandwiches, each fighter was served a handful of dried fruits and another cup of coffee. The doctor looked around with a suspicious squint. He asked no questions and was asked none.

After the meal and a cigarette, Kamil turned to the doctor and said, "We are a group of Jewish partisans. We have decided to take our fate into our own hands, and we have now been joined by a group of men, women, and children whom we rescued from a death train. These survivors spent five days in locked cattle cars, without food, water, or air. They arrived here in terrible condition. We have brought you here, Dr. Krinitski—and forgive me for the way we did so—so you can help us heal the few who have survived the great slaughter."

The doctor narrowed his eyes and turned his head to the speaker, as if to say something, but then changed his mind and said nothing.

Kamil studied him, then said, "Would you like to help us with this holy mission?" To which the doctor replied, "This is how you bring a doctor? This is how you bring a criminal! I did no harm to anyone. I even used to have Jewish patients." It was obvious that anger was blocking his words and what slipped out was just a fragment.

"Dr. Krinitski, don't be angry with us. You know what the criminals did, also in your village."

"I am not to blame for that." He jumped up from his seat.

"We don't blame you."

"But manners, where are your manners? To wake a man in the middle of the night and kidnap him from his home? This is manners? This is culture?"

"And everything they did to the Jews in your village—this is manners? This is culture?"

"I am not to blame." He remained firm.

Kamil did not continue to argue. After a few minutes, he looked back at the doctor and said, "From a doctor we expect a little consideration, a little humanity. You saw with your own eyes what the criminals did to the Jews, how they abused them, killed them and their children."

"I am not to blame," he repeated.

Felix, who stood to the side, could not contain himself and shouted, "We don't expect you to be considerate or humane or to identify with us. We expect you to be a doctor, to suppress your feelings and do your duty as a doctor. If you act with negligence or malice, we will set up a tribunal to judge you. We are Jewish fighters, and I advise you to act wisely."

The doctor understood that he had best keep quiet, and he did so.

Danzig returned to the children and spoke with them. They were suffering from malnutrition, but their curiosity was undiminished. One of them asked if we would always stay in the land of the Jews.

"We'll really try," he said with a chuckle.

Karl brought sweetened porridge and began feeding the hot food to the children. The children are so thin that it's frightening to look at them, much less touch them. Ever since he was wounded, Danzig has been sensitive to every sight and gesture. "God, teach us to take care of these little birds," he cried out in a voice not his own. "Teach us what to say to them, what songs to sing to them. Teach us how to be parents, grandparents, and uncles. They are so thin, so weak."

52

Salo and Maxie sorted and arranged the medical supplies brought by the fighters. Isidor and I brought pots of boiling water. Karl and Hermann Cohen cleaned and disinfected the male survivors and changed their clothes. Tsila and Miriam washed the women.

The activity was conducted with meticulous concentration and care. For the first time I saw Big Karl in action: power and dedication combined.

In the meantime, Werner's condition worsened, and Dr. Krinitski came to inspect his wound. "As I already told you," he said, "this requires surgical intervention."

"We brought all the instruments from your clinic."

"There are no sanitary conditions here."

"We'll provide them."

It belatedly dawned on Dr. Krinitski that he was a prisoner, and he agreed to operate on the wounded man. Salo and Maxie assisted him. It turned out that the damage to Werner's internal organs was not severe. If he could survive the loss of blood and the infection, he would pull through.

Salo thanked him.

"You should not have treated me the way you did." Again he could not restrain himself.

"What could we have done?"

"And you will give me back my instruments?"

"As soon as the war is over," said Salo, with his hand on his heart.

"The Jews have so many doctors; where are they?"

"I think there's an obvious answer to your question."

"The Hebrews are generally a well-mannered people," Dr. Krinitski said, avoiding the word "Jews." And for a moment it seemed that he didn't believe his eyes. Jews, who only yesterday were being abused and killed, had captured him and were now his masters.

DANZIG RECOVERED but not completely. He doesn't go out on missions but helps wherever he can be useful and devotes much attention to Milio. At first it seemed that Danzig's injury would induce Milio to speak. There's no doubt that he is keenly aware of everything that goes on around him, including the arrival of the survivors. But his speech is still blocked. Earlier on, Danzig would find excuses for this. After he was wounded, he became convinced that Milio was just developing in a different way. At his own pace. His intelligence was beyond doubt. Presumably he would soon overcome his impediment, open his mouth, and words would emerge.

Dr. Krinitski examined the survivors and declared that two of them were sick with typhus and must be quarantined. Some were suffering from malnutrition and needed to be fed very carefully.

The hope that the survivors would recover within a week or two was dashed. Their recuperation will take months, said Krinitski. Kamil knows this. The big, critical missions still lie ahead, but Kamil's morale is undiminished. He recognized a schoolmate among the survivors, and every few hours he goes over to him and whispers, "Bruno, you are in good and loving hands. Soon, with a bit more effort, you'll get through this."

AT NIGHT I DREAM that among the women we rescued lay my mother. A long pink scar crosses her face, but this is definitely Mama. The mouth and forehead are hers, as is the way she moves her head.

I kneel down and want to call "Mama!" but I don't dare. The women beside her have lost consciousness and don't move. Finally, I can't hold back and cry out, "Mama!"

Mama opens her eyes slightly, looks at me, and closes them immediately. I don't remember this facial gesture, but her collapse is familiar to me. She sometimes lay in this position on the sofa in the afternoon. In my childhood I would study her every movement and expression.

"Mama," I repeat. Mama again opens her eyes and says, "What do you want of me?" Her words sting me, but I get over it. "Don't you recognize me?" I ask.

"Even here I get no rest," she responds without opening her eyes.

I stand up but stay where I am.

Again I study her: This is without a doubt my mother. Among the debilitated women her face had lost its uniqueness, but most of its features confirmed that this is Mama.

"Mama," I again call out, although I know it's best to leave her be. She needs rest more than talk. Her face is shrunken, and the pain that had subsided as she slept has clearly returned. She places her hand over her mouth. I know that gesture well, for whenever she was distressed, she would cover her lips. I am glad. Any doubts are gone; this is Mama coming back to me. I kneel down again, but awkwardly. I hurt myself, and I wake up.

53

D r. Krinitski refuses to accept his situation. He keeps muttering angrily to himself. Now and then he asks Salo and Maxie, "When will you let me go? I have a family, a clinic, and patients."

"At the end of the war. You are performing a great humanitarian service."

"Admit it—an involuntary service."

Victor knows Dr. Krinitski. He's a notorious anti-Semite, a close friend of the German officers. He plays poker with them and attends their wild parties. Victor often heard Dr. Krinitski praise the Germans for eliminating the Jews from Slavic lands. "The Slavs will breathe free from now on," he said.

WERNER IS OUT of danger. He sleeps most of the day. His friend Karl visits him often and whispers into his ear, "Dear Werner, we must struggle a bit longer; victory is not far off."

The raids continue with great intensity, night after night. Ever since the refugees joined us, we have needed more food, especially nutritious food. "More fruits and vegetables," implores Salo.

We avoid eating meat.

In one of the raids, before the snows began, the raiders brought a cow. "Free it!" Kamil ordered at once. The thought of slaughtering the cow and eating its flesh repelled many of us. The raiders set her free, but the cow just stood there without moving, and for many days she grazed at the base, as if she knew we would not harm her.

More and more we are eating fish. Tsila and Hermann Cohen have become experts in grilling fish—which, in Salo's opinion, keeps us healthy.

The great peril: the cold. We have a number of stoves, but they cannot heat the tents. We saw and chop wood from trees, but the fresh logs are smoky and suffocating when we burn them.

Krinitski complains that he is cold at night and will soon fall ill and require treatment. He does not inspire trust. Salo and Maxie are suspicious of his advice. He insults the elderly. "It's impossible to save old people in their condition," he claims. Salo dismisses this opinion and has informed Krinitski that we will care for the elderly the same way that we care for the young, and with even greater attention.

After a week of devoted care, we see the results. Several of the survivors have raised their heads from their blankets, and their eyes light up. "Where are we?" they ask. There has also been improvement among the children. For the time being, Milio and Michael are not permitted to come near them.

Milio doesn't speak, but the sequence of sounds that he utters makes Danzig happy. Danzig prefers not to push him. The way Milio observes things and people proves that he is thinking, gathering information, and the day will soon arrive when he will surprise us.

"What sort of surprise are you expecting?"

"One doesn't ask about surprises," Danzig replies with a smile.

"You have a hunch?"

"I do, but I won't reveal it to anyone."

Maxie, on the other hand, is very pleased with Michael's

accomplishments. At the end of the war, when Michael returns to his parents and school, he will skip at least two grades.

EVERY TWO DAYS I go out on a raid. Even while walking I get drowsy and sometimes doze off. Mostly I go out with Felix. Felix doesn't express his beliefs or opinions. He is all about action, but during breaks on the way back to the base, he hums entire symphonies. His musical memory is extraordinary. I sometimes think that if someone brought him a cello he would sit in the middle of the snow and play. His physique fits the cello; the music is in his body. Speech and the written word do not move him. When he is not humming symphonies, he is silent. He steers clear of arguments as one would avoid fire.

"What is there to say when there's nothing you can do," he says, quoting a famous author.

One of our patrols detected a squad of trackers, opened fire, and captured one of its scouts. When interrogated, the Ukrainian tracker disclosed that the Germans were planning a mortar attack, and his squad had been sent to reconnoiter the area.

But the Russian radio is again broadcasting news of the German retreat on all fronts and is calling on partisans to hunt them down.

"The Germans are in retreat. Why would they attack us now?" asked Kamil.

The tracker was not fazed by the question. "Killing the Jews is the first priority," he replied, as if it were obvious.

After Kamil was done, Felix interrogated the man as well. He told Felix that at least once a week, on Tuesdays, a train passes through that is filled with Jews whose screams pierce the heavens. When Felix asked if any Jews still live in the area, he replied, "Not a single one," in a tone that was hard to evaluate.

Here's the dilemma: According to Kamil's original plan, we are to go down every Tuesday, blow up the railroad tracks, and rescue Jews. But our plans are delayed by harsh weather and many logistical problems. The survivors are recovering, but it will take several more weeks before they can stand on their feet. The big question is, where will we house new arrivals in this bitter winter? Where will we get food to feed them? Above all, there is the looming threat: the German attack on us.

Victor also believes that the Germans' top priority is to kill Jews. They are bursting with motivation. More than once, we've seen them pursuing a single Jewish child, not giving up until he was caught.

In Kamil's opinion, we must prepare for the attack and at the same time continue our regular raids, continue to go down and rescue as many Jews as we can from the boxcars. There is no purpose to our existence without saving lives. Felix agrees with Kamil and adds, "The survivors are not a burden but a clear justification for all that we do here."

Last night, Isidor chanted Sabbath and High Holiday prayers. The survivors, who had never heard praying like this, were stunned, and they wept. Tsila also cried, but these were tears of relief: she was able to contribute to the survival of the saved.

Only now are we discovering relatives and acquaintances among the survivors. I found Emil, my classmate, who excelled in the exact sciences but found it hard to memorize poetry. The math teacher admired him and often asked him to show us how to solve problems. Within minutes Emil would write the equations, fractions, and square roots on the blackboard, as if this weren't a math problem but an amusing quiz. The numbers flowed magically from his fingers.

While for the majority of students schoolwork was a burden and having fun was most important, Emil was busy supporting his family. His parents were blind from birth, and Emil not only supported them by giving private lessons but also took them to the park every day to breathe some fresh air and listen to the songs of the birds. And in the summer he often took them by streetcar to the river.

His parents were among the first to agree to leave the ghetto for "agricultural training," where everyone, it was promised, would work according to his abilities and receive what he needed, the blind and elderly included. But in fact these were the first *aktionen*, the deportations to the death camps. Emil was transferred to various work camps and finally taken to the train station and crammed into a suffocating railway car that he was sure he would not survive.

I haven't seen Emil in about a year. To my surprise, he has not changed much externally and probably not internally, either. His face, wonderfully bright-eyed and childlike, is the same as ever as he lies on the mat of twigs. Emil was all innocence and kindness. In the *gymnasium* he had suffered due to his exceptional intelligence and innocence. The rowdy boys and girls mocked him, called him names, and loved to taunt him, as if to show him that excellence in math did not make him superior to them. On the contrary, in their eyes he was below average in practical matters.

Emil speaks to me with difficulty; his astonishment has made him lose his words.

FELIX CONTINUED to interrogate the Ukrainian tracker. "Did you volunteer," he asked, "or were you forced to serve?"

"I volunteered." He did not deny it.

"Why?"

"The pay is high and there are benefits. Our family is poor, and things improved for everyone after I signed up. Papa says it's better to join the Germans; they are fair and won't cheat you like the communists do."

"You weren't afraid to kill Jews?"

"I didn't kill anyone," he quickly replied. "We just rounded them up and brought them to the forest."

"But on the way you whipped them and shot the weak or the ones who tried to escape."

"Those were the orders."

"And you didn't fear God?"

"I did, but I was more afraid of disobeying orders."

"I understand," said Felix and let him be. Felix doesn't know how to restrain his emotions. If it were up to him, he would punish the Ukrainian not only for what he did but for what he said.

"Are you going to kill me?" The Ukrainian was openmouthed with terror.

"We'll see," said Felix without looking at him.

"I have three little children. Don't kill me." His lips trembled.

"When you killed Jews, did you think about *their* children?"

"I didn't kill any Jews," he repeated.

"Don't lie; we punish twice as hard for lying. I ask you now, and give me a simple answer: Did you kill Jews?"

"I did."

"Now we'll see what punishment you'll receive."

"I regret what I did," he said, weeping.

55

Ever since the Ukrainian tracker reported that the Germans were planning to attack us, we've stepped up our missions and preparations. The only rest period during our day is the radio hour. The German Army is retreating on all fronts, the newscaster unequivocally declares.

I have nothing but admiration for the comrades who care for the survivors: They are not reluctant or squeamish. They wash and rinse the emaciated bodies, the wounds oozing pus, all the while singing songs of the Bund and youth movements. Miriam and two fighters do the laundry. I am in charge of the fire and the pots of boiling water.

The snow that had fallen continuously for many days suddenly stopped. The wetlands are now the land of ice. The temperature is ten below zero. The heavy clothes of the gendarmes protect us, and Hermann Cohen added two more stoves to the tents. Unfortunately, we lack enough dry firewood. The wet wood is smoky.

My friend Emil is feeling better. He's very thin and can barely stand, but the light is returning to his eyes. He loves Tsila's soup and savors it slowly. He also gets a piece of fish and two potatoes every day.

During our last raid, we found a pantry full of oil, salt, sugar, and many spices. The sight of the little jars made us especially happy because it reminded us of kitchen cupboards back home.

Tsila has promised that from now on the meals will be tastier. Everyone praises her cooking and calls her the "magician." She is an inspiration to us all. Every day she surprises us with a new dish or a familiar one with a new taste.

Kamil is focused on anticipating the enemy's next moves and on preparing two expanded squads to blow up the railroad tracks. We must stop the trains carrying the Jews to their death. Kamil impresses this urgency upon us every minute of the day, and we are eager to follow his orders.

Hermann Cohen informs us that there are no more tents and no more metal to make into stoves. The bunkers are full to capacity. This argument does not deter Kamil. According to information we have gathered, a death train will pass by in two days, and we will do our duty and derail it.

At one time there were quite a few who opposed this action. Now it's clear to everyone that these are indeed death trains. Whoever does not suffocate in the trains will die in the camps.

AGAIN I SEE PAPA and Mama standing before me in their overcoats. Mama is as pale as plaster. Papa shares her paleness; his face is drained of color. At this brink of disaster I failed the test. I was not thinking of them. Every time I see Emil, I am afraid he will ask me about my parents and about Anastasia.

Emil is exactly my age, but his experiences have been worse than mine. He was in three work camps before he was sent to the railway station.

"How did you overcome the hunger and the cold?" I asked him, immediately regretting my question.

"I thought about my parents the entire time and asked God to bring me back to them."

"Are you a believing person?"

"No. But one time something strange happened in a work camp

that affected me. I don't know who was behind it. On one of the unbearably cold nights, I thought my end was near. At first I hoped that Leon, the oldest one in our barrack, would come and cover me with a blanket. He didn't come. I was sure I wouldn't last till morning, and I shut my eyes as I suffered from great pain. Suddenly a voice spoke to me and said, 'Emil, don't be afraid; your life is not over. There's much more you will do.' At first I thought it was my father's voice. I was wrong. It was a different voice but directed at me. Again I said to myself: soon Leon will come and cover me with a blanket. Leon didn't come and the voice did not return, but I miraculously overcame the cold."

"Who, then, spoke to you?" I asked cautiously.

"I have no idea. Someone who grew up with religious faith perhaps expects revelation. I have no such expectations."

"But the voice strengthened you nevertheless."

"Yes. And I waited for it to come back, but it didn't. I don't put much stock in hearing voices. I don't relate to things that are beyond me."

"Man is alone in the world?" I couldn't help but say it.

"Apparently so."

I felt sorry for my friend, whose face was filled with light and wonder but who ignored the voice that called out to him.

56

Then came the order to get ready to leave; fortunately, I hadn't returned my clothes to the storeroom after the last raid. Kamil thinks we ought to wear lighter clothes and not the gendarmes' uniforms, which slow down our walking. But this time he doesn't insist, owing to the bitter cold.

When Kamil is excited by an action or mission, he easily passes his excitement on to us. He seems to shove aside his darker, depressing thoughts and doesn't show them.

So it was this time. We lined up to be counted; there were sixteen of us. The password for the operation was *hayahid*, the individual. This is a precious word; the world depends upon it.

Kamil sometimes uses lofty language, but his words, as we've learned, are not for show. Every sentence is quarried from deep within. People here are attuned to words; even the ones who for years spoke in slogans now try not to rely on them. Kamil sometimes qualifies what he says. "Forgive me if I sound flowery," he would say. "I haven't yet found the right words, so I need to dress them up a little."

In the *gymnasium* we learned: style makes the man. Kamil is allergic to an excess of words. Also to wisecracking and feigning innocence, not to mention hypocrisy. He bites his lip over every extraneous word. His language is clear but always seems to hide a secret. Before we go on a mission, he will sometimes intone,

"Remember, there is no earth without heaven." Felix knows him going back to their time at university. Even then Kamil saw the world with different eyes. He didn't take part in ideological debates, but his whole manner affirmed that this life, be it ever so evil and ugly, has meaning. There is beauty and tenderness on the inside. The wicked must be vanquished, and the inner beauty must be zealously protected.

When Kamil was a student, he learned fencing and boxing, and Felix often heard him say, "We'll beat the hell out of the bad guys so they won't ruin our lives." He gained his first religious insights from a monk named Sergei. He would visit his monastery once a week. Kamil never denied those visits. On the contrary, he would often say, "Sergei taught me what religion means, but I also searched for the Jew in me—for the books that would nourish the Jew in me and for the people I could connect with." Later on he discovered Martin Buber and Franz Rosenzweig. He wanted to follow Rosenzweig's path toward religious observance, but it just didn't work out.

Before each mission, a new Kamil is revealed. This time he wore a thick cap with a visor that made him look like a fisherman. Many dangers await us, and we do not take our mission lightly. If we manage to save a handful, our battle against evil will not have been in vain.

Kamil recited the psalm "The Lord is my shepherd." His reading was charged and tense, like a strike on hot metal. I asked Isidor if Kamil's reading is traditional or his own version. Isidor didn't know how to answer; he said only, "In the synagogue of the Hasidim they didn't read it like Kamil does."

57

The upper crust of snow has frozen in the bitter cold; fortunately, we are equipped with walking sticks. The sticks help us keep our footing and not slip. In this season, the steep descent to the railroad tracks takes about three hours. Hostile patrols and ambushes must be taken into account, as well as sprains and fractures. Salo and Maxie are equipped with splints, bandages, disinfectants, and medicines. Still, there were no end of surprises; as we snaked down from the mountain, we discovered a young German officer sprawled on the ground, nearly frozen. We could have simply moved on, and there were good reasons for doing so, but Kamil felt we should leave him a little food and water and pick him up on the way back. Capturing a German officer is no minor matter.

After we gave him a cup of water, Karl questioned him as to how and why he was separated from his unit. The officer admitted that he collapsed from weakness and apparently fell asleep. About the operation itself, he said, "We went to survey the area and get ready to attack the Jews who escaped from the ghettos." He didn't know about the German retreat from the Eastern front, or didn't want to reveal it.

"Are you Jews?" he blurted out in shock.

"That's right."

"And you're not killing me?"

"No."

"Thank you. That's unusually gracious of you."

"Why?"

"Because we killed Jews indiscriminately."

"What do you mean by 'indiscriminately'?"

"We killed them only because they were Jews."

"Are you sorry about that?"

"It was an order, and orders are obeyed. Yes, it was unpleasant work, and sometimes even horrifying, but it was an order. You obey orders and think about it later."

"You say this was unpleasant work. What do you mean?"

"Killing day after day."

We could suddenly see how young he was, twenty-three or twenty-four. He was obviously weak, and it seemed that the words he spoke surprised him, too.

"And if the same order were given again, would you obey it?"

"It's hard to imagine myself refusing an order."

It was strange; he could have pretended, lied, or blamed his superiors. But he preferred not to betray the oath of loyalty he had sworn at the end of officers' training.

"Do you have parents?" Karl changed the course of interrogation.

"Yes," said the young officer, surprised by the question.

"Where do they live?"

"In Düsseldorf," he said with a smile.

"Are you married?"

"I'm engaged." He smiled again, more broadly.

"What does your father do?"

"He's a pharmacist."

"What were you thinking when you killed Jews day after day?"

"I didn't think. Obeying orders comes before thinking."

"And what about human feeling? Jews are also human beings."

"Yes, but they are said to be different."

"In what way different?"

"They are dangerous to mankind."

"Can you explain?"

"They are profiteers," he said, barely containing his smile.

"You are an educated young man. I assume you graduated from high school and studied the German classics. You listened to classical music, went to the theater, but you speak like a despicable murderer. Who made you a murderer? Do you understand my question? Let's assume that the Jews are profiteers; is that a reason to murder them?"

The young officer apparently realized he had gone too far and didn't reply. Karl waited a moment and said, raising his voice, "Tell me, did you study Goethe's lyric poetry?"

"Yes," he said quietly. Then he suddenly looked up and asked, "Are you going to execute me?"

"We'll see," Karl said dryly.

"I ask permission to write a short letter to my parents and fiancée."

"And what will you write to them?"

"That I was loyal to my oath until the last moment of my life."

"You're less than a man," said Karl with a scornful glare.

We all felt the officer should be shot. But Felix thought he should be kept alive, picked up on our way back to the summit, and interrogated more thoroughly. We took away his shoes and his rifle and left him a blanket.

Without another word to him, we went on our way.

WE HAD TWO HOURS to spare. I forgot the dangers awaiting us and was happy to be out on a mission; my feet were warm and dry, my body pounding. I carried a new weapon, I had five magazines and four grenades, and I was with people I could depend on.

I remembered my arrival at the base, meeting Kamil and Felix,

Salo, Maxie, and Karl, who struck me as people with a big plan for the world, a plan to which they were devoted, body and soul. They were armed but not violent. Their movements were quiet and restrained; they spoke little, and what they did say I didn't always understand.

I also remembered the first drills: running, crawling, and rope climbing, the breaks between drills, the sandwiches and ten o'clock recess. I didn't know this was also mental training for the days to come. I didn't yet know how to rid myself of egotism and bond with my new comrades. Little by little I learned from them how to be silent, how to be ready to help and be helped.

58

We continued on our way without mishap and arrived about an hour ahead of the train. From within the woods we could see the tracks. Maxie and Karl prepared the explosives and went to set them in place; we fanned out, poised to attack.

I was glad Isidor and I were together again. Although he works wonders in his weekly prayers, Isidor is utterly free of arrogance or condescension. His prayers inspire awe but not gratitude. I sometimes think people are afraid of them. After praying, he lights a cigarette, withdraws, and leans against a tree. I've often heard it said, *What is the nature of his prayer? Should it be considered prayer at all?*

The train arrived at precisely 2:00 a.m. The explosives were detonated, and the earth shook. Two cars were derailed and the guards, when they regained their senses, began shooting. We were ready, and our fire was better aimed than theirs; within minutes we finished them off.

People began to emerge from the open cars, and we approached them. Many dead bodies lay on the ground or in the cars. We went from car to car to see if anyone else was still alive. The operation took no longer than half an hour, but it seemed like forever.

This time there were dozens of survivors, not just twenty-eight. We asked each young survivor to assist an old person or a child. Each fighter took responsibility for two or three people.

Karl led with the sick and wounded, and Kamil assisted those who could plod along on their own. Salo and Maxie went from group to group, tending to the wounded. An old man I helped to walk murmured a blessing: "You are an angel from heaven."

The procession came to a halt before dawn, and Kamil announced, his voice shaking, "We have covered a lot of ground, and now the fighters will hand out sweets. There are tents and food at the camp; we will eat and rest when we get there." Kamil, who knows how to talk and instill faith, spoke in practical terms this time. He described our situation in the forest and the weapons we collected for self-defense. Finally, he said, "Dear brothers, thank God we are now able to help others. Worthless thugs deprived us of help and love. From now on we will support one another, advancing slowly, the weak and wounded going first. And if we hear shots, we will lie down on the ground and not raise our heads."

The German officer we had left on our way to the tracks saw us and was sure he was done for. He raised his hands and said, "It appears I will not live." Karl promised that if he behaved properly, obeyed orders, and told us everything he knew, we would take that into account and reduce his punishment.

The officer revealed at once that he had been in a special unit that, among other things, executed Jews. He remembered the names of the villages and forests where they were murdered.

"And you weren't afraid to kill women and children?"

"That was the order."

"I didn't ask you about the order. I asked if you were afraid," said Kamil, raising his voice.

"When you obey an order, you are not afraid."

"Are you afraid now?"

"Yes."

"What were you looking for here?"

"The shortest and best route, from a military standpoint, to reach the places where the Jews are entrenched. A hostile patrol discovered us, and we had to retreat."

"Don't say 'hostile patrol.' Say 'Jewish patrol.' "

"It's hard for me to say that," he said without looking up.

For this he was slapped.

59

In the light of day we saw how gaunt and exhausted these people were, beyond hunger and thirst. Were they happy to be
returned to life? It was hard to know. Their faces, which for so
very long had known no joy, remained sunken and frozen, without expression.

Kamil watched over the groups in the rear, so we were ready
for any surprise attack. The fighters went from person to person
to extend a helping hand; they carried those too weak to walk.
Karl carried three children on his big body. Kamil had prepared
us for this moment. We had drilled day and night, and it showed.
We were chained to this caravan of survivors.

In the afternoon we saw from afar four people carrying two
large pots. We knew they were bringing tea and cookies baked
by Tsila. We called out to them, and they shouted back. We were
happier to see them than the survivors were. They were too weak
to be happy. We fed them spoonfuls of tea and cookie crumbs.
Consuming even this little was hard for them.

We could tell at a glance that among these suffering people
some were alert, and their lips were taut with amazement. The
look on their faces said, *We never imagined we would ever again see
compassionate people.*

We set up two campfires and filled the pots with snow to boil
the tea. Kamil raised his large head and spoke. "The world stands

upon the individual," he said, "and we will protect and preserve each one. In the eyes of the enemy we are numbers, subhuman. They didn't just want to kill us but also to demolish the image of God that is within us. Thank God, we have returned to what we used to be, and that is no small thing. We are the children of parents and the parents of children. Brothers and sisters, from now on every one of us will go by his first and family names, which have been handed down for generations. It is forbidden to change these names for any reason. We will make sure to call everyone by name. Help us renew the covenant between us and our names."

The people looked at one another and could not believe their ears. They had not heard words like these for a long time. And it was good that Kamil was the leader of this operation. If Felix had been in command, he would have kept silent. A hard-won victory deepens his silence.

The fires, tea, and cookie crumbs did their quiet work, and it's good that we are walking in small groups. First-aid workers go from child to child, to each of the elderly, bandaging wounds, splinting sprained ankles, dispensing pain medicine, and all the while learning people's names.

Kamil had wanted to keep moving at night, but the wind and cold prevented it. The campfires and big pots didn't warm the area much. Just before dawn the wind died down, and we continued on our way.

In the meantime, a squad came down from the mountaintop to help us carry the wounded. Kamil was happy to see them and quickly gave each one an assignment. Our worries and doubts subsided. The job allowed no room for that. Felix is right when he claims, "Let the job do what only it knows how to do. The solution is in the doing, not the wishing."

———

I WAS SUDDENLY SAD for the loss of the intimacy we had developed among ourselves: the heart-to-heart talks, the study evenings, watching the sunset and sunrise, Tsila's delicious cooking, the wide-open eyes of little Milio, and the passion of studious young Michael. From now on, Kamil says, "We are devoted to all, and we thank God, who has given us the privilege of this mission. We are not able to stop all the death trains, but what we can do, we will do. We will not sit and do nothing."

60

By midday we reached the summit with all the refugees. Danzig has not been on a mission since he was wounded, but he helps Tsila and Hermann Cohen. His hands are not what they were, but they're still strong enough to lift objects of medium size. And when he hugs Milio, his fingers, stained with tobacco, tremble.

Among the survivors Hermann Cohen discovered Teresa, the daughter of his younger sister. She's sixteen, but her bony face makes her look older than her years. Hermann Cohen knelt down and asked if she recognized him. The girl answered yes and closed her eyes. Hermann Cohen could not control his emotions and covered his face. Salo hugged him and said, "The girl will recover, and in a few days you'll be able to talk with her."

It's hard to rely on our prisoner-doctor. He constantly complains and claims his capture was illegal. He was rebuked by Kamil, but he holds his own. Salo despises him but requires his help. Two surgeries were urgently needed. Krinitski was taken to see the patients and showed no goodwill. Kamil warned him then and there that the unit would hold a tribunal and try him for refusing to obey an order. During wartime, the penalty for that refusal is death.

Krinitski apparently understood the gravity of his situation and went to work, but he announced before beginning the surgery that he could not be held responsible for its outcome. Kamil stood firm and warned him that if he was derelict in his medical duty, he risked his own death.

Felix grinds his teeth in anger. In his opinion, we should set up a tribunal right away and put Krinitski on trial. A doctor who does not treat the sick willingly, from a sense of duty, is a criminal.

The next day Krinitski operated on two more patients. There are several more who will require surgery, but we will first see how these people recover.

The German officer was taken to the summit, but before he could be interrogated, he fell ill with typhus. He ran a high fever and mumbled in his delirium that he was faithful to his homeland and did not violate his loyalty oath. His presence and his screams were a burden for us, and we probably should have left him where we found him. In any event, what's done is done.

THAT NIGHT WE WENT on a raid. We are running out of food. We now number one hundred and seventy-three people. If we don't stock up immediately, the survivors will die of hunger. Hermann Cohen brings semolina and flour to the kitchen in rationed amounts. Ever since the survivors arrived and he saw his niece, he has not been the same. He chain-smokes. Once or twice a day he goes into the tent where his niece lies and looks at her. This strong, stable man, who withstood great stress and was a brilliant logistical planner, is collapsing. Kamil hugs him and says, "We have come a long way, and we will do more. The coming days are the most critical. The Red Army is on its way to us. The question is whether we can last another month. Without you, I am certain, we cannot do it." Hermann Cohen doesn't respond to this compliment. He covers his face with both hands.

61

Before we went out on the raid, Kamil spoke to us. "Our fate, my dear ones, is in your hands today. Our camp—which grew, thank God, beyond expectations—is battered and suffering, and if we do not feed these people, they will die. The base is in desperate need of food, tents, and metal to make stoves. We must save these tormented bodies so their souls can return to them. Once we were few, but today, thank God, we are many. You are God's faithful in this land, performing a righteous mission."

When Kamil speaks, you feel that you are not alone in the world. You are surrounded by loyal people, and you rise to the challenge. Kamil does not use the word "sacrifice." He has rejected that word on several occasions. "We seek not death but life. Our togetherness is a wondrous unity." Kamil does not blame God for not imposing justice on the world; he blames instead people who do not deserve to be called human.

"Thoughts, even exalted ones, make no difference. We must focus on actions," says Felix. This severe outlook comes naturally to Felix, but it's difficult for me. Ever since the new people came to us, a part of myself disappeared. I haven't yet connected to these people.

During the day, I'm responsible for boiling water, and I help Salo, Maxie, and Karl bathe the emaciated bodies of the survivors. I must admit, I am repelled by these human skeletons. They look like scary ghosts. Your hands find the strength to do their duty, but your heart, almost defiantly, refuses to identify with them. These people exude death and despair, and your heart lacks the strength to say, *These are my brothers and sisters, and I must be happy that they are here.*

Danzig's huge presence pulls the survivors from their despair, and they lift their eyes to him as to a savior. But most effective in their revival, believe it or not, is Victor. He's not repulsed by urine and excrement. He teaches us the meaning of brotherly love.

Victor stays close to the sufferers and does all he can to relieve them. He has clearly undergone a great change. The Ukrainian farmer in him is still evident, and in the cornfields he would be no different from the rest of his tribe. But here, among us, some of his gestures bring to mind a monk who has forsworn selfishness and is devoted to all mankind.

Kamil asks him now and then about his village and the neighboring villages, and about the Ukrainian and his lady friend who were killed and the daughter who was abducted. Victor tries hard to remember but cannot recall more than he has already told us.

"Paul, Paul, where have you gone?" I once heard Kamil moan. I suddenly pictured Paul, tall and agile, a fighter whose every graceful move was precise and silent.

62

We are raiding every day and bringing food, utensils, clothing, fabrics, and sheepskins to the base. Sometimes a fancy shirt or household items used only by Jews turn up in the haul. In one raid we found a pair of candlesticks inscribed with the words *Shabbes Kodesh*, Holy Sabbath.

It's impossible for many reasons to raid a house we've already raided. So we go farther out, to isolated houses on the hillsides or tucked away in the woods.

Kamil wants to go down to the flatlands every week and derail a train carrying Jews to the death camps. But for the time being, we are unable to do so. We continue to patrol and to lie in ambush. A gloomy feeling has taken hold among us, that from now on our sole activities will be theft and looting. And eventually the farmers will band together, join the Germans, and surround us. They hate us no less than the Germans do, and they have plenty of weapons.

My friend Emil has recovered. He can stand on his feet and go to the toilet, but he still appears listless and confused. He didn't ask about my parents but told me about his blind parents, who barely supported themselves by weaving baskets and rugs. Emil has helped them since childhood, but it was only after his bar mitzvah, when he began giving private lessons, that the specter of poverty was lifted from his home.

Emil's parents were among the first to be deported from the ghetto. When he talks about his parents, it's clear that he's tied to them with every fiber of his being. He doesn't speak of them in the past tense but says, "Mama is so conscientious. Every rug she makes is flawless, without any imperfection. Papa likes to talk while he weaves. For this reason he makes mistakes, and his merchandise sells for much less money."

Emil has been observing his parents since his childhood, and something of their blindness has rubbed off on him. Even now.

It's strange how we—as well as those who've come to us lately—don't talk much about the families we left behind. We're busy with daily needs, we listen to the radio, but we don't delude ourselves that life will soon return to what it was before.

THE TENTS ARE CRAMMED with agony. Salo and Maxie lack the drugs to ease the suffering of those in pain. The captured doctor grumbles and blames his captors, who took him away from his home and his patients. Felix has warned him again several times that if he continues to make accusations he will be executed, even without a tribunal.

"I don't care; I'm not afraid," he says, without looking Felix in the eye. It's hard to comprehend this audacity, until you realize that for Krinitski taking care of Jews is humiliating, a deep insult to his dignity. He would rather die than be a prisoner of Jews and care for their sick.

Victor says not to despair. There is a pharmacy nine miles away, which happens to have belonged to a Jewish pharmacist. It's still functioning, and we should raid it without delay. Kamil spreads out the map and finds the exact location.

The German officer continues to blaze with fever. We have no medicine, but we give him an extra blanket. All night long he calls out loudly, swearing his allegiance to his homeland and leader, berating his fiancée, who doubts his loyalty. He wants his parents to denounce her to her face. He bellows other delusional commands regarding personal issues and questions of honor.

MY FATIGUE WON'T LET GO of me. I sleep standing up, while walking, any chance I get. My sleep is not peaceful, and it's a good thing the images vanish when I open my eyes.

Last night I imagined, as clearly as I could, Anastasia, in full. But her tall, cylindrical body was covered in brown fur. I wanted to go touch her but realized she was likely to bite me. Indeed, she turned her head toward me and flashed her big white teeth.

"Anastasia," I called to her, "don't you recognize me?" She stared at me with a feral gaze. I couldn't tell if this was a threat or a promise of intimacy. I asked again, "Don't you recognize me?" Hearing my question a second time made her smile. I thought she was about to ask me something. I was wrong. She looked at me defiantly, as if to say, *What are you doing here? By all accounts you had gone away and would not return.*

When I awoke, I remembered the dream vividly. I thought that the squads had gone off and left me behind because I'd overslept, and I wouldn't be able to catch up with them. But I went into the kitchen and found the fighters relaxing on the mats of twigs, drinking tea and smoking, and I felt relieved.

63

We urgently need supplies. Though we know quite little about the pharmacy, it has been decided to raid it anyway. The spirit was upon Kamil, and after announcing the password, *rofeh holim*, healer of the sick, he reminded us that the mission was to save lives, plain and simple. "We are not now able to go down to the lowlands and derail the trains from their tracks. But if we can get drugs, we will help those in pain."

Snow was falling, and the cold burned the skin. Kamil's clear voice echoed in our ears from far away. We were visible to the patrol that would come to our aid if we were ambushed.

It must again be said—with a measure of guilt, as always—that it's easier to go on a mission with Felix than with Kamil. When Felix is in command—with his silence, his rhythmic pace, his keen alertness—you're confident that the operation will go exactly as planned, that we'll return to base without cries of joy and uplifting words but satisfied with what we did.

The way there was shorter than we'd imagined. We stood about two hundred feet away from a small darkened building with a sign in front that said PHARMACY. The name of the owner was blotted out, but with some effort we could make out AARON SHMULEVITZ. The surrounding houses sat peacefully amid mounds of snow.

The moment before a break-in is like a dive into dark water.

The body shakes, but the hands fill with power and will soon overcome the fear.

We broke in through the back door without making noise. We made our way in the darkness and quickly began filling the sacks we'd brought. We did this methodically, shelf after shelf. Half the squad was positioned outside, standing guard. After half an hour, all the medicines were loaded into seven sacks. We left and closed the door.

Felix was pleased. But he, unlike Kamil, doesn't show his satisfaction. The sacks were full but not heavy. They smelled like medicine.

WHEN MAMA LAY SICK in bed, Papa ran from doctor to doctor, from pharmacy to pharmacy, and if he was able to buy medicine, he would run home and arrive out of breath.

The money ran out. First Papa sold his gold watch and then Mama's jewelry. The doctors were inconsiderate and charged the full amount. The pharmacy owners also didn't give any discounts. We had been an affluent family and became poor overnight. Papa's hands trembled on the table.

I didn't take part in this pain. I was wrapped up in my uncanny happiness and refused to share my parents' desperate struggle.

Then, suddenly, I saw my father as I had never seen him before: Sitting at the table, his fist blocking his mouth, he abruptly raised his head, looked at me, and wordlessly asked, *Edmund, what wrong have we done to you that you cut us off like this? We're not asking for your help; your happiness is important to us. But if you'd take a minute to ask how Mama is, that would be very kind. She's very ill and about to undergo surgery; a good word will perk her up.*

I felt Papa's imploring look throughout my body. But I hadn't the strength to do what he wanted. I escaped his gaze and ran outside to meet Anastasia. Anastasia conquered me instantly with her big eyes. Only later, under the tree whose top was bent to the ground, did I see Papa's look clearly. The burning passion stored in my body was snuffed out, and my toes were seized with cold.

ISIDOR HAS TOLD ME that he, too, is now uncertain about whether he did the right thing when he escaped and left his parents behind. Isidor's words are painfully clear. His prayers, which move people so deeply, apparently do not affect him. "The prayers are not mine," he has told me. "They are my grandfather's." I didn't want to ask too many questions. You can hurt someone even with a careful question.

A while ago one of the fighters let out a heartbreaking shriek when he was asked a thoughtless question. Even solid, quiet Karl snapped at someone who innocently asked how long he had been in the ghetto. We have learned it is better to be silent.

64

We arrived back at the base before dawn. Our lookouts, positioned a few miles from the summit, saw us. They called out to us, and we shouted back the password—*rofeh holim*.

Salo and Maxie, who had not come with us, unloaded the sacks and were delighted with every drug. We even brought a directory of medications.

It's so good to be back at the base. The pack drops from your shoulders, and a sandwich and cup of tea await you in the kitchen. True, we also got sandwiches before leaving, but the long hours of the night, the load we carried, and the high alertness all starve the body. This sandwich tastes of all the seven flavors, and the cigarette is a tonic.

And, as always, there is news, good news and less good. Russian radio again announces that the German Army is in panicked retreat and urges partisans to blow up railroad tracks and chase away the occupiers. "We should be happy," I heard Salo say. But our actual situation has its ups and downs. There is a group of survivors who are recuperating, who wear clothes and can drink tea standing up. They stare into space, and their movements are unsteady, but they have begun to ask, "Where are we, and what will we do when we get well?" But most of the survivors are still feeble and sick. Salo and Maxie and their assistants Karl and Victor and Hermann Cohen are in charge of hygiene and food; some of the sick understand that they are in good hands and thank the medical team with tears in their eyes.

Dr. Krinitski sees the sickest patients every day but thinks that without blood tests and the right medicine they don't stand a chance. Krinitski has been with us for several weeks but has still not come to terms with his capture by the Jews. He continues to insist that his detainment is illegal and insinuates that the Jews do not respect the laws of the land. "I know the Jews well. They lived among us for many generations."

Even as a prisoner he is unafraid to express his opinions, and he told Kamil, "Armed Jews do not frighten me; it's out of character for them. They seem to be masquerading." Felix was furious. In his opinion, such anti-Semitism in the wake of mass murder is an intolerable crime. When Felix is furious, he doesn't raise his voice; instead, his lips tighten, and he looks like he will leap and strike at any moment. Kamil reminded Felix that three urgent surgeries are scheduled, and only afterward will we settle our score with the doctor.

We brought many different types of medicines. They are now stored in the bunker. The owner of the pharmacy, Aaron Shmulevitz, could never have imagined where his medicines would end up. God bless him, too, for his chocolates, coffee, and cocoa. Now we can make the children happy.

The German officer burns with fever, and his hallucinations make him cry out loudly at night. He swears again and again that he was loyal to his homeland and his leader. Krinitski examined him and declared that his life hangs by a thread. In a day or two he will be dead. Krinitski stands beside the officer's mat with an ironic smile, as if to say, entire villages were subject to the whim of this junior officer; now he lies here like a corpse.

65

The skies thundered. At first we thought the thunder meant new snow, but among the survivors were veterans of the Great War who knew at once that this was artillery fire.

It became clearer by the hour that artillery was indeed hammering the horizon. Kamil ignored the obvious omen. He continues to claim that we will soon be attacked and that we must be ready. Felix agrees with him.

This makes no sense, people argue. While the Red Army attacks and advances and the Germans are in retreat, it's hard to imagine they'll keep on killing Jews.

"You're wrong, dear boy," Kamil told one of his persistent challengers. "For Hitler, killing Jews is a sacred calling. Yes, it contradicts military logic, but their war against the Jews comes from their evil core, and we will never fathom their motives."

The more opponents Kamil has, the stronger and sharper he gets. He's at his best in battles of the few against the many. He sparkles with cleverness when fighting over dreams and ideas.

At night the radio reports on the locations of the German retreat. It's clear as day that the Red Army is beating them and getting closer to us. Felix has calculated that they are about 150 miles away. This news doesn't affect our readiness: squads are training while other squads patrol. The daily raids continue. Victor never stops reminding us: "Killing Jews is their ultimate desire. Their fanaticism knows no limits; don't look for rational explanations."

The snow is about three feet deep now. Going up and down the mountain is a huge effort. Even the fittest fighters return exhausted from the raids. But what can we do? The raids are a necessity. We have to feed dozens of people.

I GOT A NIGHT OFF and fell into a deep sleep. In my dream I am on my way home. The anxiety and emotion slow my steps. I can see that in the neighborhood everything is as it was. The two poplar trees by the house stand naked. The rustling, silvery leaves I loved to look at had fallen off while I was far away. Smoke billows from the chimneys of the Ukrainian neighbors' homes. I know this serenity. When I came home from school, I would stop here and absorb it. We are neighbors, though different; in our yard there are no cows or fowl. Our yard is carpeted with grass and rows of flowers. In late afternoon we sit on the veranda or in the yard. It's an hour of silence and grace, the light streaming through the acacias and blending with the shadows.

I stop near my house. The gate to the yard is closed but not locked. I open it and stand still: the grass has gone brown at the edges, the acacias are bare, and Nicky's doghouse is empty, a sign that he's lying down in the living room. I sense that a big surprise is in store, but what kind I don't know.

Many months have passed since we left the house in a rush. I hesitate, afraid to enter. In the yard, at least, nothing has changed. Is Nadia looking after the house? I assume so. She is very devoted to Mama. She took care of her when she was sick, and unlike other housekeepers, she stayed on the job even when working for Jews was forbidden.

I knock on the door. There is no reply. I knock again and inadvertently open it. The foyer is the same as ever. Our three coats hang on the hooks. My visor cap and Papa's are beside them; perhaps the house was not abandoned, and Papa and Mama have come back and are resting now.

I proceed cautiously. In the living room, something has changed. Instead of the drawings by the famous artist Rosenberg, three icons are hanging. This surprise, for some reason, does not frighten me. Other things are in their regular places, including the record player. An icon is hanging in my parents' bedroom, but the bed and its cover and pillows are as usual. There's no icon in my room; everything is in order, the schoolbag at the foot of the desk.

"Mama!" I call out, my voice cracking. I go back to the living room and sit in my favorite chair. All is in place, I again tell myself. But in my heart I know that the quiet is not the quiet we left behind.

And the truth is quickly revealed: In the doorway to the kitchen stands Nadia. She looks younger, and wears Mama's apron.

"Nadia!" I gasp.

"Who are you?" She recoils in shock.

"Edmund," I say softly. "Don't you recognize me?"

She squints at me, takes a closer look, and finally says, "It's you but not you."

"I'm Edmund, nobody else," I say, startled by my own words.

"They said the Jews would never come back," Nadia says in her familiar voice.

"Who said?"

"Everyone."

"And you believed it?" I say indignantly.

"Till now not even one Jew has returned."

"So you won't let me into my house?"

"No," she says flatly. "This is my house now. I worked here more than twenty years, and I am the rightful heir. The municipality recognized my rights."

"And I?"

"You belong elsewhere; your place here has been revoked. May I remind you: At the time of the ghetto you were busy with Anastasia. You couldn't spare even fifteen minutes to sit by your sick mother and share her pain."

"And you won't let my parents enter the house?"

"How do you know they'll return?"

"I assume they will."

"Leave! And, anyway, you have no rights here. A son who kept distant from his sick mother has no right to inherit her house. That's obvious. Moreover, all your parents' property now belongs to the municipality. I advise you and also your parents, if they come back, not to be stubborn about this. Fate has decided who will live and who will die."

"I'm alive," I say and cock my rifle.

"Don't shoot me!" Nadia screeches, waking me from my sleep.

66

There's still what to be glad about: every day, two or three more survivors recuperate. They are pale and can barely stand, but they stare in amazement at the training exercises and the fighters leaving for raids and ask, "When will we also be able to do our part?"

"Your job is to get stronger," says Kamil. "It's too bad we don't have more nutritious food, but not to worry, tomorrow morning we're going to break the ice on the lake and bring back fresh fish. Tsila will make us a feast fit for a king."

It's hard for the stoves and campfires to overcome the fierce, biting cold at the summit. If we'd hoped the bunkers would be warm, we were mistaken. The cold bites us there, too.

Dr. Krinitski doesn't stop complaining. "Why did you bring me here? Why did you snatch me from my home? There are no medicines or sanitary conditions. Take me back home; if you don't, I will die of the cold."

"And you can't empathize at all with those who suffer?" asks Felix.

"What are you talking about? How is it possible to empathize with a hundred and seventy starving, sick, and exhausted people?"

"We should leave them to die?"

"That's their fate; what can we do."

"If you can't empathize with those who suffer, we'll do it for you. We'll bathe them, and we'll feed them with what we have. We'll warm the tents with the stoves we improvised. We'll protect every one of them. Our faith in humanity, thank heaven, has not expired."

"Am I to blame?"

"From my standpoint you are no longer a member of the human family. A man without human dignity or the dignity of a doctor is an insect. A worm."

"Jews don't talk that way," protested Krinitski.

"How do Jews talk? Come on, tell us, so we'll know."

"Jews accept their fate quietly."

"Not here, not in these mountains, not under my command. Here we are on a sacred mission: to judge people as people. We will love the good ones and condemn the despicable."

"You're going to execute me?" Krinitski looked up fearfully.

"First you must judge yourself."

"I don't care about anything anymore. I am done for," he said and rested his hands on his knees.

I LOOK AROUND ME and know: these are the last days on this wondrous mountaintop. Everything that happened here, and all the people—the commanders, my friends—will stay with me even if we are far away from one another. The summit broadened our minds, if I may say so. Everything I saw—and I saw a great deal—will be with me like a warm coat.

I feel bad about all the equipment we carried here on our backs: every pot and spoon and fork, every cup, not to mention the tripods, the various metal scraps that we hammered and welded into stoves, every utensil I ate or drank from—they are part of me, and it hurts that we will soon leave them behind.

Edward comes and latches onto me. Ever since the dog arrived as a wonderful guest, everyone wants to be near him. The closest are Maxie and Michael. Maxie talks to him a lot and reminds him of the days at home: in the summer he slept in the doghouse and in winter in the house. It sometimes seems like Maxie is fishing for information about the fate of those who were sent to the work camps.

Edward excites us whenever he hops into view. One thing can be said for sure: After Edward came, Maxie changed. His steps became small and cautious. Sometimes he stands as if straining to hear a sound, or he stares ahead with wonder. More than once I heard him ask Edward, "How did you know how to find me? I always knew you were loyal and had a rare sense of smell."

67

Russian radio is on the rampage, calling on even women and children to assault the retreating army—shoot them, beat them, all is permitted.

The cannons roaring day and night are proof that the army that bragged of conquering the world is retreating in disgrace. The communists among us rejoice and sing Russian marches, shout the names of Lenin and Stalin, confident that justice will speedily arrive.

Our patrols confirm that most of the trains are filled with soldiers; civilian transportation is suspended, and only trains carrying Jews are headed eastward. Kamil grinds his teeth: The snow keeps falling; many of the sick are burning with fever. What's the point of going out to bring more people? How can we house and feed them?

The patrols bring ominous news: a company of well-armed soldiers is practicing drills at the train station. Kamil has no doubt that they intend to attack us. Whoever disagrees on logical grounds fails to understand the supreme goal of the Germans in this war. It's good that it keeps snowing day and night; this will delay them. But to ignore the soldiers in training would be a terrible mistake. Kamil is getting the base ready for combat.

Joy and dread are thus mixed together. In the meantime, we monitor the daily progress of the Red Army. Felix reckons they are not far away, perhaps one hundred miles. The roar of the cannons grows louder by the hour.

Some of the recuperating survivors have asked to train for the fateful battle, but Kamil refuses. Ten or twenty people rising from their sickbeds will not make the difference. We must not put them to the test again.

The tension is high, but our routines endure. Tsila and Miriam and their support staff are cooking day and night. The fighters attached to the medical team are responsible for hygiene. Salo and Maxie dispense the medicine we have, talk to the sick, and say, "It's good that we are able to help one another." The raids continue, despite the many dangers.

I'm unhappy that our lives will soon change drastically. Kamil, Felix, and the squad commanders are preparing us for days of emergency. Were it not for the constant snow, we might be able to surprise the soldiers below and prevent the attack. This possibility is not lost on Kamil, but we are unfortunately too few to risk dividing our forces. Our commanders finally decided to house the survivors along the wall of the old Turkish fortress, to protect them from enemy fire.

FELIX HAS HEARD some good news: the Red Army has stepped up its advance and is now fifty miles away. But our supplies are dwindling. Tsila stands by the stove and says, "What can a cook do without staples? The soup is thin; the porridge is tasteless. God, give me ingredients and I'll make good, nutritious dishes. It's hard to watch the suffering of sick people." Her voice is strong, as if not asking but demanding.

In the midst of raiding, fortifying the base, and helping the medical staff, I go into the kitchen and pour myself a glass of tea. In recent days I've felt a whiff of farewell in everything I touch. I sit next to Werner, and for a moment he looks like Paul before he walked into the woods. The way he sits, the cigarette he rolled and now holds in his fingers, his sips of tea, his tall, agile body—he could be Paul's twin brother. It seems to me that he, too, is about to leave us, and I won't see him again.

"Werner," I say, but I don't know exactly what to tell him.

"What?" He looks at me.

"Do you realize what we're facing?" I ask, knowing the question is pointless.

"No," he replies.

"Victory is near," I say, knowing it's only make-believe.

"Let's hope so," he says, and a warm little smile crinkles his lips. I'm sure he doesn't want to contradict me or argue.

68

On Friday, Isidor prayed in a voice full of longing. A few of the survivors, only just rising from their sickbeds and realizing for the first time that they'd been rescued, cried like children. Somehow I had the sense that Grandma Tsirl was sitting with us, listening to the prayers with her eyes closed.

One of the communists, driven crazy by the praying, stood up and shouted, "Stop this blind ritual; let the joy of victory ring out in human language!" Fortunately, Karl intervened and asked him not to disrupt our camaraderie at this fateful hour. Who knows what lies before us.

After Karl's intervention, things calmed down, and Kamil spoke about preparations: the sick and recuperating would be housed by the fortress wall, and the fighters would secure their positions. There were questions, and Kamil answered them quietly and deliberately. The question repeated ad nauseam was whether it was remotely possible, now of all times, with the German Army in retreat, that they would attack us. Instead of answering, Kamil displayed a military map that had fallen into our hands. The map marked all the villages where Jews lived. Even a village with one Jewish family was marked as a target.

MICHAEL HAS FALLEN ILL, and the entire base holds its breath. He burns with fever and doesn't utter a sound; when he feels pain, he closes his eyes and bites his lip.

"What is it, dear fellow? Tell me what hurts," says Maxie, getting down on his knees.

At first it seemed that Michael had caught a cold, but aspirin didn't reduce his fever. He keeps burning up.

"Typhus," declares Salo, his face going pale as he speaks. He suggests that Krinitski see to him, but Maxie refuses. "I have no faith in such a man."

Michael is the light of our lives here. Sitting quietly on the crate, copying out passages from the Bible, solving math and geometry problems, he is a vivid reminder of the life we lived not long ago, as we sat reading, writing, preparing nervously for quizzes and exams.

Michael was torn away from his parents, but his parents are always present in his good manners and respect for his elders. He no longer talks or asks about them. He sometimes dreams about them and tells his dreams to Maxie. When we go out on raids or patrols, he stands there and watches us for a long while. As time went on, Michael learned not to ask too many questions. His politeness and quiet study endear him to everyone. When Maxie goes on a mission, Tsila and Miriam keep him company.

Now, as Michael lies on a bed of twigs and burns with fever, we gather by the infirmary tent, holding cups of tea and cigarettes, trying to reach out to him. If Isidor could lend us one of his prayers, we would stand there and pray. Because we have no prayers, we surround the infirmary tent and do not move from that place.

69

Last night I dreamed: Mama, Papa, and I have returned to Baden, near Vienna. Incredibly, everything is the same. The tall conductor wears a cap with a blue visor and stands on the station platform; the blond girl is at her window in the kiosk, ready to serve lemonade. But what makes me happiest is the carriage driver, standing in his usual spot, wearing his faded uniform. When he sees us, he claps his hands with excitement, for we had managed to do the impossible. Papa greets him with a wave. The carriage driver runs toward us, picks up our two suitcases as if they weighed nothing, and puts them in the back of the carriage.

The town seems the same as ever, peaceful and pleasant, showing no signs of shock or upheaval. The people walk at their usual relaxed pace. For a moment I wonder if they don't know what I know. Mama looks around and says, "It's good we came back." Papa doesn't react to that remark. He looks around suspiciously, checking every corner, a thin smile trembling on his lips.

The owner of the pension is a refined Czech gentleman who for some unknown reason had settled in this area and built a perfect guesthouse. We love him and his little hotel: here you soak up health and relaxation to last an entire year.

"Where were you? We were worried about you," the owner asks Papa.

"Far away, not worth discussing."

"We were worried about you," he repeats.

"Better we shouldn't talk. The less said the better," Papa says, regaining his familiar voice.

"Your room is ready for you," says the owner, shifting his tone.

Two porters we don't know grab the suitcases and fly up the stairs.

Our old room, number 25, is also unchanged. Everything is in its place: the tidy beds, the night tables and lamps, the desk where Mama loved writing long letters to her mother and sister. The full morning light peeks through the blinds the way I remember.

"Breakfast, children!" Papa says in a hearty voice. He shows no signs of our long night of travel. Mama, on the other hand, looks pale and pained: better I should get into bed, stretch my legs, and rest a bit, she says. Papa dismisses her request and insists: we have to eat breakfast.

The headwaiter recognizes us and greets us happily. We see at once that a table by the window has been reserved for us.

"We were worried about you," says the headwaiter in his fatherly voice.

Papa and Mama eat fried eggs, and I have a soft-boiled egg in a cup. The fresh, golden rolls are in the wicker basket, the cream is in the porcelain pitcher, the cherry jam is in the long-necked jar that I like, and the waiter is standing with the coffeepot in his hand.

"Good that we came on time," Papa says, pleased that life here is unchanged.

Papa is pleased, but the secret we carry remains hidden. Each of us has a secret, but we cannot talk about it. Not among ourselves or with those around us. They apparently guess that we carry a secret, but they don't dare ask.

For our breakfast dessert we are served forest berries in cream, a delicacy I adore. Papa lights a cigarette. I love the tiny gestures involved in lighting a cigarette, and the smell of the tobacco and the bluish smoke that rises. A cigarette after a meal is a type of dessert permitted only to grown-ups. The children watch with an eye to the future.

Time for bed, say Mama's eyes; *I'm falling over.* Papa shoots her a skeptical look, as if to say, *The weather outside is wonderful; it's a glorious morning. How can we pass up a little walk in the Hapsburg Park?*

You're right, dear, but what can I do. I'm tired and my whole body aches. I can barely move, Mama replies wordlessly.

"Try just a little spin, and then we'll have a nap. You can sleep as long as you like; no one will disturb you." Papa's voice is gentle and filled with goodwill. Mama tries to stand up but can do so only with Papa's help.

In the doorway Mama says weakly, "Don't forget, dear; I underwent a difficult operation, and every little move hurts me."

"I know, my dear; I just wanted you to see, if only for a minute, the Hapsburg Park in full bloom."

The hotel owner, observing our dilemma, comes over and says, "How can I help you this morning?"

"We're going for a moment to the Hapsburg Park. We love the park in the morning. My wife doesn't feel well today, but I'm sure she'll be better in a day or two," Papa says apologetically.

Mama sits on a bench, her weakness apparent even while she is seated. Papa sits beside her, marveling at the colorful flowers but saying nothing.

Only after a few minutes does he say, without looking at us, "How wonderful; nothing has changed here." It's hard to assess the tone of his voice; is it wonder or irony?

"Right," says Mama. She has no strength to utter more than this word.

Several couples walk past us. I remember them from previous vacations, but I don't recall their names. They are caught up in themselves and ignore us.

"It's strange," says Papa.

"What's strange?" asks Mama.

"It's hard to say the flowers have changed—of course they haven't changed, and neither have the trees. But why do I feel that these aren't the trees that I knew?"

"You're imagining it," Mama says, in her voice from before the surgery.

Mama's strength is ebbing. She wants to go to bed and rest her head on the pillow. The chambermaid, Louise, greets us at the door to our room. She recognizes us right away, hugs my mother, and says with excitement, "Where were you? Where'd you disappear to? I was worried about you. I was used to seeing you every year, and suddenly you disappeared. I haven't seen you for a few years." Her voice chokes and tears flow from her eyes.

"Dear, dear Louise, there is so much to tell but not now; I can barely stand on my feet. After I rest, we'll talk. We'll talk for a long time."

"Come in. If I had known you were coming, I'd have brought more flowers from the garden. Flowers always make the heart happy." Louise used to say that a lot, as I recall.

"I won't disturb you; go rest," she says and retreats to the corridor.

"Louise hasn't changed," Papa says.

Papa takes off Mama's shoes. Only now do I see how pale she really is. The paleness has worsened since I left them at the train station. Papa lays Mama down on the bed, and suddenly, like a magician, he reveals the huge bandage, tied with laces, that covers Mama. He loosens the laces, removes the bandage carefully and expertly, and right away I see the yellow-red stains. Papa quickly lifts Mama up and puts a new bandage underneath her, folds it like a diaper, ties the laces, and says, "I tried hard not to hurt you."

"Thanks, sweetheart," Mama says, almost silently.

It's now clear to me that these big bandages have enabled Papa to save Mama. I always knew Papa was talented in many areas, but I didn't imagine that he was also an excellent medic. I keep watching him. Some of his old movements are gone, replaced by new ones, unfamiliar to me.

Having finished the job, Papa stands by the window and doesn't budge. I fear he will turn to me and ask where I've been ever since I left them at the railroad station.

Papa doesn't ask. He's planted by the window. My fear keeps growing, and finally I can't hold back. "Where were you, Papa?" I ask.

"Why do you ask?" He answers with a question, surprising me.

"I'm curious."

He apparently doesn't approve of the word "curious." He purses his lips and says, "Why do you use the word 'curious'? Don't you know it's not used anymore?"

"What should I say, Papa?"

"Whatever you want, just don't use the word 'curious.'"

This remark seems odd to me. Are there words that must not be used? If a word helps us understand something, why not use it?

Because of Papa's puzzling remark, I don't ask anything else. Papa suddenly seems weighed down with sorrow. I sit on the chair and my eyes close of their own accord.

70

I woke up and immediately realized that I had been away from my tasks for a long time. I was ashamed that at a critical moment of our life here I had evaded my duty. It felt like I had slept for many hours. Karl, who woke me, informed me that Michael's condition had improved. He had opened his eyes. Isidor and Sigmund brought the pots with boiling water. Salo had asked that they let me sleep, and he now greeted me warmly. "It's good that you slept," he said. "We expect a grueling night." I was touched by his concern and said, "I'm sorry."

I went to the wardrobe tent, and Hermann Cohen gave me military winter pants and a thick farmer's sweater, and I also took a short coat. I had already learned the hard way: better to suffer from cold than clumsiness.

The evening meal was delicious: corn porridge with cheese and pickles, coffee, and a slice of cake. I lit a cigarette and enjoyed the rush of the smoke. Just a few months ago cigarette smoke still choked me; now I enjoy every puff.

Leaving the camp this time was not as per usual, and there were even a few conflicts over trivial matters. But Felix's briefing was quiet, clear, and to the point, and everyone calmed down.

Were it not for the diminished supplies, Kamil would not have approved this raid. Kamil is increasingly convinced that we will be attacked in the days to come. The small number of hostile patrols doesn't mean they won't carry out their evil plan. In his opinion, we would be able to hold out for a week, even more. By then, we can assume, the Red Army will arrive.

We went out on the raid at one in the morning and reached the target at 2:30. It was a small farm with three buildings: a house, a cowshed, and a storeroom attached to a silo.

We broke in and woke the elderly couple. They did not scream. They stood by their beds in their long nightshirts, illuminated by our flashlights. On hearing our request that they willingly give us food and used clothing, they smiled awkwardly, as if we were pulling their leg or had lost our minds.

Felix told them we were partisans. No point in bargaining, just give generously. And when the Red Army arrives, they will get special recognition for their help in the war effort. The couple didn't move. The dumb smile spread across their faces.

Felix didn't prod them. He allowed for the fact that old people awakened in the middle of the night are in shock and must be given a moment to recover.

Finally, the man came to his senses and said, still smiling, "Take what you want. Just consider that this is winter, the roads are blocked, and we won't be able to go out and get supplies." He spoke reasonably, his dignity intact.

Because of this simple, human request, we took about half the supplies in the pantry. In the cellar were apples and pears; we took them as well as two old coats and a few sheepskins, and that was enough.

As we were about to leave, the old man asked us, "Where are you from?"

"We are partisans fighting the enemy's rear flank," Felix said simply.

"We were afraid you would empty our house," said the old man, still smiling.

"We take only what we need and don't intend to ruin other

people. An army is supplied with food and clothing. Partisans must take care of themselves," said Felix in the voice of a sensible farmer.

"There are bottles of vodka in the cupboard. Take a few."

Felix went to the cupboard, took three bottles, and said, "God bless you; there are still people in this world in whom the light of God has not gone out."

"God protect you, too."

After putting the bottles in a sack, Felix handed his flashlight to the old man and said, "This is for you; maybe it will help."

"Many thanks, you are good people."

This peaceful encounter, the likes of which we had not experienced since we began our raids, instilled faith in us that all had not been lost, that there were still people who can be trusted.

The food and clothing we took were heavier than we had estimated, but we moved quickly and in good spirits, and we were pleased that this time we would bring supplies that were given to us willingly. And there was another reason we were happy: we could hear the thunder of the cannons and smell the fires that broke out not far from us. We were not afraid of this friendly fire. For some reason we were confident that it would not strike us. We sang the Russian marches we'd learned from our communist comrades and envisioned the Russian Army liberating the towns and villages at the foot of the mountains.

When we returned to the base, our friends welcomed us joyfully. Only Kamil was not himself. He spoke with the fighters and with Hermann Cohen and with the survivors and explained that the danger has not passed: a wounded army is often an irrational army, likely to rashly send its fighters to their death.

We were not the only ones to return in a good mood; the reconnaissance patrol commanded by Karl came back and reported that the streets of the towns and villages were empty of occupiers, and everyone awaited the arrival of the Red Army.

Kamil and Felix huddled in a tent to plan the relocation of those who were sick and recovering to the wall of the Turkish fortress.

Heavy snow falls without respite. Some of the fighters think our preparations are excessive. Kamil again argues, "Never forget: the goal of the enemy was and remains the destruction of the Jews."

71

We had no idea how right Kamil was. In the early hours before dawn, we were hit by a hail of shelling. At first it appeared to be a "softening up," to be followed by an attack by the company that was training down below. Kamil didn't say "I told you so." He was glad we had moved the sick and recovering to a relatively safe place.

The shelling intensified, and luckily all the shells did not reach the summit. Salo and Maxie took care of the wounded, and it was a good thing that our positions were deeply entrenched and that the fortress wall provided protection.

The shelling got heavier and lasted about two hours—in fact, until daybreak. When we poked our heads out from our positions, we were stunned by what we saw: many fighters were lying on the red snow, doubled over in pain, calling for help. Salo and Maxie went from person to person, trying to stanch the bleeding and bandage the wounds. The tents had collapsed, and there were no fires or water.

Werner had taken a direct hit and was lying with outstretched arms, soaked in blood, no longer breathing. Not far from him lay Big Karl. His tall body was crumpled, and it looked like he had suffered terrible pain before dying. Quiet, devoted Miriam had been struck in the face by shrapnel as she emerged from the bunker; her head was now hanging down on her shoulder as she lay motionless on the ground. A distance away, legs spread apart, lifeless, lay Kamil.

There was silence, and it was red. And for a moment it seemed that Salo and Maxie, who were busy saving lives, would look up and berate us for standing and doing nothing.

It had stopped snowing, and the sun shone brightly on the summit; not a whisper was heard. Salo and Maxie moved on their knees from person to person, trying to revive them. Victor was at their side to help. He carried the box of medicines and bandages and a pail of water. His beard had grown since he came to us, and he looked like a man completely devoted to other people.

We didn't know what to do and just stood. We saw the dead lying there and the blood spilled on the snow, and we did not absorb the magnitude of the disaster.

Felix was the first to regain his bearings and told us to set up the stoves and the tents to prevent the wounded from freezing. Tsila wept bitterly, beating her head with both hands. The fighters tried to console her, to no avail. Her whole body shook. "Why were they killed now, a moment before the liberation?" she wailed.

"They died like heroes," a young fighter said gently.

"I don't want them to be heroes; I want them alive. For whom will I cook? For whom will I make soup? I want the hands that took plates from me; I want the faces that smiled at me. They were younger than I am. I should have died, not them."

The young fighter withdrew, as if chastened.

As we started to put up the tents, to arrange the tripods and the stoves, as we saw Hermann Cohen carrying a bundle of wood and Felix's penetrating gaze, we knew we must not delay. We had to take care of the many wounded and ease their pain.

Dr. Krinitski seized the opportunity and ran away. He had done nothing of his own free will, only under duress. Words and gestures had no effect on him; he never stopped complaining and blaming and speaking ill of everyone. It was good that he was gone, and it would be good, too, if he were to end up buried in the snow.

This small discovery did not pull us out of our shock. The disaster spread as the sun rose higher. We had not seen such a sun for months. The great light exposed the damage and the death. We were afraid to approach the dead and cover them. Felix, who was now in command, reasoned that the silence coming from below indicated more than anything else that the German Army was in retreat and the Red Army was flanking it on all sides. But we should not risk going down; instead, we should first ascertain that the Red Army had reached the train station.

Without delay, a patrol went out to check the area, and we watched as it disappeared from view.

72

Then we picked up the bodies. We laid them in a row and covered them with blankets. It seemed for a moment that they were still alive, only sleeping, and would soon wake up.

It was strange, how quickly we put up the tents, fixed the stoves. The wounded had been moved and were lying on boards padded with twigs. Several were badly wounded, and Salo and Maxie didn't leave their side. But the burning stoves and the water boiling on the tripods reminded us of our old routines, when everyone was active and satisfied by the activity.

Hermann Cohen now took Tsila's place in the kitchen. Salo, who saw how Tsila was suffering, gave her a sedative, and she stopped wailing. There were still sandwiches and tea for breakfast, and anyone who ran out of cigarettes could ask Hermann Cohen to advance the next day's packet.

During the shelling, Milio clung to Danzig's chest and went completely mute, but then he began pounding with his hands and making loud sounds. Danzig explained to him that we'll soon go down below, but that there's nothing to be afraid of; the war is over and there will be no more shellings.

Then Felix stood up and asked to speak. His distress was apparent, his fists clenched close to his body. He began by saying, "I'm sorry Kamil is not standing here instead of me. He led us day and night. He knew these mountains not from maps but from his footsteps. He saw things we did not see. It hurts so much that this great commander is not with us." He was clearly dissatisfied with what he said and was about to apologize. Fortunately, Danzig, holding Milio tightly, spoke up and reminded us of Karl's love for his fellow man, a love that had led him to communism. His communism was pure. How terrible that his wife and small children would not see their father return home. Danzig suddenly burst into tears, and we silently clung to one another beside the covered bodies, the question of why they died and we were alive unanswerable.

Then we moved the wounded and weak to the tents, and the line dividing the living and dead became sharply drawn. We grabbed the tea and cigarettes; these were our hold on life at this hour of need.

Michael, despite his weakness, knew what had occurred and asked what would happen now to the dead who lay on the ground. Maxie answered very simply: there is no need to worry about our heroes; they have gone to heaven, and in time we will go up there, too, and be with them.

"And we'll be together, like here?"

"Presumably."

Michael is very familiar with the word "presumably" and has the feeling that it conceals something important, but he asked no more questions. He saw that Maxie was distracted and it was best not to burden him.

More survivors have recovered and some stood up, wanting to know where the kitchen was. Everyone is hungry. Hermann Cohen, replacing Tsila, distributed small portions of sweetened porridge.

No one asked what we will do with the dead who lie before us, where we will bury them and when; as in every war, hunger is stronger than grief. A man hides his head in a plate and savors every spoonful of hot porridge.

73

A mid all this, the patrol returned with the news that the Red Army had indeed captured the train station and the surrounding military camps and was running wild, looting and singing Russian marches.

Oddly, this news we had awaited for years did not make us happy. It was as if the river of time had frozen solid. The sedative paralyzed Tsila's face, and her eyes bulged from their sockets, wishing to pull free.

Salo, Maxie, and Victor treat the wounded and exhausted without a moment's pause. No one goes near the dead, as if it has been agreed that they are cut off from us and now live their own silent lives. The question of when we will go down to witness the victory is not being asked. The medical team feels that for now we must save the sick and wounded and not move them.

Felix, who has taken command, announced that two squads will go out tonight to raid distant houses, and the others will prepare stretchers so we can carry down the sick and wounded when the time comes.

Patience has run out among some survivors; they want to descend right away. Felix found the right words and explained that there is mutual responsibility at the summit; people help one another, protect the weak and wounded, and obey orders. We will not return to the days when every man cared only about himself. The survivors listened and did not respond.

Felix is alert and focused yet addresses the people quietly. Unfortunately, he sprained his right foot and is walking with a stick. His new walk and tight lips suggest a man of determination, free of self-pity.

Were it not for the dead covered in blankets, life at the summit might return to the routine established by Kamil and Felix. Kamil's spirit hovers over us with great intensity. One of the fighters, preparing for a raid, said in passing, "I'll be sure to do exactly what Kamil taught us."

An old man went to Felix and said, "It is forbidden to leave the dead lying here."

"What should we do?" asked Felix.

"We must bury them."

"Soon we will go down and bury them in the Jewish cemetery," said Felix and moved aside, as if he had not encountered a man but a ghost. The old man, who could barely stand on his feet, kept standing, as if wanting his words to be heard and carried out.

AND THEN I SAW a spectacular vision of Kamil standing tall: his chest wide and arms outstretched as if protecting us all. But his chest is too narrow to include everyone. Kamil does not give up. He broadens his chest and lengthens his arms. And it's a miracle; now he's a giant, and more people are shielded in his shadow. Kamil is pleased and wants to express his satisfaction in words, but the words defy him, are stuck in his mouth. This strong man, who knew how to inspire life even in the darkest hours, now stands at full height with the words trapped within him.

Why don't you speak?, one of the fighters asks him.

As he hears the fighter's question, Kamil breaks out in a smile as if to say, *There is no need for words now. A tight bond requires no words; let us stay silent, as we know how.*

Kamil's face is so powerfully expressive that even his opponents don't dare contradict him. Because they do not speak, Kamil maintains his silence, which tells us: we will always be together. Everyone who was at the summit will take it with him everywhere. He will carry the living with him, and also those who passed away: Paul, the noblest of men, whom we could not save; Miriam, from whose hands everyone received not only a bowl of soup or mended clothes but also a part of herself; Werner, whose comments when we studied at night were now hidden inside us like an eternal light; and Karl, beloved by all of us. Grandma Tsirl said again and again that the partition between life and death is very thin; today we are here and tomorrow we are there. Not to fear, our togetherness is like a walled fortress.

THIS VISION STAYED with me a long time. Isidor, who had not uttered a sound since the shelling, came by and asked me if I felt all right. I didn't know what to tell him. It's hard to talk about visions. He bent down and said, "Thank God I'm not being asked to pray. Prayer has been taken away from me."

"I understand you," I said.

"Thank you," said Isidor.

"Don't be afraid. People will not force you to pray."

"But the dead are waiting for the prayer to protect them," he whispered.

"Say whatever you can; no one will blame you."

"Thank you," he repeated.

I wanted to tell him, we are beyond good and bad; we are in the world of silence. But I didn't say so.

74

The squads returned before dawn, loaded with supplies but in a foul mood. They had raided a house filled with women and children. The women, unfortunate and insolent, threw things at them, screamed and cursed. Threats and hand-cuffs only increased their screaming. The children had to be locked in another room.

It was a poor home, and yet the squads managed to score a sack of potatoes, a medium-sized sack of flour, some corn, red cabbage, apples, onions, and garlic. Asked by Felix what had happened, one of the fighters replied, "It's very unpleasant to fight with women and children. What was unavoidable a month ago is now indefensible. The time to go down is now."

Tsila went into the kitchen and served sandwiches and coffee to the squads. She is still not herself. Death has lodged in her face. She speaks slowly, as if fearing her own speech.

Hermann Cohen is also not the man he was yesterday. Every time the radio plays marches, he contorts his mouth. His niece wasn't wounded in the shelling, but ever since then, she's been shaking, saying things no one understands, and once an hour she asks her uncle to take her to the toilet.

"You'll be cold," begs Hermann Cohen.

Hearing his plea, she smiles and says, "What can I do?"

BUILDING THE STRETCHERS CONTINUES. Felix figures we'll need at least forty stretchers, and they should be prepared as quickly as possible because the food is running out.

Color has returned to Emil's face, and his sense of wonder, too. Were it not for his weakness, he would walk out of his tent and stand there looking at the spectacular view. Yesterday he emerged and stood for a few minutes. His eyes filled with tears.

Kamil would always say that as long as we're alive it's possible to do good. Until the last moment of his life, Kamil was full of action. But at the same time he was devoted to big ideas that governed his daily life.

Now Kamil lies in the snow, covered with a blanket. For a moment it seems that he's about to take off the blanket, arise from his frozen state, and say, *What happened to me? Why didn't you wake me?* Most nights Kamil didn't sleep, but he would often lie down in the middle of the day and sleep for an hour or two.

Once he asked me, "What kind of career do you want?"

"It's not clear to me yet," I replied.

Kamil then revealed that his twin brother was the first violinist in the Brussels Philharmonic Orchestra. From the age of five, he and his family knew that he would be a violinist; even then he strove for perfection. There were days when he was happy with the sounds he made and days when he was gloomy, closed off, and angry. Their mother, who was very close to him, would try to ease his inner tension, but she rarely succeeded. It was hard for him to describe the flaw in his playing to his mother, but by age seventeen he had very nearly overcome it, and his face lit up. People loved him and would come from afar to hear him. Success smiled upon him, but he knew that a bit of that flaw still nested within him and that he had to try harder. It was a Sisyphean struggle that began in the morning and ended at night. "I saw his struggle but didn't know how to help him," said Kamil. "To my ears his playing was perfect. And when I told him so, he said, 'You're wrong.'"

Again I picture Emil standing by the blackboard, casually solving a problem. Everyone is amazed, envious, making jokes, interrupting, and realizing that none of them will ever reach his level. *What good will his genius for math do for him?*, they finally say. *He's as innocent as a child and can easily be duped.*

I want to tell him, *Emil, many great achievements await you. You are only at the beginning of the road.* But I quickly understand that these words, spoken at this time, would only make things worse. Now he needs to lie down on a mat, close his eyes, and be one with his body.

75

Isidor doesn't pray at night anymore. Since he stopped praying, we pay less attention to ourselves. The pain of the survivors comes first. No one is more devoted than Salo and Maxie. They know all the survivors by name and by their wounds. Victor, his hair uncut and wild, is regarded as a doctor by some survivors. Victor sometimes apologizes and says, "I'm not a doctor or a doctor's son; I'm a farmer." But his dedication is total. Sometimes he says, "Forgive me; I speak only Ukrainian. It's a limitation that's hard to overcome."

We listen to the radio and get ready to go down the mountain. The elderly survivor again warns that it is forbidden to leave the dead unburied. Felix's repeated assurance that we will soon go down and bury them in a Jewish cemetery does not set his mind at ease. The old man's warning sows disquiet. The teams building the stretchers try to speed up their work.

In a day or two we will make our way down. The sick and the weak, who were supposed to have recovered, have not yet done so. Yes, the fish we catch in the lake, which Hermann roasts with great artistry, have put several survivors back on their feet, but most are weak and a few seem lost, asking over and over, "Where are we? When will we go home?"

In my heart of hearts I'm afraid of going down. The months

we've spent together in the wetlands, and especially at the summit, are written in my body: the patrols, the ambushes, the raids, the rescue of the survivors. My high school years seem awkward and strange after the challenges of the wetlands. True, there were teachers at the *gymnasium* whom I admired, but none of them can compare with Kamil, Felix, Hermann Cohen, or Tsila.

Isidor eagerly anticipates meeting his parents, and if he doesn't find them at the train station, he will return to the city and wait for them. I am fearful of his expectations and want to tell him, *Let's wait and see*, but I don't say a thing.

A PATROL RETURNED bringing supplies that the Red Cross is providing to the locals. The bottles of vodka and the cigarettes were particularly gratifying. They met a few Jews who had been in the camps but who refused to answer questions.

That night Felix announced that we would begin our descent the next morning, in the following order: First we will bring down the dead and bury them in the Jewish cemetery. After we get settled below, we will take down the sick, then the weak and exhausted, and finally we'll remove Koba and Grandma Tsirl, and two other fallen comrades, Mark and Gabriel, from their graves and give them a Jewish burial. The descent will take at least three or four days. Two squads will carry the sick and wounded, and two squads will protect the base.

We spent the last night at the summit almost without words. We drank vodka and ate the black bread and cheese brought by the patrol, and we smoked a lot. It's doubtful that anybody expected miracles. But we were mourning the days of being together that were fast disappearing; soon each person would be for himself, without closeness and camaraderie.

Isidor, who is not used to drinking vodka, drank two glasses and burst into tears. The weeping came from deep inside him, without words, and shook his body. I didn't know what to tell him, so I said, "Soon we'll go down." His body kept shaking, and I doubt that he heard me.

76

We rose early and ate breakfast together. It was strange; there wasn't much emotion. After the meal, I lit a cigarette and sat down.

At exactly 7:00 a.m. Felix announced that the stretchers were ready and that everyone should go to the stretcher to which he had been assigned.

We stood by the stretchers, and Isidor was asked to read "The Lord is my shepherd," the psalm Kamil had loved. Felix handed over the command to Danzig.

We lifted the bodies onto the stretchers. Kamil's stretcher was carried first, and after it came the one bearing Karl. Isidor and I carried Miriam, and on the last stretcher was Werner.

We knew there were rules and customs for funerals, but no one among us knew them. Werner, a man of broad education and intuition, lay on the stretcher, gone from us.

Felix, suffering from his sprained ankle, had changed overnight, appearing restless and apologetic. "I know little about rituals and prayers," he said, "but I ask of you, look after yourselves and be careful. The German Army may have retreated, but gangs of Ukrainians are surely swarming in their hideaways."

He stood in place and kept an eye on us for a good while. We felt his presence even in the distance.

It was a sunny day; the snow glittered and the water trickled in brooks. There was a first whiff of early spring, when the double windows would soon be dismantled, with Mama standing in the living room and saying, *Spring is almost here.*

Men and women were clearing the piles of snow that had accumulated beside their homes and on the sidewalks. Everyone spoke in new voices: Finally, the cold and dark have passed, soon the doors and windows will be opened; children and old people will stand in the gardens.

As we carried the stretchers, careful not to trip, we heard shots. Danzig ordered us to take our positions. We lay in readiness beside our dead. Kamil and Karl, fighters of great stature, always seemed to keep death at a distance. Now they lay on stretchers, covered by blankets, deathly silent.

After an hour of listening for gunfire, we continued on our way. We kept apart from one another and walked in a crouch. The thought that Kamil would not be with us and that we would have to live without him had actually sunk in only now. And for a moment it seemed we were escorting not only Miriam to her eternal home but also her father and mother, her husband and children. They lived with her the entire time she was with us, and now, when she is not mending clothes and not serving soup, they accompany her to the next world. I wanted to share this thought with Isidor, but I couldn't find the right words. I was wary of being misunderstood and said nothing.

WE ARRIVED at the railroad station. It was filled with people, including some survivors. There was no fear, just restlessness. We made our way to the cemetery by means of a sketch Felix had given Danzig, and within half an hour we stood at its ruined gate.

Some of the tombstones had been broken and vandalized, and many were uprooted, leaving empty cavities. We looked for a plot to bury our dead and didn't find one. Finally, we found a corner at the foot of an old poplar and started to dig; fortunately, we had spades and hoes and baskets made of rope. Danzig, who had not recovered from his wounds, apologized that he couldn't take part in the digging. Immersed in the work, we temporarily forgot our sorrows. We didn't think about what our hands were doing.

Before we put them in the ground, Danzig spoke. "Kamil, my esteemed commander. We never imagined that at the moment of victory you would not be with us. You were a father and brother to us; you trained us step by step and turned us from ordinary people into fighters. We walked scores of miles together, and with every mile you taught us the duty of a Jew at this time. Forgive us; we didn't always understand what you meant, and forgive those who argued with you. You had a vision and you wanted to guide us by its light. I assume that more than once you were sick of us. You withdrew to your tent, and what you went through in your despair we will never know. You knew what each one of us needed. We, for our part, didn't always make the effort to understand your best intentions. We loved you: the way you stood and spoke, the way you taught us what matters. Now you are leaving us. Where are you going, dear man?" The last words choked him up, and he became pale.

Our spirits plummeted. We stood beside the bodies and the graves, exposed in every direction. Manfred, Karl's friend and ideological ally, did not hesitate and spoke directly to him: "You were like your famous namesake, loyal to your comrades and to all mankind. You did not discriminate between people. You left us a great legacy: love. Your love is planted in every one of us. Long live world communism, long live true communism."

The last blunt words spoken by the fighter roused us from our stupor. Next Isidor spoke up. "We didn't know anything about Miriam," he said. "Do we know anything about the lives of angels? They appear at the hour that we need them. Everything you served us, Miriam, everything your hands made for us, was steeped in your love. Rest now, my dear one; you deserve perfect peace." Then he fell silent.

One of the fighters who carried Werner on the stretcher lowered his head and said, "I didn't know you, dearest Werner, and I didn't know your life story, but every word and sentence that came from your mouth was pure. You are taking this purity with you to heaven. All those who met you in this world got from you more than they deserved—I did in my case, anyway."

We delayed no longer. We buried them one after another. I had grown weaker in recent days, and it showed: I trembled, and my hands could barely hold the spade. Isidor worked his wonders yet again. He said Kaddish in a quivering voice beside every grave.

We stood a long time by the filled graves. We knew the friends we buried deserved greater praise and glory, but our sorrow produced no words. We stood bereft of all we once had and walked with bent heads through the broken gate of the cemetery.

77

We got moving without delay. We carried the empty stretchers at intervals of one hundred feet. Luckily, we encountered no rioters. The path was rough for walking and seemed longer than it was. We didn't reach the base until late at night.

We saw at once that our friends hadn't sat on their hands. They set up more tents to house the sick and wounded. Salo and Maxie looked drained and could barely drag their feet. Maxie hugged me and said, "I don't dare ask what it was like. Thank God you got back safely. And thank you for doing the most painful duty of all." It wasn't Maxie talking but rather his grief and fatigue.

Hermann Cohen greeted us in the kitchen and served everyone a sandwich and cup of coffee. I was hungry and thirsty and ate with a great appetite. At the same time I hated myself because only a few short hours ago we had buried our friends in the ground, and now I was enjoying food and a hot drink.

Emil also hugged me and said, "I'm happy you returned safely." I didn't know how to respond. "We did our duty," I said, "and it was lucky Isidor was with us. When words fail us, it's good to have prayer to hold on to." That's wasn't exactly what I wanted to say, but I was glad I was able to string a few words together. Emil told me that the medical team stays close to the wounded, bandaging and splinting as necessary. The wounded don't stop thanking them. In the camps where he had been, people didn't help each other. Whoever got sick knew the end was near and that no one would prevent it.

Danzig wrapped Milio in his arms and told him that Kamil, Karl, Miriam, and Werner had gone up to the sky and were resting there now. Milio listened with his mouth open, not making a sound. Tsila, who cared for him when Danzig was away, looked at him with loving eyes and said nothing.

I was tired and wanted to close my eyes, but Felix asked to speak. He began: "We thank the squads headed by Danzig, who brought our friends to their proper burial. This was a difficult mission, and you performed it with perfection; it's good that you are with us."

That's how Felix is. He's good at not talking, but when forced to, he relies on convenient words like "mission" and "performed." Only this time, they weren't the right words. I was tired and oversensitive, so I paid attention to the way he spoke. I knew that criticizing a friend's language at a time of pain is either foolish or wicked. I learned that from Kamil, who was famously precise when it came to speech.

After a short pause, he continued: "Our hold on the mountaintop is about to end. We have enough food for a few days. There's no point in more raids. We'll go down and see what we have to do."

"And what about our equipment?" somebody asked.

"We won't take the tents. We'll take the blankets and sheepskins. Also pots and pans, personal items, plates and cutlery and cups. And of course all the books."

"And everyone will go home?" asked a survivor who recently recovered from illness.

"We'll have to see what the conditions are. We must not rush. The descent must be orderly and secure." Felix's dry, logical words filled me with melancholy, and I sat down.

Salo approached me. "What's the matter?"

"It's hard to return to everyday life," I said.

"At this moment, dear fellow, we can't be weak. We have to bring the survivors to a safe place. Let's pray that the worst didn't happen and that most of the people who were taken to the camps will return. Our mission is not over. Our beloved Kamil surely wants us to bring the survivors to their families."

Again I didn't know what to say, so I just said, "I'm sorry."

"There's no reason to be sorry. You are a wonderful fighter, a loyal friend, and devoted to the survivors."

I knew he wanted to appease me. "Soon I'll come to help the medical team," I said.

"Rest a while; the medical team is well staffed."

The survivors are recovering, and some of them are eating hungrily and asking for second helpings.

SUDDENLY I HAD a vision of Kamil as I'd never seen him before, collapsing with anguish. Many a time he would leave the big tent and seclude himself in the small command tent. It sometimes seemed he was angry with us. Only later did we learn that, among other reasons, he would seclude himself out of depression. Kamil was a strong man, and when he fell, he fell hard. Once, in a moment of great enthusiasm, he said, "We will be together from now until forever!" His tone of voice attested that he had just emerged from black despair. Kamil never spoke about this hidden wound. Now it came to me in a flash: all his life he battled the abyss.

78

Again I'm boiling water, bringing the pots into the big tent, and helping Victor bathe the sick. They look at us with admiration and don't stop thanking us. Once in a while one of them props himself up on his mat, looks at us, and says, "Who are you?"

The snow has ended, and it is raining. We can hear avalanches of snow detaching from the summit. Michael came over and asked if the uncles and Aunt Miriam have reached heaven yet.

"I guess so," I said.

"Why do they have to be buried before they go up to heaven?"

"That's how it's done." I couldn't find other words to explain it.

"Will they appear to us?"

"In dreams, I assume."

"If they are going up to heaven why do we mourn for them?"

"Because they are far away from us."

"Will we see them in dreams the way we used to see them?"

"I assume so."

Michael stands beside me and looks like an angel who hasn't yet grown wings. I remember him sitting on a little crate, copying verses from the Bible or sitting hunched over and solving math and geometry problems, totally focused. His questions are startlingly sharp. Grandma Tsirl loved him and would answer him with serious attention.

The delicate fabric we wove among us is unraveling. We are left bare, and the few words that served us in the past no longer do us much good.

It's impossible not to keep seeing Karl—his height and broad shoulders and magnificent smile. Always ready to give of himself, always fishing in his pockets to find something sweet or funny. When he doesn't find anything, his smile widens with embarrassment.

We remember fondly the study evenings when he would recite some Marxist teaching and remind everyone that he was a communist and the son of communists and that until communism ruled the world everything was flawed. Despite the clichés, you couldn't be angry with Karl. When he spoke, you could see the child in him, and many fighters wondered how that cruel ideology had infected this man who wanted only to do good. Sometimes he would ask Danzig's permission to take Milio in his arms. Milio would look at him with wonder, as if to say, *Your height, Karl, you're a giant, but I'm not afraid of you.*

Milio's face is so expressive. You can understand him with no effort. I sometimes think he grasps our situation better than we do. Now and then I detect pity in his face.

After the shelling, he covered his eyes with both hands. Danzig asked him to uncover them, but Milio did not respond. Now, too, he keeps closing his eyes. Milio's existence is a perpetual riddle. I look at him with the fear that he will soon utter a sentence that will shock us all.

79

One more day, two more days, remain in our stay at the summit. The time grows shorter. The coffee has run out. We drink tea and roll tobacco in newspapers. Whoever is not treating the sick and wounded is building stretchers.

The disquiet that we had suppressed all along now rises to the surface. Stinging words never heard before unsettle the atmosphere. Felix asks for restraint and reminds us that during our entire time here, we had never vented our anger. Every fighter must do exactly as Kamil ordered. Now that he is gone, we must follow his orders with even greater diligence. Nobility means obligation, says Felix, repeating a motto of Kamil's. In recent days Felix has often relied on Kamil's words. Truth to tell, they don't suit him and sound awkward. Felix should stay Felix, even when there's a need for words and maxims.

We already have the stretchers that will take the first people down tomorrow morning. What will happen? How will we carry on? I can't form a picture in my mind.

Emil is on his feet and feeling well, but he won't be among the first to make the descent. His hope of finding his blind parents has not abated. He speaks of them all the time, as if trying to inform them that he's not far away.

Tsila doesn't budge from the kitchen. Hermann Cohen brings her whatever he still has in storage, and she makes tasty meals from it. The fighters help and encourage her and continue to promise that no one will ever forget her cooking; it is stamped into every cell in our bodies. It seems to me that a secret has been conveyed to her. "I know. I understand," she mutters to herself, which is more frightening than her weeping.

Felix speaks to her tenderly. "Your job is not yet over," he says. "You will stay with us for many days to come. We cannot do without you. When we go down, we'll still be together. We have the sick and wounded, and we all depend on one another."

She looks up. "And we won't split up?"

"Absolutely not. We'll stay together. We have a great responsibility. Kamil spoke of this a lot. Our togetherness is ingrained in us."

"When will we go down?"

"Soon. We'll go down carefully, and within a few days we will again be together, and with all the equipment we've used. What we did here we will do down there. Life at the summit was a preparation for the days to come. Kamil left us a great legacy, wonderful teachings, and we will protect it vigilantly."

"And we won't split up?" she asks again.

"God forbid. Our strength is our togetherness. The summit lifted us up from the dunghill. We will descend together as people who did what they had to do."

I've never heard Felix speak so fluently, and I strongly feel that Kamil's words have attached themselves to him. I long for the silence locked inside him. Now it's gone, and he will never be what he was.

I look around and try to collect the vessels of life, which are hard to pack: Danzig hugging Milio. Milio not speaking as we'd hoped, but his face aglow with the will to absorb what surrounds us. Danzig speaks to him as to a son that he raised. "You will remember more than we do," he says to Milio. "We were busy with raids and stakeouts and didn't preserve what we saw. You, my dear boy, sat and watched and packed vision after vision into your soul. When the time comes, you will tell us everything you saw."

Not far away, on a pile of twigs, sit Maxie, Michael, and Edward the dog. Ever since Edward's sudden arrival, our togetherness has had a secret ingredient. Michael's progress in the past month has been remarkable. Now he's learning French with the same diligence that he applied to his study of arithmetic and geometry.

Karl always stands ready to lend a hand or to run and pick up a person who has fallen down. If all communists were like him, the world would be redeemed without delay. In the ghetto there were greedy people who hoarded food, deaf to the cries of those dying of hunger. The evil and malice that surrounded us penetrated every one of us, and only a few, the chosen ones, remained unblemished.

Karl remains at his post. He exudes good-heartedness, but we do not feel inferior to him. On the contrary, each contact with Karl elevates us. Sometimes he sits down, but even when he's seated, his stature is high.

So the eye drifts from image to image: from those who are with us to those who have gone on to another world.

80

A t night we said goodbye to Victor. He decided not to return to his home but to enlist in the Red Army. We opened a bottle of vodka in his honor. The fighters were joined by the survivors Victor had cared for. We sang Russian marches, and our elation was mixed with melancholy.

Felix began by saying, "You have been a brother to us in every sense of the word. It never crossed our minds that a true Ukrainian would come to us and become a cherished brother. If we were an army and not a unit of partisans, we would decorate you with a medal of brotherhood. But not to worry, when all this is over, we will remember you, dear friend. And the name Victor Marshevicz will live on inside us."

Victor was embarrassed. "Dear brothers," he said. "I leave you today with love and sorrow. The days I spent with you were days of purification and transcendence. When I came to you, I didn't know how you would receive me. The people of my village did not treat their Jewish neighbors with humanity. They witnessed the cruelty and stood to the side, but you accepted me as a brother; you included me in your activities and thoughts and gave me a home among you. I didn't feel like a stranger. Sometimes I felt like your thinking was my thinking, as if we had been brothers for generations. You suffered so much, each of you alone and all of you together; now the time has come when God will turn to you, to you especially, and heal your wounds. The war rages on, and I've decided to enlist in the Red Army. We are commanded to fight against evil. I will go down with you and help you get organized, and then I'll go and meet my destiny. I'll hold on to my days with you as a precious gift."

"Why don't you come with us?" asked one of the fighters.

"Everyone performs his mission in this world in the place meant for him. God intended for me to fight in the ranks of the Red Army. In the Red Army I will do what I learned from you: from Kamil and Felix, from Salo and Maxie, and from the survivors I took care of. I learned from you that not everything in this world is debased."

Were it not for Tsila, who suddenly burst into tears, we would then have all gone off to our mats of twigs. Her tears this time were bitter and burning, as if things hidden from us were revealed to her. Salo and Maxie knelt down and tried to comfort her. "Thank God we are not descending alone; dozens of people are going down with us. You played a big role in this tremendous rescue. We weren't able to derail more trains, but we did what we could."

Tsila seemed to absorb what Salo told her, but she could not dam up her tears. Salo finally gave her a dose of liquid sedative, and she stopped moaning, as if her weeping had been cut with a sharp knife.

Just a few days earlier, Werner had said, "The days at the summit are over; now it's each to his own suffering. In truth, I have no desire to leave this place. Flaubert is certainly an important author; I have read a lot of his work and about him. At one time I was sure that he was the greatest writer ever. Now he strikes me as a pedant, with his merciless depictions of detail. I can't connect with him anymore."

Ever since we heard about the attacks by the Red Army, we talk less and less among ourselves. Only those sick who have not recovered keep on mumbling, confessing their failures, and wondering about the punishments that await them in the future.

81

The next day we rose early and were each given a slice of bread spread with oil and a cup of tea. Hermann Cohen organized this meal. Maxie, Tsila, and Danzig prepared a meal for the survivors.

The first ten stretchers carrying a group of survivors set off without delay. I was happy to be with Isidor again. We carried Dr. Weintraub, the beloved teacher from the *gymnasium*. I didn't study with him, but Isidor was one of his students and admired him. When we brought him to the summit, his condition was grave. Over time he recovered and began to look like his old self.

Dr. Weintraub knew my parents well. He referred to Papa as "a smart man who represented big firms that trusted him fully. He was always attentive to those in need. He was a big donor, and once a week he came to the hospital and sat with the patients, fed them if necessary. He didn't consider this beneath his dignity."

I knew that Papa was a generous person, but I didn't know of his contributions to the hospital. Dr. Weintraub looked at me for a moment and said, "You look like your father, and also your mother."

"Is it true, Dr. Weintraub, that this was the biggest war against the Jews in history?" I asked.

"I and others like me did not foresee this war," he replied. "We were certain that within a decade or two the Jews would assimilate into the nations of Europe and disappear." Every sound he uttered was drenched in fatigue, but his words were carefully chosen and composed. Years of teaching at the *gymnasium* had shaped his voice and manner.

After an hour of walking, dodging obstacles, and a few missteps, we took a break. We gave Dr. Weintraub a slice of bread with jam and a cup of water. He thanked us and said, "I never imagined that Jewish fighters could be so disciplined. It is common knowledge that Jews are anarchists by nature, avoiding rules and public order. I'm astonished that everything here has been handled in exemplary fashion, both during the shelling and also thereafter. Who was Kamil?"

"He was a superb commander," I replied.

"Did he have a philosophy?"

"He had us read texts from the Bible, Hasidic writings, also poetry."

"He was a religious person?"

"I think so, but without rituals or ceremonies. He once called himself a religious anarchist."

"An interesting classification. Your commune has made a great impression on me. In all these years of war I did not see any brotherhood. In the ghetto and the camps we lost our faith in man. The hunger, the degradation, and the hard labor uprooted any feelings of humanity. A person became indifferent to the pain of others and ultimately to his own pain. Your commune, the devotion of each and every fighter, has restored the image of man to the world. I'm no longer young, and a person of my age does not easily change his views. But my stay with you has changed me nevertheless. I saw with my own eyes what our people are capable of accomplishing. Even after disgrace and humiliation and abuse, people rise up from the dust to revive and help others. Thank you, dear people; I have been privileged to see the light in mankind. I have spoken too much. Now, with your permission, this old man will close his eyes and nap."

82

When we reached the train station and set the stretcher on the ground, we saw at once that Dr. Weintraub was lifeless. His face was silent, pale, motionless. The other stretcher bearers came and surrounded ours. Their faces mirrored the pallor of this man who had just passed away. Dr. Weintraub, who had been aware of the mistakes he made in life, hid nothing from us in his final hours. Now he lay still, as if he had given up on living.

We stood and waited for the next group of stretchers. The station was filled with soldiers, refugees, and abandoned dogs. Isidor wept, and I didn't know how to console him. "Dr. Weintraub died peacefully," I said. I was immediately angry with myself for saying "died peacefully." How did I know that? He didn't die in his home or his bed or in the bosom of his family. Who knows what thoughts scorched his final moments?

The group that had been delayed arrived in late afternoon, and Dr. Weintraub's death shocked them, too. Few knew him, even among the survivors, but his dignified conduct during his time with us made an impression on many.

PEOPLE WHO HAD EXPECTED to find friends or relatives who had come back from the camps found chaos. Danzig, who had taken command, did not waste time. He saw a large warehouse near the train station and claimed it for us. He ordered Isidor and me to carry the stretcher with Dr. Weintraub's body to the cemetery, and a quorum of fighters and survivors accompanied us.

About five hundred yards away from the train station, we encountered some Ukrainian youths who yelled "Jews to Palestine!" Danzig fired a few shots in the air, and they ran for their lives. The burial took place slowly because of the weeping, and one survivor fainted. There was a feeling that we were giving a Jewish burial not only to Dr. Weintraub but also to all those we had seen dead and dying alongside the death trains, who were abandoned to birds of prey.

Isidor tried to suppress his crying, but tears flooded his Kaddish and shook the rest of us.

On the way back to the warehouse there were again youths, this time shouting "Dirty Jews!" and Danzig fired shots in the air without hesitation. Reality again hit us in the face.

But despite the gloominess, there was a degree of satisfaction: the third group arrived in the evening and was allotted space in the warehouse. A joyful smile crossed Danzig's lips; Milio clearly spoke a word that everyone heard. "Papa!" he cried out. "Papa!" Danzig hoped for one more word, which was not late in coming: "My Papa, my Papa!" The words pushed Danzig past the brink of emotion: tears streamed down his face, and he hurried to wipe them.

Not far from the big warehouse, we found a smaller, empty one, and we moved into it. Fortunately, we had brought the blankets and sheepskins.

Felix, who oversaw the descent from the summit, sat down, drank tea, and smoked a cigarette. He knew well that the battle was not over and that tense days awaited us, but like any commander worthy of his name, he needed a moment to collect his thoughts.

83

The next day, the fourth group arrived, commanded by Sontag. Sontag was astounded by the teeming train station and the soldiers in the streets. When he got over his shock, he told us the descent had not been easy. No one had ambushed them, but several survivors couldn't handle the hardships of the journey and had to be carried. In the end, brotherhood prevailed.

Sontag constantly surprises us. This muscular man, sometimes prone to visions and hallucinations, is an outstanding fighter and commander. Now he stood with all of us, amazed at the new life that had begun to blossom here.

The survivors came to him and thanked him, and he returned their compliments. Finally, he said, "We protected everyone, and everyone is still with us," but he was embarrassed by the words he had spoken.

Yet again, hunger saved us from fear and anguish. Tsila, Hermann Cohen, and many of the fighters and survivors joined in to prepare dinner. We peeled potatoes and boiled them in five large pots, on Primus stoves we found in the small warehouse. The noise they made was music to our ears.

That night Victor left us to enlist in the Red Army. Before he left, the survivors hugged him and asked him to stay. But Victor was determined to join up, come what may. "If they don't take me because of my wound, I'll come back to you. It's not easy for me to leave you," he said with tears in his eyes.

And then, for a moment, it seemed as though Paul was nearing the train station. But it was just an illusion. The tall, well-built man, who from a distance looked like Paul, was a local. He paused, briefly puzzled that we were looking at him, and then he went on his way.

ONCE A DAY a military truck appeared and distributed supplies. We stood first in line and stocked up on bread, salt, sugar, canned food, and cigarettes. We also got a big package of tea.

When we were leaving the summit, we thought our lives would change overnight. We would cheer the liberating soldiers and greet those who returned from the camps; our hearts would be as one, and joy would blend with the sorrow.

On the final night on the summit, I dreamed that Tsila's family had returned and that Tsila fainted, overcome with emotion. But when she recovered, her face lit up and she said, "God Almighty, how can I ever thank you."

THE ISOLATED REFUGEES who turn up at the train station are mainly men who had hid in the homes of farmers or pretended to be Ukrainians and managed to survive. Now, because they had not spoken for years, they can barely utter a word.

One of them approached us and asked, "Where were you?"
We told him.

He looked at us suspiciously and moved aside. When we asked him where he had been, he made a strange gesture with his right hand, as if to say, *Why does it matter? It's not worth telling.*

And there was one refugee, of medium height, who was proud that he had been able to fool the Germans. Once he even masqueraded as a priest. He seemed like a grown-up child who sticks out his tongue and brags, "I won. They didn't catch me." But the rest of the refugees walked around mutely, with blank expressions, dragging their feet and looking for a corner where they could rest their weary bodies. Only the young soldiers of the Red Army were alert and energetic. No full-bodied young woman escaped their attention.

FELIX AND THE VETERAN FIGHTERS feel that for the time being we should wait here for those who will return. The place is a crossroads, and in the coming days the trains will start running again. There were several survivors who ignored the commander's advice and went on their way. Felix didn't try to persuade them. "If they want to go," he said, "they're entitled."

It's strange: These survivors, whom we carried on our shoulders, whom we fed, and whose wounds we bandaged, didn't say a word of goodbye. No one, in any event, said a thing to them. They went off without a backward glance.

THE SPRING REVEALS its beauty anew each day. From the train station we can see the flowing river and the flowering gardens, the cows and sheep grazing in the meadows, as if the horrible war had never happened.

With the help of the fighters and survivors, Tsila and Hermann Cohen prepare two meals a day. The meals are spare but still taste a bit like the food at the summit.

The days of the summit grow more distant from us, but it sometimes seems that we will return there one day, together with Kamil and all the comrades who died. When Felix mentions the summit, a little smile flits across his lips, as if to say, *Those were, in the end, clear days with no fog and no illusions. We knew what to do and we did what we could.*

84

Felix has decided that the time has come to move the dead we had buried in the wetlands to the Jewish cemetery. Two squads equipped with digging tools, stretchers, and blankets went out early in the morning.

The wetlands at this time of year are a muddy mess. Danzig, who led the squads, knows the territory well, but we were forced to diverge from the familiar route to avoid swamps and streams, and the extended journey took four hours.

Before ascending to the summit, we lit a bonfire. Hermann Cohen had supplied us with round bread and cheese, dried fruit, and tea. We were very hungry and finished everything. For a moment I forgot the solemn mission to which we had been assigned. The days we had spent together passed before my eyes—the patrols, the ambushes, and the raids—and I was sad that this close friendship was coming apart. Soon everyone would be facing his own fate.

We did not tarry and climbed to the summit. This exalted place that we had clung to now stood naked and exposed to the winds. Several tent canvases were strewn on the ground, crumpled and abandoned. Our former bunkers bore undeniable testimony to the tough, determined lives we led here. But what can you do? Nature is always stronger than human life. In another month or two these remnants will be erased, and the summit will again be what it was—an inseparable part of the Carpathians.

Without delay we began to dig around the grave of Grandma Tsirl. Soon enough the shovels touched her sedan chair. In a group effort we lifted it up and placed it on the stretcher. Suddenly we had a vision of Grandma Tsirl coming back to life as we had known her: her gaunt face, her neck wrapped in a thin scarf, her eyes blazing as she seemed to whisper, *The body is gone, but the soul is part of God above*. There's no point in doubting this pure truth. For good reason our hands trembled as we tied the sedan chair to the stretcher with ropes.

We brought the stretcher down from the summit carefully, step by step. Next we began digging around the grave of Koba, our first casualty. I didn't know him, but Danzig, a classmate of his, knew him well and valued him greatly. Buried on either side of him were Gabriel and Mark.

The fallen were still wrapped in faded police uniforms. I remembered that Mark had been buried in his uniform; it had seemed right to me that we didn't bury him in his tattered flak jacket. The uniform would protect his body until his soul departed from it.

We loaded the bodies on the stretchers and went on our way with a sense of urgency.

When we reached the cemetery, it was already evening. We dug graves beside the graves we had just dug for our other fallen comrades. The digging took a long time because of the soggy ground and our fatigue from the journey. Isidor recited the Kaddish and the *El Maleh Rahamim* prayer. What would we do without him at a time like this? Whom else could we turn to for words? He knows the words that were spoken by the forefathers and he speaks them.

Afterward, we sat down and had no strength to get up and

walk. Danzig didn't rush us, but when a group of young people passed by and shouted, "Jews, the Germans will soon be back," we chased after them. They ran away, but we were quicker. We caught most of them. They pleaded for their lives, but we didn't let go until they kneeled down and swore to God that they would no longer threaten or curse us.

85

We spend the days at the train station, standing around restlessly or sitting on the doorstep of the warehouse, doing almost nothing. Military trucks arrive daily at the station square, and soldiers hand out food generously. We take what we need but do not hoard. Several survivors who have recuperated hoard cigarettes and sugar and barter these in secret. Felix eyes them disapprovingly but doesn't say anything. The will to live that had once made us flexible and nimble has suddenly been cut off. Overnight we have become idlers. We fall asleep in the middle of the day. No one asks what we should do or where we are going.

Michael woke up and asked, "Who are we waiting for?"

"The train," Maxie replies absentmindedly.

"And where will we go?"

"To one of the big stations, I presume."

Michael looks at him as if to say, *What does "I presume" mean this time?*

Refugees have stopped coming. Once in a while one of them shows up, stares into space, and disappears.

Every few days we visit the graves of our friends, and Isidor softly chants the Kaddish.

The abandoned cemetery is now our secret haven. We stay there a long while, wandering among the desecrated headstones, but we don't bother to erase the swastikas and hateful slogans.

Finally, filled with anger and confusion, we fire our guns in the air and return to the warehouse.

Felix is again not what he was. He sits at the entrance to the warehouse, drinks tea, and chain-smokes. Sometimes the commander in him awakens, and he stands us in a row, checks our guns and ammunition, and repeats that the war may be over but not for us. Gangs lie in wait for us; if we're not alert they won't fail to surprise us. They are no less fanatical than the Germans. The guns need to be cleaned and the bullets kept close at hand. This clear warning doesn't pull the fighters out of their apathy; they sit in front of the warehouse, smoking and staring into space.

Refugees are not to be found. Sometimes a person or a couple who look like refugees turn up, but they are just poor people from the area. For this reason there are fighters who believe we should head south and reach our city and the surrounding villages as soon as we can, without further delay. On the other hand, there are fighters who say that this railroad station is an important hub, and it's best to wait.

Felix doesn't express his opinion. He has gone back to being Felix: a man of few words. Kamil's absence is felt at every moment. I sometimes imagine I hear his voice, see him stooped over as he hunts for a word or a slogan, and then it's clear that nothing comes easily to him; he is always digging deep inside. Only one person is content: Danzig. Milio adds a new word every day, sometimes two. Last night he pointed at the sky and said, "Sky."

Days of inactivity have stunted our speech. Disorganized thoughts and fantasies race through our minds but not one logical idea. Last night I saw from a distance a man and a woman slowly shuffling along, and I was sure they were Papa and Mama, who had come back; I ran toward them. Then reality hit me in the face. They were a local couple and were startled by my running.

I see Felix grumbling about those recovered survivors who are busily bartering goods. "It's unbecoming for people who endured the seven circles of hell to peddle their wares at the station," he says. "You would expect their conduct to be more dignified."

Danzig is less harsh than Felix. "We didn't take the survivors up to the summit to correct their values," he says. "So long as there are people who suffer, we will do whatever we can for them. They don't owe us anything."

In truth, we no longer argue; we just quibble over this and that. We have easily gotten used to our idleness; nevertheless, we're tired and exhausted, and whenever possible, we lean our heads against the doorpost of the warehouse. Last night Emil thought he saw his father and mother exiting the station and approaching him. He ran toward them. They were in fact a blind couple but not his parents.

So the days go by. Were it not for guard duty, we would sleep all the time. One squad patrols the warehouse area, and another is ready if needed. This is not a whim of Felix's. Suspicious people are hanging around the station. Some of the survivors have recuperated, and some have left to search for their families, but we still have about thirty-five sick and frail people who depend on us.

Michael suddenly got back to business, solving math and geometry problems and reading a book by Karl May. Maxie promises Michael what he has already promised: he will skip at least two grades at school. Maxie's words encourage him, and he asks for more difficult exercises. Once in a while Michael picks his beautiful head up from his notebook, as if to say, *I believe that God will bring my father and mother back to me.*

Tsila keeps cooking. The Primus stoves make a deafening noise. Not long ago her hands juggled pots and pans with ease. Now she cooks everything with a sort of perpetual bewilderment. It's hard to know what she's thinking. She asks nothing, and no one asks her anything. Her kitchen at the summit teemed with life and appetite; now it's bare and empty. Once in a while a survivor approaches her and says, "God will bless and repay you for all you have done." Tsila does not respond to this blessing.

Salo and Maxie continue to care for those in need. Each day, two or three survivors rise from their beds and say, "We need to go." They eat breakfast and leave. We watch them walk away and feel that part of us is going with them.

I close my eyes and see the summit blanketed in snow, the brilliant light, and all of us in heavy coats and boots and the thick stocking caps knitted by Reb Hanoch. The night before, we had been on a raid. All the food, blankets, and household goods we brought have already been arranged in Hermann Cohen's storeroom. He takes careful inventory of the loot, and whenever he comes upon a Jewish item, he smiles, as if to say, *What was lost has returned to its owner.* Then comes the meal in Tsila's kitchen: the generous sandwiches, the coffee and cigarettes, and not long thereafter, you are wrapped in sweet, deep sleep.

Our evenings of study and poetry also came to mind. Kamil taught us to use words precisely. More than any other activity, our studies by candlelight and flashlight reminded us that we were free men seeking to connect with texts that can nourish the soul even in days of disaster.

The entire time we spent in the wetlands, especially at the summit, the books that we'd brought from that abandoned house were our secret sustenance.

"I CAN'T CALM DOWN," Isidor tells me. "Ever since we stopped going on raids, I have nightmares and I prefer not to sleep."

"What are you thinking about?" I ask him cautiously.

"I don't think. I see things. It's hard to banish the things I see."

I understand exactly what he means and ask nothing more.

We're sitting at the entrance to the warehouse, and our lives are coming apart. Not long ago we fought using the stratagems Kamil taught us. True, we were defeated more than once, but there were also battles we won and from which we came away with booty. Now Kamil is gone, and we've grown weaker. Felix apparently has things to tell us, but he is bound up inside himself, and what we hear are mumblings that are hard to understand.

One of the survivors whom we had brought half dead to the summit approached Felix and said, "Commander, permit me to thank you in my name and the name of those you took up to the summit for giving us life. It's hard for us to thank God." Felix listened and looked at the man as if to say, *What do you expect me to say?*

We're again sitting in front of the warehouse. I'm peering into the depths, and my face and my friends' faces are reflected in the water. One time I see Felix and another time Kamil, and another time Danzig hugging Milio. Hermann Cohen is also in the depths, not budging from his niece Teresa. And, suddenly, Karl and Werner and Miriam are floating in the cold deep waters. *Why are we drowning in the abyss?*, I ask myself. *Why are we not extending our hands to others? We are well trained in climbing and bending metal bars. Why now of all times is it hard for us to move from place to place?*

We go to visit our friends buried in the cemetery, and we can see that the desecration of the gravestones has continued. Several more stones have been shattered and several have been uprooted. Danzig believes it's our responsibility to set the stones upright and erase the graffiti, to ambush the desecrators and beat them up.

We're very angry, but to be practical, what's the point of erasing the graffiti? We're leaving tomorrow, and the cemetery is open and unguarded. The vandals will just repeat their acts. But Danzig insists. "It is our duty to do this," he says. "Not every action brings immediate benefit. For our friends who are buried here, we are obliged to remove the blasphemy and protect what remains."

Felix eventually orders the squads to stand in a row, and he asks Isidor to say Kaddish. Isidor recites the Kaddish in a quavering voice and nearly chokes up. Felix orders the squad to cock their weapons and raise them. Then he says, "In honor of our friends buried in this holy ground—fire! In honor of our glorious commander, Kamil, who led us through the wetlands to the summit, who did not live to see the victory—fire! In honor of our loved ones who were taken to the camps and for whom we will wait forever—fire!"

The gunshots deafen the ears and shake the heart. We hurry to leave. Felix marches in the lead with quick limping strides, and we follow a short distance behind him. There is a feeling that we should not have parted this way from our friends. We should have sung a quiet song or remained silent, but what was done was done.

When we reach the train station, we learn that a gang of rioters has surrounded the warehouse and is about to burst inside. Sontag, in charge of the squads, attacks swiftly. The rioters withdraw, leaving three wounded men in the area. A large mob begins cursing and demanding revenge. The fighters keep shooting, and the crowd disperses.

Felix assesses the situation and orders the women and equipment to be moved to the train station. The squads quickly do so. Within an hour a military train enters the station, and we are packed together in one carriage, pleased that we have managed to transport both the survivors and the equipment.

One of the survivors, who stands beside Felix, asks, "Commander, where are we going?"

"Home," he answers right away.

"Which home?" asks the survivor.

"There's only one home we grew up in and loved, and we're returning to it."

The survivor is astonished by Felix's answer. A smile, thin and unintended, spreads across his face.

A NOTE ABOUT THE AUTHOR

Aharon Appelfeld is the author of more than forty works of fiction and nonfiction, including *The Iron Tracks*, *Until the Dawn's Light* (both winners of the National Jewish Book Award), *The Story of a Life* (winner of the Prix Médicis Étranger), and *Badenheim 1939*. Other honors he received include the Giovanni Boccaccio Literary Prize, the Nelly Sachs Prize, the Israel Prize, the Bialik Prize, and the MLA Commonwealth Award. *Blooms of Darkness* won the Independent Foreign Fiction Prize in 2012 and was short-listed for the Man Booker International Prize in 2013. Born in Czernowitz, Bukovina (now part of Ukraine), in 1932, he lived in Israel from 1946 until his death in 2018.

A NOTE ON THE TYPE

Pierre Simon Fournier *le jeune* (1712–1768), who designed the type used in this book, was both an originator and a collector of types. His services to the art of printing were his design of letters, his creation of ornaments and initials, and his standardization of type sizes. His types are old style in character and sharply cut. In 1764 and 1766 he published his *Manuel typographique*, a treatise on the history of French types and printing, on typefounding in all its details, and on what many consider his most important contribution to typography—the measurement of type by the point system.

Typeset by Scribe,
Philadelphia, Pennsylvania

Printed and bound by Berryville Graphics,
Berryville, Virginia

Designed by Cassandra J. Pappas